The Stiger Chronicles
Originally published as
Chronicles of an Imperial Legionary Officer

Book 1

STIGER'S TIGERS

BY
MARC ALAN EDELHEIT

FANTASY
The Stiger Chronicles
Originally published as Chronicles of an Imperial Legionary Officer
Book One: **Stiger's Tigers**
Book Two: **The Tiger**
Book Three: **The Tiger's Fate**
Book Four: **The Tiger's Time**
Book Five: **The Tiger's Wrath**
Book Six: **The Tiger's Imperium**
Book Seven: **The Tiger's Fight (Coming 2023)**
Book Eight: **The Tiger's Rage (Coming 2023)**

Tales of the Seventh
Part One: **Stiger**
Part Two: **Fort Covenant**
Part Three: **A Dark Foretoken**
Part Four: **The Kingdom of Thresh (Coming 2023)**

The Karus Saga
Book One: **Lost Legio IX**
Book Two: **Fortress of Radiance**
Book Three: **The First Compact**
Book Four: **Rapax Pax**
Book Four: **Brothers of the Line (Coming 2024)**

A Ranger's Tale
Book 1: **Eli**
Book 2: **By Bow, Daggers, and Sword**
Book 3: **Lutha Nyx (Coming 2023)**

The Way of Legend: With Quincy J. Allen
Book One: **Reclaiming Honor**
Book Two: **Forging Destiny**
Book Three: **Paladin's Light**

SCI-FI
Born of Ash
Book One: **Fallen Empire**
Book Two: **Infinity Control**
Book Three: **Rising Phoenix (Coming 2024)**

Guardians of the Dark
Book One: **Off Midway Station (Coming 2024)**

Nonfiction
Every Writer's Dream: The Insider's Path to an Indie Bestseller

Stiger's Tigers Book 1: The Stiger Chronicles. *Originally published as Stiger's Tigers Book One: Chronicles of an Imperial Legionary Officer.*

Third Edition.

I wish to thank my agent, Andrea Hurst, for her invaluable support and assistance. I would also like to thank my beta readers, who suffered through several early drafts. My betas: Jon Cockes, Nicolas Weiss, Melinda Vallem, Paul Klebaur, James Doak, David Cheever, Bruce Heaven, Erin Penny, April Faas, Rodney Gigone, Brandon Purcell, Tim Adams, Paul Bersoux, Phillip Broom, David Houston, Sheldon Levy, Michael Hetts, Walker Graham, Bill Schnippert, Jan McClintock, Jonathan Parkin, Spencer Morris, Jimmy McAfee, Rusty Juban, Marshall Clowers. I would also like to take a moment to thank my loving wife, who sacrificed many an evening and weekend to allow me to work on my writing.

Editing Assistance by Hannah Streetman, Audrey Mackaman, Winslow Eliot

Cover Art by Piero Mng (Gianpiero Mangialardi)

Cover and Formatting by Telemachus Press

Visit the author website:
http://www.MAEnovels.com

ISBN: 978-1-942899-16-7 (eBook)
ISBN: 978-1-942899-39-6 (paperback)
Version Third
10 9 8 7 6 5 4 3 2

*To Peggy Edelheit (mother and published author),
who inspired in me a love of reading.*

CONTINENT OF ILOSTA
WORLD OF ISTROS

EASTERN OCEAN

NORTHERN REACH

ELVYN LANDS

CASTOL MALLARA

KINGDOM OF THE RIVAN

IRAN TIBER

FOREST OF ARATH

INLAND SEA

MALZETHIN EMPIRE

MOGUL ZETH

SERRAL ZETH

THE WILDS

CYREN

KINGDOM OF TABOR (CLIENT STATE)

BARRENS

MOTIAN (CLIENT STATE)

SENTINEL FOREST

OCCUPIED SOUTHERN PROVINCES

ERAWAN

INDEPENDENT KINGDOMS

NARROW SEA

CYPHAN CONFEDERACY

ORA STEPPE

CARTOGRAPHER: PIERO MNG

Excerpt from Thelius's Histories, The Mal'Zeelan Empire, Volume 3, Book 2.

The Mal'Zeelan Imperial Legion
Pre-Emperor Midisian Reformation

The imperial legion was a formation that numbered, when at full strength, 5,500 to 6,000 men. The legion was composed of heavy infantry recruited exclusively from the citizens of the empire. Slaves and non-citizens were prohibited from serving. The legion was divided into ten cohorts of 480 men, with First Cohort, being an over-strength unit, numbering around a thousand. A legion usually included a mix of engineers, surgeons, and various support staff. Legions were always accompanied by allied auxiliary formations, ranging from cavalry to various forms of light infantry. The imperial legion was commanded by a legate (general).

The basic unit of the legion was the century, numbering eighty men in strength. There were six centuries in a cohort. A centurion (basic officer) commanded the century. The centurion was supported by an optio (equivalent of a corporal) who handled minor administrative duties. Both had to be capable of reading and performing basic math.

Note: Very rarely were legions ever maintained at full strength. This was due primarily to the following reasons: retirement, death, disability, budget shortages (graft), and the slow stream of replacements.

The most famous legion was the Thirteenth, commanded by Legate...

Post-Emperor Midisian Reformation

Emperor Midiuses's reforms were focused on streamlining the legions and cutting cost through the elimination of at least half of the officer corps per legion, amongst other changes.

The basic unit of the legion became the company, numbering around two hundred men in strength. There were ten twenty-man files per company. A captain commanded the company. The captain was supported by a lieutenant, two sergeants, and a corporal per file.

ONE

Two road-weary riders, both legionary officers, crested the bald hill and pulled to a halt. A vast military encampment surrounded by entrenchments and fortifications took up much of the valley below them in a shocking display. Smoke from thousands of campfires drifted upward and hung over the valley like a veil. After months of travel, the two riders were now finally able to set their eyes upon their destination—the main encampment of General Kromen's Imperial Army, comprising the Fifteenth, Eighteenth, Twenty-Ninth, and Thirtieth Legions. These four legions had been dispatched by the emperor to put down the rebellion burning through what the empire considered her southern provinces.

The awful stench of the encampment had been on the wind for hours. This close, the smell of decay mixed with human waste and a thousand other smells was nearly overpowering. What should have been relief at finally reaching their destination had turned to incredulous horror. Neither of them had ever seen anything like it. Imperial encampments were typically highly organized, with priority placed on sanitation to reduce the chance of sickness and disease. The jumble of tents and ramshackle buildings laid out before them, surrounded by the fortifications, spoke of something much different. It told of an almost wanton criminal neglect for the men who served the empire, or perhaps even incompetence in command.

An empty wagon, the first of a sad-looking supply train, rumbled around past the two riders, who refused to give way. The driver, a hired teamster, cursed at them for hogging the road. He took his frustration out on a group of dirty and ragged slaves sitting along the edge of the road. The slaves, part of a work gang to maintain the imperial highway, were forced to scramble out of the way, lest the wagon roll over them as it rumbled around the two travelers.

An overseer resting on a large fieldstone several feet away barked out a harsh laugh before shouting at the slaves to be more careful. One of the slaves collapsed, and yet both riders hardly spared him a glance. Slaves were simply beneath notice.

The supply train's nominal escort, a small troop of cavalry riding in a line alongside the wagons, was working its way slowly up the hill toward the two officers and away from the encampment. Much like every other legionary the two travelers had come upon for the last hundred miles, the cavalry troop was less than impressive, though somewhat better looking in appearance. Their armor wasn't as rusted and had been recently maintained.

Several empty wagons rumbled by the two, which saw additional invectives hurled their way. They ignored the cursing, just as they had disregarded the wagons and the plight of the slaves. Where they had come from, it would have been unthinkable for someone to hurl invectives at an officer, who was almost assuredly a nobleman. At the very least, a commoner would invite a severe beating with such behavior. Here in the South, such lack of basic respect seemed commonplace.

One of the travelers had the hood of his red imperial cloak pulled up as far as it would go and tilted his head forward to protect against a light drizzling rain, which had been falling for some time.

The other had the hood of his cloak pulled back, revealing close-cropped brown hair and a fair but weather-hardened face, marred only by a slight scar running down the left cheek. The scar pulled the man's mouth up into a slight sneer. He looked no older than twenty-five, but his eyes, which seemed to miss nothing, made him look wise beyond his years. The slaves, having settled down in a new spot, watched the two warily.

As the first of the cavalry troop crested the hill, which was much steeper on the encampment's side, the lieutenant in command pulled his mount up.

"Well met, Captain," the lieutenant said. The lieutenant's lead sergeant also stopped his horse.

The cavalry troop continued to ride by, the men wearing their helmets to avoid the drizzling rain but miserably wet just the same. The lieutenant offered a salute, to which the captain simply nodded in reply, saying nothing. The captain's gaze—along with that of his companion, whose face was concealed by the hood of his cloak—remained focused on the encampment below.

After several uncomfortable moments, the lieutenant once again attempted to strike up a conversation. "I assume you came by way of Aeda? A miserable city, if you ask me. Can you tell me the condition of the road? Did you encounter any rebels?"

The lieutenant shivered slightly as the captain turned a cold gray-eyed gaze upon him.

"We saw no evidence of rebels," the captain replied in a low, gravelly voice filled with steel and confidence. "The road passed peacefully."

"That is good to hear," the cavalry officer replied. "I am Lieutenant Lan of the One Hundred Eighty-Seventh Imperial Horse Regiment. May...may I have your name, Captain?"

"Stiger," the captain growled, kicking his horse into motion and rapidly moving off the crest of the hill, down toward the encampment.

The lieutenant's eyes widened. Stiger's companion, without a word or a sideways glance, followed at a touch to his horse, leaving the lieutenant behind.

The door to the guardhouse opened and after a moment banged closed like it had undoubtedly done countless times before. Stiger and his companion stepped forward, their heavy bootfalls thunking across the coarse wooden floorboards that were covered in a layer of dirt made slick from the rain. The floor had not been swept in a good long time.

"Name and purpose?" a bored ensign demanded, his back to the door. A counter separated the ensign from any newcomers. He was sitting at a table, attempting to look busy and important by writing in a logbook. After a few moments, when the ensign heard nothing in reply, he stood and turned with obvious irritation, prepared to give the new arrivals a piece of his mind. He was confronted with two wet officers, one a captain and the other a lieutenant.

Stiger locked the ensign with a piercing gaze. The ensign was old for his rank, which was generally a sign that he was unfit for further promotion. Instead of forcing such a useless man out of the service, he was put in a position where he could do little harm and perhaps accomplish something useful. It had been Stiger's experience that such men became bitter and would not hesitate to abuse what little power was available to them.

Flustered, the ensign tried again. "Name and purp—"

"Captain Stiger and companion," Stiger interrupted, with something akin to an irritated growl. The captain slowly placed his hands on the dirty counter and leaned forward toward the man. The ensign—most likely accustomed to dealing with lowly teamsters, drovers, corporals, and sergeants—blinked. His jaw dropped. He stood there for a moment, dumbfounded, before remembering to salute a superior officer, fist to chest. Stiger said nothing in reply, but gestured impatiently for the ensign to move things along.

"Forgive me, sir," the ensign stammered. It was then, as the lieutenant who accompanied the captain pushed back the hood of his cloak, that he noticed Captain Stiger's companion was not human. The ensign's mouth dropped open even further, if that was possible.

"Lieutenant Eli'Far," the elf introduced himself in a pleasantly soft, singsong kind of voice that sounded human, but was tinged with something alien at the same time. Eli was tall, whipcord thin, and very fair. His perpetually youthful face, complete with blue almond-shaped eyes and sharply pointed ears, was perfect. Framed by sand-colored hair, perhaps it was even *too* perfect.

"I have orders to report to General Kromen," Stiger stated simply, impatient to be done with the fool before him.

"Of course, sir," the ensign stammered, remembering himself. He slid a book across the counter. "If you will sign in, I will have you escorted directly to General Kromen's headquarters."

Stiger grabbed a quill, dipped it in the inkbottle sitting on the counter, and signed for both himself and Eli. He put down the quill and pushed the book back toward the ensign.

"Corporal!" the ensign called in a near-panicked shout.

The guard corporal poked his head into the guardhouse.

"Captain Stiger requires an escort to the commanding general's headquarters."

The corporal blinked as if he had not heard correctly. "Yes, sir," he said, fully stepping into the guardhouse, eyes wide. "This way, gentlemen," the corporal said in a respectful tone. It was never wise to upset an officer, and even more irresponsible to offend one from an important family, no matter how infamous. "I will escort you myself. It is a bit of a ride, sirs."

The two traveling companions followed the corporal out of the guardhouse. They stepped back into the rain, which had changed from a drizzle to a steady downpour. Eli pulled his hood back up, once again obscuring his features. Stiger left his down. They retrieved their horses from where they had secured them and mounted up. The corporal also mounted a horse that was waiting for such a purpose and led them through the massive wooden gate that served as the encampment's main entrance. Stiger was disgusted to see the sentries huddled for cover under the gate's overhang. Those men should have been on post despite the weather.

Stiger had thought it impossible for the stench of the encampment to get any worse, yet it became much more awful and unpleasant once they were clear of the gate. It made his eyes burn. He had only ever once encountered a worse smell. That had been years before on a distant battlefield, with the dead numbering in the many thousands under a brutally hot sun, rotting quicker than they could be buried or burned.

Massive numbers of tents and temporary ramshackle wooden buildings spread out before them, amongst a sea of mud flowing with animal and human excrement. The three worked their way slowly through the muddy streets with rows of tents on each side. They came upon a small stream, muddy brown and swollen from the day's rain, running through the center of the encampment. The stream was threatening to flood nearby tents.

A rickety wooden bridge, which looked as though it had been hastily constructed to ford the small stream, appeared at risk of being washed away by the growing rush of water. Unconcerned, the corporal guided them over the bridge and to a large rough-looking building directly in the center of the encampment. An overhang and porch had been constructed onto the building, almost as an afterthought, but probably in response to the rain and mud.

Several staff officers on the porch loitered about in chairs, idly chatting and smoking pipes or playing cards, as the three horsemen approached. It was clear this was the main headquarters. A rough planked boardwalk that looked like it might sink into the mud at any moment connected the building to a row of larger tents and other nearby buildings. The porch and boardwalk served the purpose of saving the officers from having to get their perfectly polished boots muddy.

A dirty and ragged slave, ankles disappearing in the muck, stepped forward to take the reins of their horses as the two officers dismounted. Stiger tried to avoid thinking about what was in the mud as his boots sank into it.

"Good day, sirs." The corporal saluted and swung his horse around, riding away before anything more could be required of him. Stiger understood that the man was relieved to be on his way. It was said that bad things tended to happen around Stigers.

"This camp is an embarrassment," Eli said quietly to Stiger. "It is very unfit."

"I hazard half the camp is down sick," Stiger responded in sour agreement. He had never seen a legionary encampment in such a state. "Let us hope we are not detained here for months on end."

The two walked through the mud and up the steps to the front porch of the headquarters building, where they hastily kicked and scraped the muck from their boots. The headquarters building was not at all what one would expect for the commanding general of the South. The finely attired officers on the porch purposefully ignored the new arrivals. Stiger hesitated a moment and then stepped toward the building's entrance, reaching for the door.

"Where exactly do you think you're going?" a young staff captain sitting in a chair demanded disdainfully without looking up from his card game. The man was casually smoking and took a rather slow pull from his pipe, as if to show he was in charge.

Stiger turned to look at the staff captain, who wore expensively crafted legionary officer armor over a well-cut tunic and rich black boots. The armor was highly polished and the fine red cloak appeared to be freshly cleaned and brushed. There was not a hint of mud or dirt anywhere on the officer. He almost looked like the perfect toy soldier. Stiger took him to be of the soft type, a spoiled and pampered nobleman, likely from a minor yet wealthy house. At least wealthy or influential enough to secure his current position. Much like the ensign in the guardhouse, Stiger had also unfortunately encountered this kind of officer before—a bootlicking fool. Stiger's lip curled ever so slightly in derision. The bootlicker, more concerned with his fawning entourage of fellow officers, did not seem to notice. Eli, however, did. He placed a cautioning hand on Stiger's arm, which had come to rest upon the pommel of his sword.

"I am ordered to report to General Kromen and that is what I intend to do," Stiger responded neutrally, casually pulling his arm away from Eli's restraining hand. The elf sighed softly. "Unless, of course, the general is not present. In that event I shall simply wait for his return."

"Oh, I believe the general is in," the captain said with a sneer. "However, you do not get to see him without my personal permission."

Several of the other officers snickered.

"Perhaps you should say … please?" one of the other officers suggested with a high-pitched voice. The others openly laughed at this.

Stiger's anger flared, though he kept the irritation from his face. The captain was likely an aide to the general, a player of camp politics, working to control access and thereby strengthening his powerbase. He was the kind of man who was rarely challenged openly. He was also someone who would most definitely hold a grudge if he was ever slighted or offended. In short, he was another arrogant fool, and Stiger loathed such men.

Suffer the fool's game or not? Stiger was new to the camp and the last thing he wanted was to get off on the wrong foot. Still, the captain's manner irritated him deeply. The man should have behaved as a gentleman, and yet he had blatantly offended Stiger. Should he continue, Stiger would be justified in issuing a challenge to satisfy honor. Somehow, Stiger doubted General Kromen would approve of him killing, or at best maiming, one of his staff officers on his first day in camp.

"Stop me," Stiger growled. He opened the door and stepped through. The staff captain scrambled out of his chair and gave chase, protesting loudly.

Inside, Stiger was greeted by a nearly bare room. The interior was intentionally darkened, the windows shuttered. Several lanterns provided moderately adequate lighting. A fireplace, set along the back wall, crackled. The chimney, poorly constructed, leaked too much smoke into the building. A table with a large map spread out on it dominated the center of the room. Three men stood around the table, while another, a grossly obese man, sat in a chair with his elbows resting heavily on the tabletop. He had the look of someone who was seriously ill. His face was pale and covered in a sheet of fever sweat. They all looked up at the sudden intrusion, clearly irritated. Two were generals, including the one who was seated, and the two others held the rank of colonel.

"What is the meaning of this intrusion?" the general who was standing demanded. He had a tough, no-nonsense look about him.

"I am sorry, sir," the bootlicking staff captain apologized, pushing roughly past Stiger and Eli. "I tried to stop them."

"Well?" the general demanded again of Stiger.

Unfazed by the rank of the men in the room, Stiger pulled his orders from a side pocket in his cloak and stepped forward. "I am ordered to report to General Kromen for duty."

"I am General Kromen," the large, seated man wheezed before being consumed by a wracking cough. After a few moments he recovered. "Who in the seven levels might you be?"

"Captain Stiger reporting for duty, sir." Stiger assumed a position of attention and saluted.

"A Stiger?" the staff captain whispered, taking a step back in shock.

The other general barked out a sudden laugh, while General Kromen went into another coughing fit that wracked his fat body terribly.

"Captain Handi," General Kromen wheezed upon recovering, waving a hand dismissively. His other hand held a handkerchief to his mouth. "It would seem," he coughed, "we have important matters to discuss. You may go."

The captain hesitated a moment, looking between the standing no-nonsense general and the seated one before saluting smartly. He left the room without saying another word, though he managed to shoot a hate-filled look at Stiger as he passed.

"A Stiger!" Kromen exclaimed in irritation once the door was closed. "Who is your companion?"

Eli reached up and pulled back his hood, showing his face for the first time.

"Hah!" Kromen huffed tiredly. "An elf. I swear, I never thought I'd see one of your kind again, at least in this life."

"Sadly, we are few in these lands, General," Eli responded neutrally, with a slight bow.

"An elf, as well as imperial officer? I thought you fellows had given up on the empire," the other general stated.

"The emperor granted a special dispensation to serve the one known here as Ben Stiger," Eli answered, nodding in the direction of the captain. The nod had an odd tilt to it that reminded everyone present he was not quite human. Human necks just did not bend like that. "The rank conferred was to help me better serve."

"You serve a human?" the standing general asked with some surprise before turning back to Stiger. "What did you do to earn that dubious honor, Stiger?"

"I, ah..." Stiger began after a slight hesitation, "would prefer not to discuss it, sir."

"The emperor," Kromen breathed with a heavy sigh, steering the conversation away from a direction that Stiger was clearly uncomfortable speaking on. "The emperor and the gods have forsaken us in this wicked and vile land."

Kromen was an old and wily politician. Stiger suspected that the general would not press him, but would instead write back to his family in the capital to get an answer. Information was often more important than the might of an entire legion. More importantly, Stiger knew that Kromen wanted to know why a Stiger, a member of one of the most powerful families in the empire, was here in the South, and that required moving the conversation along.

"Perhaps not... You asked for combat-experienced officers and men of quality. Well... here stands a Stiger," the other general said after a moment's reflection, taking General Kromen's subtle nudge to change the subject. Stepping over, he took Stiger's orders. "Were you in the North?"

"Emperor's Third Legion," Stiger replied.

"The Third gets all of the shit assignments." The general handed the orders over to General Kromen, who opened them and began reviewing the contents. Silence filled the room, and all that could be heard was the pop of the logs in the fireplace and the rustle of parchment as General Kromen read.

"An introduction letter from my good friend General Treim," Kromen breathed hoarsely as he read.

Stiger was familiar with the contents of the letter. According to the letter, the emperor had directed Treim to send a few of his best and most promising officers to the South. Stiger could imagine Kromen's thoughts as the general looked up briefly with a skeptical look. The general was finding it hard to imagine that Treim would release one of his truly outstanding officers. The politician in Kromen would scream that there was more here than met the eye. Perhaps even the general might consider this whelp of a Stiger was actually a spy for his enemies in the senate looking to gain some advantage. Though the Kromen and Stiger families were not actually enemies, they were not allies either.

"Interesting," Kromen said after a few silent minutes, and then turned to the other general. "General Mammot, it seems that our good friend General Treim has dispatched this officer at *our* request. The letter indicates more such officers of quality are on the way. Interesting, don't you think?"

"Very," General Mammot replied dryly. "How long did it take you to travel down here, Stiger?"

"Three and a half months, sir."

General Kromen was consumed by another fit of coughing. He held a handkerchief to his mouth, hacking into it.

"Impressive time," General Mammot admitted with a raised eyebrow and turned to Kromen. "Do you think he can fight?"

"General Treim," cough, "seems to think so." Kromen handed over the letter of introduction, which General Mammot began reading. After a moment, he stopped and looked up, a strange expression crossing his face.

"You volunteered and led not one, but two forlorn hopes?" Mammot asked in an incredulous tone. "Do you have a death wish, son?"

Stiger elected not to respond and remained silent. Mammot continued to read.

"Seems General Treim sent us a fighter, and the elf comes as a bonus." Kromen took a deep and labored breath, having somewhat recovered from his latest coughing fit. He seemed to make a decision. He looked over meaningfully at General Mammot, who paused in his reading and caught his look. "We were discussing a pressing issue…"

"We were," Mammot agreed.

"Well then… since we are now saddled with a… Stiger, perhaps he might prove of some assistance in resolving this irritating matter with Vrell? Don't you agree?"

General Mammot frowned slightly and considered Stiger for a moment before nodding in agreement. He waved both Stiger and Eli over to the table with the map.

"Stiger," Mammot said, "allow me to introduce Colonels Karol and Edin. They are brigade commanders from the Twenty-Ninth."

"Pleased to meet you, Stiger," Colonel Karol said, warmly offering his hand. "I fought with your father when I was a junior officer. How is the old boy?"

"Well, sir," Stiger replied. His father was a touchy subject with most other officers. He found it was best to be vague in his answers to their questions. "His forced retirement wears on him."

"I can understand that," Colonel Karol said. "Perhaps one day he may be permitted to once again take the field."

"I am not sure he ever will," Stiger replied carefully. Many would feel threatened by such sentiments.

Colonel Edin simply shook hands and refrained from saying anything. Stiger could read the disapproval in the man's eyes. It was something the captain had grown accustomed to from his fellow officers.

"Now that we are all acquainted," General Mammot began, directing everyone's attention to the map on the table, "we have an outpost four weeks' march from here, located at Vrell, an isolated valley to the east with a substantial population." Mammot traced a line along a road from the encampment to the outpost for Stiger to follow. "Specifically, the outpost garrisons one of the few castles in the South. We call it Castle Vrell. The locals call it something different."

"We have not heard from them for several weeks," Kromen rasped. "We have dispatched messengers, but none have returned. It is all very irritating."

"The castle is a highly fortified position," Mammot continued. "There are over nine hundred legionaries defending it and the valley. Vrell is an out-of-the-way place, surrounded by mountains and a nearly impenetrable forest. We think the castle unlikely to have fallen to enemy forces." With his hand, Mammot traced a new line on the map, well south of Vrell. "The rebels control everything south of this line here ... There are no roads traveling to rebel territory from Vrell. Beyond the mountains, it is all thick forest for about one hundred miles to rebel territory. The only road to Vrell moves from the encampment here, westward, through the Sentinel Forest and terminates at the valley. It is our opinion the enemy has simply cut our communications with a handful of irregulars."

"The garrison commandant, Captain Aveeno, has been complaining for months of rebels harassing his patrols and stirring up trouble," Colonel Karol spoke up. "Then suddenly, nothing ... no word."

"The garrison is due for resupply," Kromen added, taking another labored breath. "Normally we would send a simple cavalry escort. However, with the road apparently infested with rebel irregulars, a foot company appears to be the more sensible approach."

"The Third has been heavily involved up north in the forests of Abath," General Mammot said. "We would appreciate your expertise on the matter."

"Sounds like a difficult assignment," Stiger said, non-committally. "How are the rebels equipped in this area?"

"Poorly." Colonel Edin spoke for the first time. "This terrain presents a very difficult obstacle for the rebels to overcome. We have only ever encountered light units, mostly conscripted farmers... the equivalent of bandits."

"What is the condition of the road?" Stiger leaned forward to study the map more closely. Eli stepped closer as well. The map was a simple camp scribe copy.

"Poor, but passable for wagons," Karol admitted. "Imperial maintenance crews repaired it just three years ago, so there should be no significant problems for the supply train."

"I don't see any towns and villages." Stiger found that odd for such a long road.

"There are—or were—a handful of what you might call farming communities," Edin admitted. "Really the remnants. I personally would be surprised if you discovered anyone left."

"Reprisals?" Stiger asked, looking up at Edin. He already knew the answer.

"That was my predecessor's work," General Kromen answered carefully. "A nasty business, though he did a good job in clearing the bastards out. There should be no one left to support the rebels, at least we think, until you get to Vrell. The valley's population is not with the rebels. For some strange reason, they seem to think of themselves as imperials, or at least descended from imperial stock. That said, they are not exactly friendly, at least according to Captain Aveeno's last reports."

"Captain Aveeno could have sent a force to break through, could he not?" Stiger asked.

"Not very likely," Mammot answered with a heavy breath. "Captain Aveeno, the garrison commandant, is a bit cautious. He likely would have put everyone on short rations and kept them in defense of the castle and valley, rather than take the risk of losing additional men."

"Aveeno comes from a good family," General Kromen wheezed, speaking up in defense of the man. "However, he is a timid sort, which is why he is commanding a garrison instead of leading a line company."

Stiger nodded, understanding what had not been said. General Kromen was likely Aveeno's patron, hence his defense. "A good company should be able to get through, then," Stiger said, looking down at the map once again. "Should the rebel forces operating in the area prove superior, a company will likely be able to get word out or at least fight its way back."

"Excellent," Kromen said, looking from Eli to Stiger. "How would you like the job? I have an absolutely terrible company that just became available. With your experience, you are perfect for working it into shape!"

Stiger was surprised he was being given a mission that would take him away so soon after arriving. Though marching with unfamiliar men into territory overrun by rebels was not a terribly appealing idea to the captain, his initial impressions of the legionary encampment led him to believe that such a march would be preferable to risking an untimely death by lingering sickness. He knew that the command he was being offered was most probably, as the general said, a truly terrible assignment. If the men had been idle for months, as he suspected they had, they would be sick, poorly equipped, and out of shape, and discipline would be lacking. So it all came down to risking potential death from slow, lingering sickness and disease or possible death by sword ... Stiger intentionally drew out the silence, as if he were mulling it over. Surely there were other, more effective companies that could be more readily chosen. The two generals, he knew, were also making light of the assignment so that it seemed too easy ... too good. That bothered Stiger, and he wanted to know why, but could not come right out and ask.

"I would need to outfit the company for a hard march into the wilderness," Stiger said.

"You can draw anything you might require from supply," Kromen responded, almost a little too quickly, which surprised Stiger.

What wasn't he being told?

Stiger had known that his arrival might be a headache for General Kromen. Stiger's family had influence. His presence here might be viewed as the attempt to place a spy within the Southern legions, a spy who was possibly reporting directly to the emperor or Kromen's enemies in the senate.

"We need to open communications with Vrell," Mammot added. "We can issue your company fresh arms and equipment. I will also assign some of our most experienced sergeants to help you work them into fighting trim."

"Could I meet and approve the sergeants first?" Stiger asked. He had known some pretty terrible sergeants, from ass-kissers to sadistic bastards. Instead of being dismissed from the service, such men were frequently transferred from one unit to another.

"Of course," Kromen said.

"How long until the supply train is ready?" Stiger asked, thinking about the training of his men. He needed time to become acquainted with them and to work them into

18

shape. All legionaries received the same basic training. It was a matter of restoring discipline and finding out how rusty they had become.

"Two weeks," Mammot said. "At least, we hope the train will arrive within two weeks, but certainly no more than four. It is due to leave from Aeda any day."

"Good, that would give me some time," Stiger said. He looked at General Kromen, thinking hard. "I would want to train the men my way, with no outside interference."

"Acceptable," General Kromen said with a deep frown. No general enjoyed being dictated to, especially by a young, impudent captain, even if he was a Stiger. Still...Kromen seemed to put up with it, and Stiger decided to push for more.

"That would involve training outside the encampment and living beyond the walls," Stiger added. "I would need space to prepare the men...construction of a marching camp, route marches, arms training..."

"If you are willing to brave a rebel attack outside the protection of the walls, you can do whatever you flaming wish," Kromen said, his dangerous tone betraying a mounting anger. "Anything else you require, captain?"

"No, sir," Stiger said, pleased at having escaped the confines of the encampment so easily. In all likelihood, whatever he had been set up for would prove to be a real challenge. "I will take the job."

"Very good." General Kromen flashed an insincere smile. "Colonel Karol will arrange to have you introduced to your men. He will also see to outfitting your needs." Kromen waved dismissively, indicating the audience was over.

Stiger saluted along with Colonel Karol. They turned and left, emerging onto the porch with Eli in tow. Stiger found Captain Handi resting in the same chair. The captain shot Stiger a look that spoke volumes. Doubtless Handi would be looking for ways to get his petty revenge. Stiger simply ignored him.

"You have a tough job ahead of you," Karol admitted. "The men I am giving you are in truly terrible shape and have been poorly led. Their previous commander was executed for gross incompetence. His real crime, however, was excessive graft and insufficient... shall we say, *sharing*."

"I have always enjoyed a challenge," Stiger replied softly.

"Let us both hope this particular challenge does not kill you," Karol responded. The colonel glanced to the side at the lounging officers toward Handi, who was aiming a smoldering glare at Stiger. "Captain Handi, be so good as to personally fetch Sergeants Blake and Ranl. They should be working over at my headquarters."

"But, sir, it's raining," Handi protested, gesturing at the steady rainfall beyond the cover of the porch.

"I rather imagine that the emperor expects his legions to operate in all types of weather," the colonel responded rather blandly. "Have them report on the double to the officers' mess."

Colonel Karol turned away and stepped out into the rain. He led them along the improvised boardwalk system toward another smaller ramshackle wooden building with a chimney billowing with soft blue-gray smoke.

"Wouldn't want that spoiled bastard to get his fine boots muddy now, would we?" Karol asked once they were out of earshot. Stiger found himself beginning to like the colonel.

TWO

The officers' mess was packed with officers seeking shelter from the rain and an escape from the constant boredom of life at camp. The talking ceased as the three entered, with all eyes going toward Eli as he pulled back his hood.

The colonel led them to a table in the back near the fire and politely ordered the current occupants to find a new table. Stiger and Eli removed their traveling cloaks and hung them on hooks near the fire. Once seated, the drone of conversation at once picked up, with much whispering about the elf.

"We have a real problem," Karol said quietly, so only they could hear. "This is the rainy season, and the legions are being eaten away by sickness and disease. It happens every year, but this year it is worse. This damned weather. It rains and rains. We've seen more than usual and, well, disease is sweeping through the ranks. Unfortunately, the enemy seems to know it. They are more active, and General Kromen expects the main rebel army to make a move as soon as the ground is firm. The rebels are becoming better armed and more aggressive by the day.

"It is possible," Karol said after a slight pause, "that the Cyphan Confederacy has decided to move from supporting the rebellion to becoming more heavily involved."

21

Stiger frowned at this. The Cyphan Confederacy was a trading power across the Narrow Sea to the south. Tensions between the empire and the confederacy had been on the rise ever since the empire pushed south forty years before and annexed the current lands that were now in open rebellion.

"The general has consolidated much of the power of the Southern legions here. Our allies, the auxiliaries, have been sent to man the forward outposts to the south that the legions once held. We were losing men to pinprick attacks. The consolidation was ordered to avoid losing any additional men to these attacks; however, we are now losing far more to sickness than we ever did to the enemy."

Colonel Karol leaned back in his chair and was silent for a few moments before continuing. "I will not lie to you. I expect you will run into trouble on the way to Vrell. The legions, with the exception of a few cavalry patrols, have been confined to the encampment. This has given the rebels free reign in the countryside. I don't think you will run into any real organized resistance. It is likely you will face nothing a good company could not handle. However, the last supply train that got through was hit hard. There are rebel sympathizers everywhere, and much starvation, which foments additional ill will toward the empire. Expect word to spread. Wagons full of supplies may be just too tempting a target."

Stiger said nothing.

A female slave brought a tray of hot tea and some small rolls to the table. She sported multiple bruises and a black eye, which Stiger took to reflect the mood of the encampment. She poured each of them a cup of tea and left without a word.

"The company I am giving you is the Eighty-Fifth," Colonel Karol said. "They just came in from a border outpost within the last week. Unlike the other companies that have been camped here longer, they are not yet incapacitated with sickness. I appointed Lieutenant Ikely to temporary command until a suitable replacement could be found. He is new as well, with no real experience, but seems to be a good man. He will make a good executive officer for you, I think."

"I see," Stiger said, taking a polite sip of his tea, which was terrible. He grimaced with disgust. Eli had not touched his and looked reproachfully at his captain. Stiger decided that he would refrain from having more. There was no telling where the water had come from, and with the condition of the camp, it could easily be diseased.

"I have removed the company's sergeants," Karol explained. "The two I sent for are veterans. They are among my best and should be able to help you rebuild a proper company."

Stiger took that to mean he could not reject them, no matter what Kromen had agreed to. Should he protest to the general, Stiger would likely make an enemy of Karol, who seemed to sincerely want to help. Stiger simply nodded, knowing that he was now stuck with the two sergeants, for good or ill.

"You can promote anyone else within the company you wish. It is yours to do with as you like."

"Yes, sir," Stiger said. "Do you have any detailed maps of the countryside between the encampment and Vrell?"

Karol nodded. "I will speak to General Mammot and arrange to have a set of maps sent to you." He looked sourly down at his own tea, which he had yet to touch. "You can ask for anything reasonable you may require from the depots."

"Written orders to that effect may help, sir," Stiger suggested hopefully. He had encountered more than one supply officer who believed his job was to accumulate supplies rather than distribute them.

"Your formal orders should be arriving from General Kromen shortly," Colonel Karol said. "If there is one thing the general does efficiently, it is the delivery of formal orders. That said, I will send you an amended set later this evening, authorizing you to requisition anything from the supply depots you reasonably require. Will that be sufficient?"

"Entirely." Stiger was very satisfied. At least he should not want for supply.

The door opened and two sergeants entered. Once again, the conversation stopped. Several of the officers nearest the entrance looked as if they were about to protest in outrage. This was officer country, and a refuge from the brutes. Colonel Karol called for the two sergeants to join him, and with that, any potential protest died. They approached the table and snapped to attention.

"Sergeants Blake and Ranl, I would like to introduce your new commanding officer, Captain Stiger," Karol announced. Conversation in the mess erupted at the mention of Stiger, with many officers turning to get a better look. Karol shot them an irritated look.

The two sergeants were older men, both in their late thirties. They had the quiet look and an air of competence that came from hard service. They appeared tough old salts and showed no emotion at being introduced to a Stiger.

"I am transferring you both to the Eighty-Fifth," Colonel Karol said. "You are to help whip the men into shape."

The two sergeants said nothing, but continued to stand at attention.

Colonel Karol turned to Stiger. "They can show you to your new company. Questions?"

Stiger had some, but decided not to ask anything at this time. He would need to get to know Colonel Karol better before probing for answers. Besides, there were too many interested parties in the mess.

"No, sir," Stiger responded. "I believe I have all I need at the moment."

"Very well...I will leave you to them, Captain. Congratulations on your new command. I wish you the best of luck. Oh, and welcome to the Twenty-Ninth Legion." With that, Colonel Karol stood. Stiger and Eli politely stood as well. Karol nodded slightly, then turned and left without another word.

"Please sit," Stiger said, resuming his place at the table. The two sergeants sat as directed. They showed no discomfort at sitting at a table in the officers' mess with a Stiger and an elf. Perhaps the colonel had given him good men after all. Based on how he had handled Captain Handi, the colonel definitely did not seem the sort to tolerate fools. "This is Lieutenant Eli'Far. Have either of you served with the High Born?"

"Aye, sir," Sergeant Blake admitted in a rough voice. "Both of us served in the Wilds, with the Able Legion."

Stiger nodded, pleased. Among the legions, the campaign in the Wilds was the stuff of legend, having taken place a little over twenty years ago. The elves had joined the empire for the campaign. It was the last time the nations of the High Born had fought alongside humans before retreating within their own borders. It had been a very difficult campaign, nearly shattering those legions that had been involved. If these men had survived that ordeal, they were likely very good and, more importantly, had had their share of hard experience.

"Do you know the Eighty-Fifth?" Eli asked.

"Aye, sir," Ranl admitted, a sour expression crossing his face. "We were asked to look them over. They are a terrible bunch. Discipline is awful and they have lost their self-respect."

"Well, the Eighty-Fifth is now ours," Stiger growled. "We are going to reform them."

The sergeants said nothing. They did not look terribly thrilled.

"Can both of you write and manipulate numbers?" Stiger asked.

"We both can," Sergeant Blake confirmed.

"Who is better with numbers?"

"That would be Ranl, sir," Sergeant Blake said quickly, nodding at the other sergeant. Ranl shot Blake a half-mocking sour look. Stiger could tell both men were old comrades and good friends.

"Ranl, you will keep the company books," Stiger ordered.

"I was afraid of that, sir," Sergeant Ranl said with a lop-sided smile. "I was cursed with an affinity to numbers."

"We will go see the men," Stiger continued. "I want the company packed to march as soon as possible. We will be leaving the encampment today."

"Today?" Blake asked, obviously surprised. "Sir, it is already mid-afternoon and will be dark by the time we can get them organized to leave."

"We are leaving," Stiger said firmly, lowering his voice so only those at the table could hear. "This encampment is a deathtrap. I think we will be safer outside it than in."

Blake and Ranl shared a rapid look before Blake nodded in agreement.

"Some friendly advice, sir...I would avoid the water if I were you." He gestured at the tea on the table, a look of disgust crossing his face. "Drinking that is sure to give you the green apple quick step."

The conversation abruptly ceased once again as the door banged open loudly. All heads turned to see Captain Handi enter, a stormy expression on his face. The staff captain briefly scanned the officers in the mess until he found Stiger.

He stalked over. "Your orders," he hissed, acid in his voice. He threw a sealed envelope down upon the table, then turned and left the officers' mess without another word. Stiger noticed that the pampered captain was dripping wet, and his once perfectly polished boots were covered in mud and muck. The hum of conversation resumed with more animation. Camp life was tedious and any drama, no matter how petty, helped to alleviate the boredom.

As they watched the pompous captain leave, Ranl flashed an evil smile. "I do believe I might enjoy serving under your command, sir," he said.

"Right," Stiger responded, scooping up the orders and standing. He would study them later. "Let's go see the men."

The men were not particularly impressive. Paraded for review, they were standing before their tents, clearly miserable under a steady downpour. Their current misery was a secondary concern for the captain. The sooner they all got out of the encampment, the better.

Stiger had just finished introducing himself and explaining his expectations, which he considered simple. In short: honor, courage, and loyalty to both unit and empire. They were the watchwords by which Stiger lived his life, and he would communicate them by example and force of will alone if necessary.

Lieutenant Ikely was standing beside him, clearly nervous at having abruptly learned that he would be under the command of a Stiger. The lieutenant was a young man, fit, with close-cropped, sandy-blond hair. He had a pleasant and positive air about him that contrasted starkly with the other officers in the encampment. Since the lieutenant was also new, perhaps he had simply not had time to become jaded. Or it may have been youthful optimism and excitement at his first posting.

Stiger was familiar with the Ikely family. A loyal and honorable house, though they lacked the prestige of senatorial rank. Not formidable enough to be powerbrokers themselves, the Ikelys were clients of the Agadow family, which made them a loosely tied ally to the Stigers, and not a direct enemy. Stiger was lucky in that respect. Having a member of a rival family as his second might have complicated things a bit.

"Sergeant Blake," Stiger called gruffly. He had thought about adding to his comments, but decided against it. There would be time for additional words later. It was time to leave.

"Sir?" Blake responded, turning toward his captain. The men wore their helmets, which kept their faces and hair reasonably dry in the rain.

"Break down the tents and gather up the mule train."

There was a collective groan at this, which demonstrated to Stiger just how far discipline had fallen. The men might typically complain to the sergeants and corporals, but in Stiger's experience, they would never dare before an officer. Such displays could prove fatal for the common legionary, as any officer had the right to flog a man to death at will for even minor infractions.

"Aye, sir!" Blake replied, becoming visibly enraged at the men's response to the captain's orders. The sergeant turned, along with Ranl, shouting orders laced with profanity and directing legionaries to their tasks. Both sergeants waded into the ranks that were falling out. Men who did not move fast enough were cuffed or shoved roughly by the two large sergeants. Ikely moved forward to help.

What should have taken less than thirty minutes consumed more than an hour. Stiger was not at all surprised. The men moved almost lethargically. Though he did not like it, he understood why. Filthy and ragged, they were living like animals. Half the men were missing proper marching sandals. More disturbing, they looked hungry—almost starved. It was a testament to the supply problems in the encampment.

Stiger recalled the cavalry lieutenant asking about conditions on the road to Aeda. Though he and Eli had not encountered any problems, perhaps the enemy was much more active than he had realized. No matter, he thought. The first objective was to get the men out of the encampment and to a place where they could clean up and get a proper meal. Then the real work of setting things right could begin.

"Sergeant Ranl," Stiger called, beckoning the sergeant over to him. Ranl came at a trot, sloshing through the stinking muck to where Stiger had been conferring with Lieutenant Ikely. "I want you and the lieutenant to go find the officer in charge of supply. Get us food for three months, extra mules, and a couple of wagons. If you are able, make sure the mules are in good shape. I also want fresh footwear and tunics for the men. General Kromen made it clear we can have anything we want."

"Yes, sir," the lieutenant said, making an effort to conceal his nervousness.

Stiger pulled out a gold imperial talon, more than a year's salary for the common legionary, and handed it to the lieutenant. "Present this with my compliments to the officer in charge. You can share my orders from General Kromen, should he require them. Colonel Karol is writing an amendment to our orders to requisition whatever we require. Make sure the supply officer understands that should he keep me waiting on the amendment, I will not be pleased. Understood?"

"Yes, sir," Ikely answered.

"Good." Stiger nodded. The lieutenant and sergeant saluted and left.

Holding the reins of his horse, Stiger gazed at his surroundings. Imperial legionary encampments were expected to be well-ordered, clean, and maintained. Kromen was a powerbroker in the senate and he was trying to increase his family's prestige by making a go of it here in the South. He had never had any real military experience and had simply purchased, called in favors, and bribed his way into his current position. Stiger saw nothing wrong with such political machinations. It had been done before and would be done again. It was expected that imperial senators would advance their careers and family interests through a successful military command and set an example for the other families by bringing glory to the empire. It was why many sitting senators had begun their careers serving with the legions in their youth. Military service to the empire was considered a pathway to future political success, which in turn usually led to the accumulation of vast wealth, power, and fame.

It was widely understood General Kromen was trying to make up for his lack of service by suppressing the Southern rebellion. Stiger suspected that General Mammot had also not served, meaning the top two leadership positions running the war in the South were held by amateurs. Both had likely also stacked the legions with their own pet officers and clients, leaving only a few hardened professionals like Karol on hand. It appeared that managing legions under their command had proved more than a match for both generals, and the evidence of that was plain.

The legionaries, who had been stuck in this encampment for months, looked like ghosts to Stiger. With no sanitation system, everything was contaminated, including the stream running through the valley from which the men drew their water. Diseases worse than simple dysentery were likely burning their way through the encampment. Hopefully, his men, having recently arrived, had not had time to catch anything too terrible, like the Yellow Death.

Stiger pulled himself up onto his horse. His mount, a stallion named Nomad, kept lifting his hooves to keep them from sinking deeper into the muck. It wasn't hard to tell he was unsettled.

"Easy, boy," Stiger soothed, absently patting his horse's neck. He continued to study the camp, from which thousands of fires smoked lazily upward into what had become a steady rain. Several scarecrows of men from other units trudged by, heads bowed against the downpour. There was a general apathy about them that Stiger found thoroughly disturbing.

The misery was awful. It was overwhelming and it offended Stiger's sensibilities as a legionary officer. Four entire imperial legions, some of the most powerful fighting formations the world had ever seen, were rotting away before his eyes. Not for the first time, he found himself angry that such good men should be treated in such a manner. At this rate, General Kromen was sowing the seeds for a disaster. The gods alone knew what would happen when winter finally arrived and the ground hardened. At that point, the annual fighting season would begin, as both armies would finally be able to move.

"So, this is what defeat is like," Stiger said to himself, shaking his head in utter disgust. In the North, under General Treim's command, he had led a first-rate company. Here in the South, his fortunes seemed to have changed drastically. The gods could be fickle, he knew, offering their fortune one moment and withholding it the next. Twisting the reins with a sudden surge of anger, Stiger resolved to set his own fate. He would make his new command into a first-rate company, very different from the rot that surrounded him. The Eighty-Fifth would become the finest company in the South. He would set an example for others to follow.

The gods had given him a challenge. Anger boiling his blood, Stiger ground his teeth and swore he would accept their challenge and succeed.

THREE

The company finally marched out through the main gate around five bells in the afternoon. Stiger sat astride Nomad, calmly watching as his two-hundred-odd men, along with ten company mules, slogged through the mud. Several nearby gate sentries watched sullenly as the company moved past. The sentries looked on with deadened expressions, as if they were only going through the motions of living. Tarnished and rusted, their armor suffered from lack of care. Their shields, a legionary's most prized possession, had also seen better days. These they had leaned carelessly against an interior wall of the gatehouse, bottoms resting in the mud. If they could, Stiger wondered idly, would the men march out with him?

The rain had returned to a steady drizzle. The weather was simply wretched and, judging by the clouds, might soon worsen. Despite the poor conditions and the inadequacy of the men, Stiger was somewhat satisfied. This new command, no matter how risky the mission, was, in reality, an independent command. He would have a free hand in developing his men.

The captain was under no illusion that his job would be easy. His command lacked self-respect and discipline. He would instill both while working to rebuild them into an effective, cohesive fighting force. They had learned to become indolent and lazy. He would drill them to exhaustion, working and pushing them to be better. Under his hand, the men would relearn what it meant to be a legionary in the service of the empire.

Though his men did not yet realize it, he cared deeply about their welfare. Stiger would devote a great deal of his personal time and attention to making their lives better. At first, they would believe he was like every other worthless officer they had known, intent on making life as miserable as possible. He would force them to change, and they would hate him for it. Yes, they would hate him, even as they began to once again respect themselves.

Judging by the sullen and hostile looks he was receiving, they were already well on their way to developing that hate. Over time, their attitude would change and eventually they would recognize the purpose behind his actions. If that didn't happen, one of the poor wretches was likely to stick him with a knife when his back was turned. It was not unheard of for unpopular officers to meet an untimely end at the hands of their own men. Usually such outrages occurred during the chaos of battle, though sometimes it happened in camp in the middle of the night. Stiger frowned. He would have to be careful, as he had had personal experience with this sort of thing in the past. A traitorous sergeant had once tried to end Stiger's life.

Eli cantered up as Stiger sat contemplating his men and the job ahead. The elf was exceedingly perceptive and, having sensed his friend's mood, said nothing as the company continued to march by. Eli knew Stiger would speak when he was ready.

"Sorry lot, are they not?" Stiger said finally, without turning. It was more of a statement than a question. The captain sighed heavily, rubbing the stubble on his jaw with his right hand while his left loosely held the reins.

"Far from the poorest I have seen," Eli responded neutrally. Stiger rather suspected his friend was being kind, not wishing to burden him with his true judgment. "I do believe, though, as you humans speak, that you have your work sliced out for you."

"Say and cut," Stiger corrected, with a slight trace of amusement. Eli had picked up the common tongue spoken throughout much of the empire, but occasionally he still mixed up his words. Eli, like all elves, strove for personal perfection in nearly every task, no matter how insignificant. It nettled the elf every time Stiger caught him mangling the common tongue. These days, however, such mangling was less frequent than it had been when they first met. Stiger wished he could speak Elven as well as Eli spoke Common.

"I found a nice location," Eli reported, clearly not wanting to admit to a human he had made such an error. "An old farmstead about four miles from this valley. The farmhouse and barn appear to have been abandoned for several years. Both will require a bit of work to keep the rain out. The barn is of good size and will provide adequate shelter for the animals. The main planting field is overgrown, but with some clearing it will provide plenty of space for the company to camp and train. There is also a small stream running behind the farmhouse."

"Sounds like a pleasant spot to begin rebuilding the company," Stiger responded, still watching his bedraggled men slog sullenly along.

"I took the liberty of instructing Lieutenant Ikely on which road to take," Eli informed his friend as he pulled the hood of his cloak up farther in an attempt to keep the drizzle out.

Stiger was silent for several moments. He looked back over at the gate. "A sad state, this place."

"I will readily admit I have not seen its like," Eli admitted, glancing over at the wooden walls of the encampment. "Whether they are keeping the enemy out or the legionaries in is, I think, up for debate." Eli paused and looked over at Stiger. "I feared for your health."

"I wish I had your constitution, my friend," Stiger sighed. He had never seen Eli with even a case of the sniffles, let alone anything more serious.

After a few minutes, the last of the men stumbled and sloshed by, followed by Sergeant Ranl and four battered, old supply wagons on their last legs. The wagons were covered and packed full of supplies. Trailing the wagons were the ten additional heavily loaded company mules, two or three tethered to the tail end of each wagon. The mules, like the men before them, struggled in the churned-up mud of the road. Sergeant Ranl handled the lead wagon himself, holding the reins loosely. The sergeant nodded to the captain as the wagon struggled past. The captain nodded in return.

Stiger waited 'til the last of the wagons crawled by before he brought Nomad to a slow trot alongside the road, where the ground was a little firmer. Eli kept pace next to him. At the far head of the column, Lieutenant Ikely steered his horse off to one side, angling the company onto the proper road. Next to the lieutenant slogged the company's standard-bearer. The red battle standard drooped, heavy from the rain. A faded numeral eight-five was emblazoned on it. Stiger thought the standard looked exceedingly sad.

For some time the two friends rode together next to the wagons, before Stiger broke the silence with a question.

"Did you happen across any rebels while you were scouting for a campsite?" Stiger would have bet two imperial gold talons that the legions were under direct enemy observation. Had Stiger been the rebel general, he would have the legions closely watched. If anyone were able to prove that theory, it would be Eli. There was no better scout than an elf.

"Yes," Eli admitted. "I discovered two concealed positions. When time permits, I shall perform a more thorough search to determine if there are any others."

"Good," Stiger replied with a slight growl and glanced over at Eli. "I will want them eliminated before we march to Vrell. They must not report our departure."

Eli gave a nod of understanding. They continued on, Stiger becoming lost in his thoughts on everything to accomplish before they departed for Vrell.

Four long, muddy hours were consumed slogging to the campsite Eli had selected. Besides the rain and mud, his legionaries were poor marchers. Stiger had been taught, from the first moment that he had entered service, that those who could not march were useless.

A legionary should be able to march twenty miles under full kit without becoming blown. A full kit included shield, armor, sword, spear (if required), mess kit, personal gear, and issued rations. Imperial spears were heavy, usually weighing around nine pounds, and his men had not been issued any. Their load was light, and yet they were having difficulty making just four miles! Had the campsite been a couple miles farther, he was confident many would have collapsed.

The sun had completely set by the time the company arrived at the campsite. Thankfully, the rain had also stopped falling. The moon, which was beginning to poke through a scattered cloud cover, provided a bit of pale light. Wet, tired, and muddy, the men staggered along, feet catching on branches and fieldstones as they stumbled into the campsite.

Sergeant Ranl and Lieutenant Ikely had thoughtfully secured and brought along a supply of dried logs in one of the wagons. They had also brought a small supply of dragon's breath, a low-quality flammable liquid made from olives, specifically used for starting fires in damp conditions. A fire was made while a search was organized for semi-dry branches and logs. These were added to the growing blaze, and soon the camp had a single large bonfire blazing away, driving back the dampness and darkness and restoring weary spirits.

Per his custom, Stiger walked the outskirts of the campsite to obtain a firsthand look of the perimeter. It was exactly as Eli had described it, overgrown and abandoned. If Eli said something was so, it usually was. Stiger had long ceased questioning his friend in such matters. As Stiger made his way around, the sergeants were busy moving about the camp, supervising the clearing of brush and the erection of tents. The company had no corporals, so Ikely was assisting as best he could.

The captain paused briefly to study the activity behind him as the men worked, then continued his examination of the camp perimeter. Though it was dark and little could be seen, Stiger had learned the hard way that wherever he camped, it was wise to have at least a basic grasp of the lay of the land. Should they come under attack, such knowledge of the ground could prove to be the difference between life and death. When the sun came up, he would do a second, more thorough study of the perimeter and surrounding terrain.

Eli had chosen well, he concluded after coming full circle on his walk around the perimeter. He was at the backside of the campsite, where the stream gurgled happily. It was a fine spot to begin the process of rebuilding the men. The site had everything he needed: running water, plenty of room for training, and, most importantly, it was secluded. A little scrub forest had grown up around the farm, the result of long-abandoned and untended lands.

The main encampment was far enough away that his company would effectively be isolated from the sickness, disease, poor morale, and resentment being bred within its walls. There would be some contact, but Stiger would do everything he could to keep that to a minimum. Stiger himself, however, was not far enough away from the petty intrigue. Along this line of thought, his right hand had involuntarily found the pommel of his sword, gripping it tightly. He was sure he had neither seen nor heard the last of Captain Handi.

Stiger suddenly became aware of a strange quiet—or perhaps a sense of disquiet—in the trees on the other side of the stream. The bugs had stopped singing their nightly tune. The captain mentally tensed, but showed no physical reaction. He casually shifted his stance, carefully removing his hand from his sword pommel, though keeping it close. He studied the tree line on the opposite side of the stream. The tension left him as he realized what it was that had set him on edge.

"It is a very good site," Stiger said quietly, shifting his stance and eyeing the dark woods beyond the stream with some amusement. He crossed his arms and cracked a smile. "Excellent try."

Eli, silent as a fox, stepped out from amongst the trees, almost materializing out of thin air. The elf carefully stepped across the stream, using a couple of large rocks to keep from getting wet. He approached without the slightest trace of a smirk on his perpetually youthful face.

"I admit, I thought I might have caught your mind wandering," Eli frowned. "You look ... shall I say, distracted."

Eli had quit the column early during its march. He had taken it upon himself to perform a more thorough reconnoitering of the area surrounding the company's campsite. As a result, he had been gone for several hours.

"How very perceptive of you," Stiger replied wryly. His heart was still beating hard, though it would never do to admit it to his friend. The two had been playing this game for years. Each would occasionally attempt to sneak up, unobserved, on the other. All elven children played the game, and Eli had introduced Stiger to it. Deeply impressed with Eli's skill, Stiger had resolved to learn all he could in an attempt to emulate the elf's nearly effortless ability to move through the forest unheard and unseen. Under his friend's patient tutelage, Stiger had become quite skilled, though he could not quite reach his friend's level of mastery. In the end, Stiger had come to the conclusion that if he had several hundred years to become one with the forest, he would be able to easily match Eli's skill.

"Thinking about Miranda?" Eli asked with a straight face.

"No," Stiger responded firmly. "I am not."

"You had a choice, you know…" Eli said. "Life at court with a beautiful lady, or in the field."

"Are there any rebels about?" Stiger growled. Though he could not see it in the gloom, he was sure there was a twinkle in his friend's eye.

"There was one who came around," Eli admitted, waving behind him, apparently giving up on nettling his friend, at least for the moment. "I was able to identify several other observation posts."

Stiger sighed. He had suspected as much. He was silent for a time as he considered the matter, turning to study the bustling campsite where the men worked.

"I think it unlikely the rebels should strike us so close to the main encampment," Stiger said as he began to walk back toward the center of the camp. Eli moved with him. Stiger suspected that no matter how low Kromen's army had sunk and deteriorated, the legend of legion prowess and power should keep the enemy cautious. He hoped so, at any rate.

"Agreed," Eli said, side-stepping a fieldstone in his path. "I saw no indication of large concentrations of rebels nearby. There is, however, significant evidence of imperial cavalry patrols."

"At least General Kromen is keeping some part of his army employed ... even if it is only the cavalry," Stiger said sourly. In Stiger's experience, most cavalry troopers were next to useless. Ranks filled with the minor nobility, who had an overly high opinion of their own abilities, the cavalry tended to be arrogant and difficult to work with. It was rare to find a cavalry officer of some worth.

"The enemy lookouts have some ... skill," Eli admitted grudgingly.

Stiger glanced sharply at his friend. Such a comment, coming from the elf, was somewhat telling, and that worried him.

"The observation posts," Eli continued, "that I have identified so far are situated in rough terrain with heavy undergrowth, perfect for good concealment."

"Where our fine cavalry is unlikely to venture," Stiger growled. Eli nodded by way of reply and Stiger shook his head in disgust. That meant that General Kromen's cavalry patrols had accomplished nothing other than exercising the horses and providing the pampered troopers a brief respite from the boredom of camp life.

"I believe we will post additional sentries to be on the safe side," Stiger said, after a moment's reflection.

"It should prove good practice for the march to Vrell," Eli offered optimistically.

Stiger stopped and turned to his friend. "Lieutenant Ikely tells me the company has ten men who are rated as scouts and skirmishers. Take them out tonight. Find out if they are any good. They are yours to work as you see fit. Weed out the ones who do not have potential and are not worth their weight in salt."

"I will do as you ask," Eli said simply. When Eli had first heard the salt saying, he had been confused. Elves typically kept to themselves, rarely, if ever, comingling or socializing with humans. As a result, human maxims sometimes tended to be difficult for an elf to comprehend. Stiger had had to explain that at one time legionaries had been paid in salt, which they then bartered for goods and services. Since elves only bartered services and goods amongst themselves, it was something his friend had easily grasped. Eli still found it odd how legionaries were paid in coin, seeing little value in metal other than what it could be shaped into.

"One other request. The men have been subsisting on half rations of rice and salt pork," Stiger said, resuming his trek with Eli toward the dilapidated barn. Salt pork was a staple for the legions in the field. "They have not had fresh meat in months, and besides... you know how much I hate salt pork."

"Perhaps I can find a nice solid buck," Eli suggested with a smile, showing off his small needle-like teeth, characteristic of his race.

Elves rarely showed their teeth. To humans, the teeth of the High Born looked more like they belonged in the mouth of a predator. Stiger had been around elves long enough that such smiles no longer bothered him.

"I crossed several game trails," the elf continued. "Surprisingly, the area around the main encampment is rich with game. One would think the legions would have sent out foragers to supplement standard rations. Perhaps this is an indication of fear?"

"Perhaps...though let's take advantage of our good fortune. A hot meal for breakfast should do the men well," Stiger said, avoiding the subject, for he knew his friend was likely onto the heart of the matter. If true, it did not bode well for imperial aspirations in the South. Stiger suspected that the rebels had convinced General Kromen that they were a real threat to his army. The general had responded by sealing himself and his legions inside the main encampment behind an imposing series of fortifications, while dispersing the auxiliaries around the countryside. Perhaps the rebels were more competent than was widely believed, or maybe it was just further evidence of General Kromen's incompetence.

They walked the remainder of the distance through tall, uncut grass in silence. At least it wasn't mud, Stiger thought. The rain had stopped. Stiger hoped that had been the last of it, though it was possible more would blow through during the night. In a few weeks, the rains would stop altogether. The temperature would cool and the ground would harden, signaling winter's arrival. Southern winters were very mild in comparison to those in the North. Yet, unlike in the North, the arrival of winter would mean the beginning of the fighting season.

As he and Eli entered the barn, Stiger briefly wondered what would happen when the rebels marched. Would the legions be ready to receive them? Would he have the time to fully prepare his men for the savage press of the line and the horror of a real battle?

He studied the interior of the barn. Several lanterns had been hung about, poorly illuminating much of the interior. The horses and mules were secured inside. With all of the animals packed close together, the barn was considerably warmer than outside. It was in terrible shape, with plenty of evidence of having leaked badly during the rains. Patched and repaired, it would prove adequate. Once again, Stiger thought, Eli had chosen well.

Several men were busily tending to the mules. Having removed the animals' harnesses, they were now in the process of brushing the animals down. The mules and the officers' horses munched happily on hay and oats as the men worked.

Stiger went to Nomad and removed his saddle, setting it on a broken stall railing. Taking out a well-worn brush from a saddlebag, he began the process of carefully brushing down his mount. Many officers chose to use their men as servants, frequently having them carry out their grunt work. Even though he had been raised with servants tending to his every need, having his legionaries do his work for him just seemed … somehow wrong. These were fighting men, not slaves. Besides, Stiger preferred to get his hands dirty. Grunt work gave him the chance to think, process the day, and prepare for the next. More importantly, he knew it was important to set a good example. He wanted his men to see that their new captain was not above some manual work. If he attended to the smallest details, hopefully his men would do the same.

Eli began working silently and meticulously on his own mount, Wind Runner. The elf's horse, smaller in stature than Stiger's, was a rare forest breed, highly prized amongst horse traders for their intelligence and sure-footedness. The two worked away, aware that the men in the barn were watching their every move. It was hardly unexpected.

Stiger could read the doubt and fear in their eyes. They did not know what being commanded by a Stiger would mean. They wondered if they were ultimately to be sacrificed for the next generation of Stiger prestige and glory.

The reality was much simpler than that. He wasn't interested in glory or fame. Stiger was simply intent on doing his duty to the empire. With duty came honor. To Stiger, nothing was more important.

He would need to work hard to gain their trust. To that end, the men would first need to once again believe in themselves. That would come after a lot of hard work.

Hate and fear him they might, yet in the end they would become his men and he would become their captain.

FOUR

Stiger ran a hand across his freshly shaved face with some satisfaction as he checked his work with a small hand-held mirror. His morning toilet had included a badly needed shave conducted while seated on a large rock alongside the stream. Shaving in the field was a near art, especially if done well, which he had. He returned the mirror to his small toiletry bag and then filled his two canteens.

He sat back on the rock and took a deep breath. He enjoyed the feeling of the crisp, cool morning air. The rain and humidity that had plagued the region for the past few days had moved on. Fall was nearly at hand, and this morning, one could tell. Though winters in the South were mild compared to the North, there was a sense that the seasons were changing.

Stiger looked up at the sky. The sun was nearly up and would soon begin making her daily climb, warming the land far below. He loved the quiet and tranquility of the early morning; it was why each day he made a point of rising early. The peacefulness would soon be shattered when the sergeants began waking the company.

The captain stood, turned, and started walking back to the rundown farmhouse, where he had spent the previous night. He held the straps of his canteens and toiletry bag loosely with his right hand, swinging them slightly as he went. Today was his first real opportunity to begin getting the men into shape, and he felt a renewed sense of purpose as he approached the farmhouse. The day ahead promised to be a busy one. It would be a real challenge.

He reached the back edge of the dilapidated farmhouse, running through in his mind what he needed to accomplish before starting work with the men. His sword needed oiling and his armor, which he had left next to his bedroll, required some attention as well. He also needed to put some time into his saddle for—

The attack came without warning as he rounded the corner of the farmhouse. Stiger sensed sudden movement to his left. Reflexes took over, honed by years of training, and he instinctively dodged to the right before he fully understood what was happening. A knife flashed past, aimed at his neck, glinting slightly with the morning light. It missed, the point lightly scraping across the skin of his neck.

The captain's left hand snapped out, striking the assassin with a hard blow to the side of the head. This elicited a startled cry a moment before the two crashed together violently. The canteens and toiletry bag went flying as Stiger fought to remain on his feet. The assassin's momentum and weight carried him farther to the right, threatening to take him to the ground.

The assassin managed to gain a powerful grip on Stiger's shoulder. Subconsciously, Stiger understood the knife was being wielded poorly. The assassin brought it around for another strike. Stiger hastily hooked one of his legs around the back of one of the assassin's. As he did so, he threw all of his weight suddenly backward and to the right, using the assassin's momentum against him, tripping him, while at the same time managing to twist away and out of the grip. In the blink of an eye, and nearly as quickly as the attack had begun, the captain was free and on his feet.

Stiger spun around, booted foot snapping out toward the assassin's knife hand. The man was stumbling back to his feet. The kick connected violently, almost powerful enough to shatter bones. The assassin shrieked in pain as the knife went flying, landing a few feet away in the dirt. The man stepped backwards, cradling his hand to his chest.

Without letting up, Stiger delivered another kick to the assassin's side. The blow stole his attacker's wind and he dropped to his knees. The captain delivered another kick, knocking the man to the ground, where he landed heavily.

Stiger mentally cursed himself for having let down his guard. This was not the first time an assassin had made an attempt on his life. The assassin rolled away and was struggling to get to his feet.

"My turn," Stiger growled, drawing his own dagger from his boot. He advanced on the assassin, intent on murdering him.

Then he blinked in shock, almost missing a step. The assassin was one of his legionaries! He had expected the possibility that at some point one of his men might make an attempt on his life, but he had not expected it so soon. He had not even been in command for a full day!

The would-be assassin froze. His eyes were drawn to the knife and then the captain's face. Their eyes locked, one set filled with newfound fear and the other with a murderous rage. Blood boiling, the captain took a halting step forward, and then another more determined one. This man must die!

Sergeant Ranl abruptly appeared, taking in the scene in a glance and deducing what had occurred. He stepped between the captain and the assassin, hauling the man roughly to his feet. Stiger hesitated again. Within moments, drawn by the commotion, a crowd of men gathered. Lieutenant Ikely arrived with short sword in hand, pushing through the press and looking nervously at the men.

"Are you all right, sir?" the lieutenant asked. The lieutenant also placed himself between the would-be assassin and his captain.

"Bennet," Sergeant Blake thundered in a voice only a sergeant could deliver, shoving men aside as he made his way through the crowd. He retrieved the man's knife from where it had landed in the dirt. "A bad business, this. What in the seven levels were you thinking, man?"

Stiger was breathing heavily, adrenaline pumping through him. He was furious. He had initially suspected the attack was political in nature, an attempt to strike a blow at his house from another house...but so soon from one of his own men? With great effort, he forced himself to calm down. Experience had shown him that in stressful situations, it was best to think clearly.

Sheathing his dagger, Stiger glanced at the faces of the men crowded around. Assaulting an officer was a capital offense, with an immediate sentence of death. The concern written across many of the faces present was plain. Stiger concluded that the would-be assassin was a respected man amongst the rank and file. Otherwise he would not have warranted such concern.

Stiger turned back to Bennet, held securely by Sergeant Ranl. Bennet was big, strong, and tall—a near mountain of a man—just how the legions preferred their legionaries. His face had gone deathly pale. Bennet knew his own personal doom was at hand.

Stiger's eyes narrowed as he studied the wretch. He wanted nothing more than to string this skulking shitbag up by his entrails and let him die a slow death. The man had meant to take Stiger's life, and to the captain there was nothing more personal. Having succeeded, Bennet would have denied him the opportunity to continue to serve his family and the empire with honor. Stiger's rage toward Bennet blazed hot and he almost took a step toward the man, ready to just end it now. Once again, and this time with great effort, he forced himself to calm down. As reason returned, he realized there might be an opportunity to turn this to his advantage.

Stiger took a deep breath, bringing on the studied calm that he had learned to project during battle. Sparing another look at the concerned faces of his men gathered around, he became convinced that there was indeed an opportunity to manipulate the situation to his gain.

"Are you all right, sir?" Lieutenant Ikely asked once again, voice firm. The lieutenant was not looking at Stiger, but at the men around them. His sword was still out. "Sir?"

"Lieutenant, I am fine," Stiger affirmed, loud enough for those gathered to hear. "Bennet here simply asked for a demonstration in my knife fighting technique. I guess you could say things got a little spirited. He is larger than I am and strong as an ox. I am confident Bennet can now attest to the fact that skill and technique will win any day over brute strength."

"A demonstration?" Sergeant Blake asked, turning a skeptical look on his captain, clearly not believing a word of it. He fingered the sharp edge of Bennet's knife. "Are you certain, sir?"

"It looked as if he tried to assassinate you, sir," Sergeant Ranl stated, still retaining his vice-like grip on Bennet. As big and strong as the legionary was, the sergeant was the stronger man. Bennet was helpless in his grip.

Stiger stepped forward and retrieved Bennet's knife from Sergeant Blake. He casually flipped it around and offered the weapon hilt-first to the would-be assassin.

"Sergeant, had someone tried to assassinate me, I can assure you I would have cut him open like a prize pig who had failed to win at the fair," Stiger growled for the benefit of the crowd and to discourage any future attempts. For added emphasis, he used the hilt of the dagger to trace a line from Bennet's navel to his sternum, looking the would-be assassin meaningfully in the eye. Bennet shivered in apparent terror as the captain casually retraced the line back down.

Satisfied that he had made his point, Stiger once again offered the knife back to Bennet. Ranl was slow to release the man. Bennet, hands shaking violently, carefully took the knife from his captain. As he did so, he never took his eyes from his captain's gaze.

Stiger turned his back on Bennet and addressed the crowd of legionaries. Nearly the entire company had gathered around, absent those on duty. The looks of concern had changed to expressions of relief. The men never enjoyed seeing one of their own put to death. At the very least, such acts reminded them of their own mortality.

"Hand-to-hand fighting is a very critical skill to learn." Stiger raised his voice. "I was taught to handle a knife by one particular sergeant, a real mean, dirty son of a bitch. The kind who never fights fair.

" 'Stiger,' he said to me, 'when it gets to knives … there is you and him … better him go than you. How him dies matters little, as long as it's him.' "

A chuckle ran through the crowd. They had heard similar statements from training sergeants and had not expected to hear such from an officer.

"That training has saved my life on more than one occasion." Stiger looked from man to man. He paused a moment to let that sink in. They were not stupid. No matter what fiction he had just presented to them, they understood that Bennet had just tried to kill their captain. Bennet, clearly a respected man, had failed. Amongst the legions, strength and fighting prowess were respected above all else. It was becoming apparent their captain was not some pampered fop who had purchased his commission to impress the ladies.

"We," Stiger gestured at the two sergeants, "are going to teach you how to fight and fight dirty, so that if it comes to knives and fists... the other poor bastard is the one who ends up fodder for the crows."

Stiger took a quick breath. The adrenaline was still pumping through his veins, and his hands were shaking ever so slightly. Caught up in the moment, the men did not notice. He saw Eli, who had most likely just returned from hunting and evaluating the scouts, at the back of the crowd. The elf's youthful face was an unreadable mask, concealing any emotions. Eli simply nodded in greeting, though Stiger thought he could read a slight note of disapproval in his friend's eyes.

"I moved us out of the main encampment because it is rife with disease," Stiger continued. "Within a few weeks' time, had we remained, many of you would have become sick and died. Today... well, today we clean up. We set up a proper camp, a clean camp."

Stiger casually took a few steps to his left, moving away from Bennet, allowing his words to sink in. Several of the men nodded. He had wanted the men to understand why he had moved them. He also intended to clearly lay out his expectations. If the men knew what he wanted and why he wanted it that particular way, things would go easier.

"I don't know about you, but I am sick and tired of salt pork," Stiger said, gesturing toward Eli at the back of the crowd. The men turned to look. "I sent Lieutenant Eli'Far and the scouts last night on a little hunting expedition. Lieutenant, tell us what you bagged?"

"Several large bucks," Eli responded, his elven voice ringing clearly on the crisp morning air. It came across somewhat alien to human ears. "Our hunt was quite successful. We even managed a roosting pheasant and a moose to boot." They were hungry, and Stiger could tell the news was more than welcome, even if it came from an elf. In time, they would learn to trust Eli as he did. Grins broke out, followed by a ragged cheer.

"As I said, today we clean up, set a proper camp, and feast. Tomorrow we begin work, and I mean hard work. We have a job to do, and as long as we have a job to do, we stay out of that disease-infested mud pit of an encampment." Stiger paused a moment. He was not above using the men's bellies to begin winning their respect. "I will make you a promise. I will turn you into proper legionnaires. I will care for you. I will work to keep you alive and, when possible, well-fed. All I ask in return is that you do your utmost and perform your duty. I expect all of you to honor the empire and fight for your family, the company."

"If we get fresh meat," one legionary called from the back, "I will fight for you, sir!"

A cheer went up at that. Stiger smiled in reply.

"Lieutenant," Stiger said loudly, looking over at Ikely. At some point, the lieutenant, sensing the danger had passed, had sheathed his short sword. He looked much relieved.

"Yes, sir?" Ikely answered just as loudly.

"Every man is to go to the stream and have a proper toilet."

A groan went up at this statement, and the men shifted uncomfortably. A few conversations broke out amongst them. A proper toilet meant bathing, laundering tunics, and shaving. Many of the men were sporting beards.

"Kits are to be washed, maintained, and cleaned," Stiger continued.

Another collective groan.

"Yes, sir," Lieutenant Ikely responded.

"Lieutenant, see that the bucks are roasted immediately. Each man will stand for inspection. Once he has passed, he can feast and have his fill."

Another hearty cheer went up, followed by a near mad dash for the stream or back to the tents to gather up kits. So eager were they for a good meal, the men did not even wait for orders from the good lieutenant. In moments, only Stiger remained with the sergeants, his lieutenants, and Bennet.

"I am sorry for what I done, sir," Bennet said, returning the captain's gaze. He was trembling violently.

"It was just a demonstration," Stiger reinforced firmly, edging closer to the man. Stiger was impressed the man had the courage to look him in the eyes. Perhaps saving Bennet had not been such a bad thing. "I expect to hear no more of it. Understood?"

"Yes, sir," Bennet answered with a nod.

"Go get yourself cleaned up and fed," Stiger ordered, gesturing in the direction of the stream.

"Yes, sir," Bennet said, and dashed off after the rest.

"Letting that man off could be dangerous, sir," Ranl said after Bennet was out of earshot. "Examples need to be made, or it encourages similar acts."

"Agreed," Stiger said, "but then again, making an example of him may have been just as dangerous."

"Aye," Blake admitted with a deep sigh. "It could have been at that, sir."

"Let us hope this is the end of such ugly business," Stiger said carefully, bending down to pick up both of his canteens and his toiletry bag. Holding them by the straps, he slung them over his right shoulder. "Hell of a way to begin a morning," he breathed to himself with a wry smile. He brushed past the sergeants, continuing on his way into the farmhouse.

Eli joined him. Stiger knew from experience he was about to receive a lecture on carelessness. Like the recent attempt on his life, Stiger was confident the lecture likely would not be his last.

FIVE

"They will require a great deal of my attention," Eli reported of the scouts he had been asked to evaluate. Both he and Stiger were seated on a fallen snag, which had conveniently dropped directly in front of the farmhouse sometime in the last few years. The captain held his mess bowl in one hand and with the other he used a knife to eat. He chewed slowly as he listened to Eli wrap up his report of the previous evening's activities with the scouts.

"I can readily admit they are eager," the elf continued. "It is a rare opportunity, as you are well aware."

Stiger swallowed a smirk of amusement by taking a sip of water from his canteen. Eli was matter-of-fact, without even a hint of intentional superiority. He simply believed what he was saying.

Elves acted as though humans should feel privileged to converse with, let alone learn from them. Stiger supposed that had he a thousand or more years behind him, with an unknowable number ahead, he might feel the same way.

The captain shifted uncomfortably at the thought of his friend's incredible age. Eli was still young for an elf, having been born, by his own admission, just over a thousand years ago. Stiger's mere twenty-six years made him a child by comparison...a blink of an eye for Eli.

Only the youth of the elven nations ever ventured out into the wider world to mix with the other races. The elders, secluded deep in the elven realms, considered wanderlust the impetuous curse of the youthful. It was unheard of for adult elves to venture forth. Stiger had only known one other elf to venture into the outside world, and he was the appointed ambassador to the empire. Even the ambassador was a youth.

Stiger swept his gaze around the campsite. Arranged a bit haphazardly from the hasty setup the night before, the overgrown field was crowded with five-man tents, with bushes and small trees sprouting up between them. It looked very untidy to Stiger's critical eye.

The men sat scattered across the campsite in small groups, eating their first freshly cooked meal in a good long while. Having shaved and cleaned up, they looked a bit more presentable. Still, it was not enough. He had seen allied auxiliaries who appeared more professional than his men looked. Though he hated to admit it, he understood the damage done to his men could not be reversed overnight or by a single meal. It would take time and effort.

The captain noted there was plenty of lively jawing, along with scattered laughs, among the men. None of it carried the ring of the sullen, resentful, or demoralized, which had been evident on the march out. Stiger reckoned that his men viewed any change, no matter how slight, as better than what they'd had, even if a feared Stiger was behind it. Then again, Stiger conceded that the assassination attempt spoke otherwise for some … perhaps even many.

His two sergeants were making the rounds, moving from tent to tent and speaking with each group of men.

They were making sure each got his fill. Good legionaries needed to be well-fed.

At the rate his men were devouring the bucks, Stiger seriously questioned whether there would be anything left over other than bones and marrow. The company cook would likely make soup from the remains. Soup might not be such a bad thing, he mused, thinking on the ordeal that was coming.

Before the day was done, a good number would suffer from cramped bowels and intestinal disorder. He had seen such intestinal distress before, most notably after a long-running siege had been lifted. The men's stomachs would not be fit to handle the rich fare they were now consuming. He would have likely caused a near riot had he attempted to limit their portions. Like children, they would just have to discover on their own. Subsequent meals would be carefully rationed, focusing on proper portion size, until they were able to handle more.

"Plenty of healthy, fat game out there, it would seem," Stiger said thoughtfully. He took another bite, chewing and enjoying the rich, warm juices of the meat.

"Deer, wild hogs, hare…" Eli replied with a shrug. "Sadly, I find it distressing that the legions encamped here should have not picked the surrounding area clean."

"I do not wish…" Stiger began hotly, before mentally checking himself. He would not take Eli's bait, no matter how much he agreed with his friend's sentiment. He did not appreciate when others spoke ill of their superiors, and had made it a habit to not do so himself.

"Until we march for Vrell," Stiger said quietly, after a short hesitation, "I would very much like the scouts and skirmishers out and about each night. Work them hard. We need those men trained up before we march. And the company requires a source of fresh food to build strength and endurance."

"The men look awful," Eli agreed, sweeping a casual look about the campsite. "I feel confident that I will be able to conduct effective training, while at the same time providing fresh fare for the company. May I recruit additional hunters and potential scouts?"

"How many more do you feel you might require?" Stiger asked, grateful Eli had let the subject of General Kromen's incompetence drop.

"Another four or five," Eli answered without hesitation. "I think that will be sufficient for my purposes."

"They are yours," Stiger said. "When we march, I believe we will be relying more heavily than usual on your scouts as our eyes and ears."

"Captain," Lieutenant Ikely said, joining them. "You asked for me?"

"Have you eaten, Lieutenant?" Stiger asked, looking up briefly before popping another bite into his mouth. Ikely seemed to be one of those officers who saw to the men's needs before his own. Amongst the legions, such a quality was rare in an officer. Stiger respected this. He saw a bit of himself in the lieutenant. With the men gorging themselves the way they were, there would be little left. He wanted to make sure the lieutenant had his fill, too.

"Yes sir," the lieutenant answered with a pleasant smile and nod of thanks in Eli's direction. "I have, sir. I must admit, it was the best meal I have had in several weeks."

"I am pleased to hear that," Stiger said, taking another bite of meat. "Give the men an hour to rest and digest. Then set them to work on making a proper home."

"Proper home, sir?" the lieutenant asked, glancing around at the overgrown field. Stiger understood what the lieutenant was thinking. On the march, they had passed other fields that were not so badly overgrown. There were much more suitable places to camp.

"You have been instructed in how to construct a proper legionary marching encampment, correct?" Not only would he be working on the men, he would also be training Ikely to be a first-rate executive officer. Stiger would spend his evenings with his lieutenant, providing instruction on tactics and strategy. He would become the model for Ikely as to how to comport oneself as an officer and leader of men. In short, the captain would be taking the lieutenant under his wing.

"Yes, sir," Ikely replied, coloring slightly. "I have."

"Excellent, then that is what we shall construct," Stiger stated matter-of-factly, as though he did not care whether the field was badly overgrown or not. He took a deep breath, then took a sip of water from his canteen. "I don't see why we can't call this lovely spot home for a while."

Ikely appeared ready to protest, but refrained from doing so. It was clear he had no desire to get on the bad side of his new commanding officer.

"I expect we shall be here for some time."

"Ah ... yes, sir," Ikely said.

"The men need time to recover, train, and condition," Stiger continued. "This appears to be the perfect spot. Think of it as our new home."

"Home, sir, with a few, um ... entrenchments?" Ikely asked, a flicker of amusement crossing his face.

Stiger intended to recapture the spirit that was so much a part of the legionary's life and legend. Clearing the campsite would be exceptionally hard work, and hard work was what the legions excelled at. Life was far from comfortable or leisurely for the common legionary. Next to near constant training, exercises, and drills, a legionary could expect to build camps and buildings, as well as construct fortifications and roads. It was also not unknown for the legions to lend a strong arm during harvest time, should the commanding officer require it.

"Eli here has seen rebels about," Stiger added casually. "I do believe that entrenchments and a proper sentry system might just make us all feel a little more secure at night. Don't you agree?"

"Rebels?" the lieutenant asked, a look of astonishment crossing his face. He glanced around at the scrub forest, beyond the overgrown, tent-studded field. His hand involuntarily reached down to the pommel of his short sword. Stiger concealed a smile by taking another bite. In the forests of Abath, he had had some of the same feelings that his lieutenant was just now having. It was the distinctly uncomfortable sensation of being watched. "So close to the main encampment? Are you sure?"

"Their purpose is observation," Eli explained quietly, in an unnervingly ominous tone. Stiger supposed Eli was having a bit of fun with the lieutenant, though he knew that the elf was also deadly serious. "One even took the trouble to pay us a visit last night."

"I'd have thought the patrols would've kept the scum away," Ikely said, turning to look directly at Eli.

"There are patrols and then there are patrols," Eli said before offering a close-mouthed elfish smile, the kind he used when consciously trying not to unsettle humans. Stiger shook his head slightly at his friend's sense of humor and shot the elf an irritated look. Had an enraged bear been present, Stiger was sure, Eli would have poked it, just to get a reaction. Elven humor was odd, though it usually included some hint of a deeper meaning. Eli undoubtedly thought he was being fiendishly clever by taking another jab at General Kromen.

"Back to setting up a proper camp," Stiger growled, changing the subject once again, before Ikely could respond to Eli's jab. "Please ensure that the latrines are dug toward the downstream side of camp. I do not wish to be drinking someone else's piss. Washing and laundry are to be performed downstream as well."

"Yes, sir." Ikely nodded.

"Also, have the men gather plenty of firewood," Stiger continued, gesturing with his mess knife toward the rows of tents. "I want every tent to have a fire each evening, no exceptions. Understood?"

"Yes, sir," the lieutenant responded eagerly. "I will see to it."

"Lieutenant," Eli spoke up. "I would very much like to know if we have anyone who is a competent hunter. Can you spread the word and kindly ask them to speak with me, if they are so inclined?"

"I do believe there are a few men who might take you up on that," the lieutenant said with another nod. "I will direct them to you."

"Very good," Stiger said, spearing another piece of meat with his knife. He popped it into his mouth. He paused mid-chew, speaking with the side of his mouth. "Inform the sergeants of my orders."

"I will, sir." Ikely nodded and left.

Stiger continued to chew as he watched the lieutenant hurry away. After a moment or two, he returned to studying his men. They had a long way to go in becoming proper legionaries.

Placing his mess bowl down, he took a deep breath of fresh air through his nose and slowly let it out. If he had to drag them, kicking and screaming, all that long way...he would do it.

Grunting with effort, the men toiled under the sun. The cool, crisp morning air had come and gone. It had become hot and humid as the sun climbed into the sky. Shouted orders to "Lift!" or "Heave!" could be heard across the camp.

The perimeter had been carefully walked off. Stiger, Ikely, and the sergeants had marked it for the work parties. The bushes and overgrowth had been uprooted and burned in a large pile outside the camp's perimeter. Once cleared, the tents were moved closer together and better ordered, which would increase the usable space inside the camp after the walls went up.

They felled both large and small trees inside and outside the perimeter with axes. The smaller trees were cut and shaped into support columns. These were buried vertically in the ground in pairs, standing about eight feet tall. The pairs were spaced just far enough apart that the much larger trunks could fit horizontally between them, one on top of another, creating a wall that, when finished, would reach a height of seven feet. It was backbreaking work that had men straining with the effort.

Believing it was best to set an example, Stiger lent a hand. This shocked the men. Officers were almost exclusively drawn from the nobility and never got their hands dirty. Manual labor was beneath them. Yet their captain was working alongside them like a common legionary. The sergeants said nothing as they continued to supervise and also lend a hand when and where it was needed. Stiger well understood; it was not their place to question an officer. Nor would he have tolerated it had they done so.

"'Tis not right," Legionary Palla said under his breath to another as he dug a hole with a shovel.

"The captain decides what is right and what is not." Sergeant Blake, having overheard, spoke in a low, menacing tone loud enough for those nearby to hear. "Is that understood?"

"Yes, Sergeant," Palla responded after a moment, eyes downcast.

"If the captain wants to bend his back and dirty his hands," Blake continued, "that is his business, not yours. Besides, it's one more pair of hands."

"If you say so, sergeant," Palla breathed to himself.

"What was that, you pile of horseshit?" Sergeant Blake asked, taking a step closer to the legionary.

"Nothing, Sergeant," Palla answered as he continued to dig, head bent over his work.

"That is what I thought." Blake turned and walked off to the next group. He shared a brief look with Ranl, who was supervising a detail a few feet away. Ranl shook his head slightly, his eyes flicking briefly toward the captain, who was helping to lay logs for the walls. Blake rolled his eyes and continued on.

Blake's eyes fell upon Lieutenant Ikely, whom he was sure had been just as appalled as the men. The captain's behavior was very unseemly. Yet at the same time, Ikely had clearly felt compelled to follow Captain Stiger's example. Blake could almost imagine Ikely's thinking. How could he stand by while his commanding officer got down in the dirt with the men?

Ikely had joined a detail that was hauling logs. The sergeant chuckled. Most likely for the first time in his life, Ikely was stooping so low as to perform common manual labor alongside the men. It was difficult work, which would surely earn him scrapes and bruises from the rough bark. Ikely was an officer, an educated gentleman from a noble family. This was not the sort of work he was meant to do. Such labor was reserved for the lowborn, who had no hope of rising above their station. He was most probably silently cursing his captain, but he continued to toil alongside the men without audible complaint. Blake was sure it was a blow to his dignity, and that he resented it bitterly, but the sergeant knew he would get over it. Perhaps it would teach him some humility.

As the heat of the day increased, tunics were discarded. Stiger, after some careful deliberation, also removed his own tunic, revealing a hard, lean, muscular torso. A long stripe of a scar, the work of a sword, ran down his upper-left chest. The scar drew a raised eyebrow or two. However, it was the captain's back, when he turned to pick up a mallet, that drew a startled gasp from the two men working with him. They stared at their captain in horror, eyes wide. Others nearby noticed, and the reaction quickly spread. Stiger turned to look at them with a raised eyebrow.

"Have you never seen a flogged back?"

Stiger had considered leaving his tunic on, if only to conceal his shame. His honor was intact, no matter what had been done to him. Still, he felt personally disgraced. Worse, it mortified him that he had even considered concealing it. That thought made his blood boil, for he was a man who hid from no one.

Amongst the legions, a flogged back was a common sight. However, it was a punishment reserved exclusively for the ranks. Officers were never scourged in such a manner. Disgraced gentlemen were dismissed from service or, should the offense prove heinous enough, executed.

The scars that stitched their way across the captain's back were not the result of a simple flogging. The captain had clearly been flogged within an inch of his life. Such floggings were rare, and reserved for the worst crimes, like cowardice in the face of the enemy or murder of a fellow legionary. A flogging as the captain had received would usually mean the permanent crippling of the man at best. Should he survive, which was also a rare occurrence, the convicted criminal would be discharged from service and left to fend for himself. Being discharged this way also meant the forfeiture of pension, which, for a legionary, was almost as terrible as the physical punishment.

The men he had been working with were still staring at him, eyes wide.

"Have you never seen a flogged back?" Stiger asked them again, adding an edge to his tone.

The men quickly looked away and went back to work with added vigor. The captain considered them for a moment, then spat in disgust before turning back to work himself. *It is what it is*, he thought. *Soon enough, they will learn not what my scars say, but who I am.*

Stiger pointedly ignored the glances and whispers as the afternoon wore on. Word had spread throughout the camp. Even the sergeants had found an excuse to wander over. Stiger did not care. He wanted them to look now so that they would get over their shock. He did not want to build trust only to have it shaken or lost, as if he had concealed some terrible secret. Let them all take a good long look and deal with it now.

As the afternoon wore on, the walls of the encampment slowly went up. At the same time, a trench was being dug a few feet beyond the walls. When complete, the trench would be three feet deep and five feet wide. The stream had been diverted away from the encampment to permit the walls to be erected. Once the trench and walls were finished, the stream would be returned to its normal flow, which took it through the backside of the camp. A small wooden aqueduct would keep fresh water flowing through a hole cut into the wall, while a portion would be allowed to spill into the trench, eventually filling it and creating a small moat.

Several trees were positioned and carefully set to act as a makeshift bridge across the moat where the camp entrance had been constructed. Planks were laid across and firmly nailed down. The planks would ensure that the animals would not turn a hoof while being led in and out of the camp. A simple yet very stout gate locked into place with the walls, sealing off the bridge. To open and close the gate required the effort of several men.

In the space of nearly five hours, the farm was slowly but surely transformed into a heavily fortified encampment that enclosed both the farmhouse and barn. It was an impressive achievement, yet it was nothing the legionaries had not done multiple times before.

Every day that the company remained, Stiger would see to it that the camp and the fortifications steadily improved. He intended the labor to help toughen his men up, while at the same time working to restore morale. They would eventually come to be proud of what they had built.

One of the company wagons, filled with chopped firewood, rattled across the newly constructed bridge, drawing the captain's eye. While the camp had been coming together, several work details had also been busy felling trees beyond the perimeter. Company wagons repeatedly returned, heavily loaded with firewood. They had made good work of it, and already had at least three cords of wood stacked neatly next to the backside of the barn. There was already enough firewood for every tent to have a fire that evening.

With evening fast approaching, work came to a halt. The walls were firmly in place and the moat was beginning to fill. The men were dismissed and sent to clean up before the evening meal was served. The captain made a point to carefully examine the walls and moat. The work was not perfect, but it was a start, and he was pleased with what he saw. Anyone attempting to storm the camp by surprise would have a difficult time of it, though the possibility of such a surprise assault was low. Eli and his scouts would spot any significant force of rebels long before they got close. Still, it was better to be prepared.

Stiger made a short stop at the stream running through the inside of the camp to rinse off the day's sweat, grime, and dirt. Refreshed, he returned to the farmhouse and sat down on the old snag. No one had gotten around to removing it yet, for which he was grateful. He had not worked this hard in quite some time, and his entire body ached.

He and the men had accomplished a great deal on their first real day, even with half of them occasionally needing to make a dash for the latrines or bushes in intestinal distress. Yet there was much more to be done.

Mercifully, the air was beginning to cool again. Stiger had put his tunic back on and belted it tightly. After the morning's assassination attempt, he made sure his sword and dagger were within easy reach at all times. He wondered if he would ever fully be able to let his guard down.

He sat for a while, enjoying the feeling of simply doing nothing.

Eventually, duty called and he pulled out a dispatch pad and a thick charcoal pencil from a bag he had dropped by his feet. He wrote out a quick report to General Kromen and another to Colonel Karol, explaining where he had made camp. He provided a brief but vague update on his work with the company. He also requested that word be sent once the supply train was ready. He carefully added a line— *Requesting confirmation of delivery*—and then signed each. He sealed and addressed the two dispatches.

"Lieutenant," Stiger called to Ikely, who had been on his way to check on what the cook was preparing for dinner. The lieutenant altered his course and came up to the captain. Ikely looked as tired as Stiger felt. Undoubtedly, his young lieutenant was unaccustomed to such difficult manual labor. He had probably worked harder today than he had ever worked in his life, Stiger mused sadly. The captain handed the lieutenant the dispatches. "Please have one of the scouts carry these dispatches to General Kromen and Colonel Karol."

"Sir," Ikely said, exhaustion heavy in his voice. "I am afraid that all of the scouts are out training with Eli. They are expected to return in the morning."

"I see ... well then, detail a reliable man to act as courier." Stiger forced himself to keep the exhaustion from his voice. The men in his company needed to believe their captain was tireless. Stiger glanced up at the darkening skyline and frowned. His courier would be departing after it was dark. "Assign an armed file to provide an escort. Make sure the men are aware that there may be rebels about."

"Yes, sir." The lieutenant took the dispatches and left to find a detail and a reliable man. After such a difficult day, no one in that party would be particularly happy with the assignment. It was four miles to the main encampment and four miles back.

"Sergeant," Stiger called over to Ranl. The sergeant had been heading in the direction of the cook as well.

"Sir?" Ranl asked, coming over.

"I noticed stone walls beyond the camp marking off field boundaries. Tomorrow morning, see that a detail is put together to collect some of the stones. I want to build a couple of makeshift ovens for Cook."

"Yes, sir," Ranl acknowledged, scratching at his neck, which had been thickened by two decades of service. Thick, muscular necks were the sign of a true veteran. Over time and prolonged use, a legionary's helmet strengthened the muscles of the neck. The helmets were universally hated, at least until a legionary was in battle. Then the once-loathed helmet, along with all of a legionary's armor and equipment, was appreciated as it never had been before. "Fresh bread would be grand. The men have only been getting the stale stuff of late."

"There will be an inspection tomorrow morning," Stiger added, and then hesitated. "Actually, make that every morning. Allot sufficient time each evening for work on maintaining weapons, armor, and kit."

"Yes, sir," Ranl replied. "If they take care of their gear, it will take care of them."

"Good job today," Stiger said as the sergeant turned away. Colonel Karol had indeed been true to his word and given him two of his best men. "Job well done to both you and Blake."

"Thank you, sir," the sergeant replied with a slightly pleased look. "Nothing like good old-fashioned work to remind them they joined the emperor's legions."

"In the morning we will work on arms training," Stiger said, staring off into the distance, as if he was no longer talking with the sergeant, but merely expressing his thoughts aloud. "I cannot imagine how rusty they are. Work and training. We'll keep them very busy with both. That will be good for them."

"Yes, sir," the sergeant said neutrally as Stiger turned his gaze back upon him.

"We have only a few days to work the men into shape." The intensity of Stiger's distant look faded as he held Ranl's gaze. "Then we are off into the field."

"The field, sir?" the sergeant asked, clearly not daring for a second to look away. Stiger and Eli had not told anyone other than Lieutenant Ikely where the company was headed. "Where are we off to?"

Stiger stood slowly, took a step closer to the sergeant, and clapped him on the shoulder in a friendly manner. "All in good time," he said with a slight smile. He then went off in the direction of the latrines, leaving the sergeant alone.

Six

The sun was setting at the end of the company's second full day in their new home. Eli and a pair of scouts returned with a wild hog and several large hares. There was much rejoicing over the catch and the knowledge that all would once again eat well. This time, smaller portions would be issued to each man.

The hunters, proud of their handsome catch, made a show of parading it through the camp before turning it over to the cook. Colonel Karol had assigned the cook to the company on the same day Stiger had been given command. It was already clear the man was gifted at his craft.

The captain was seated on the stump of the snag in front of the farmhouse, which had been removed and reduced to firewood. He idly watched the men gather around the hog in excitement. Their lot was improving, though he was working them to exhaustion. They feared and hated him and would continue to do so. He knew that. It was a given.

Stiger's thoughts swung back to the attempt on his life. It had come very close to succeeding. How many more attempts would there be? It was fairly unlikely Bennet would try again. The experience seemed to have taught the man something. With a new lease on life, Bennet worked himself harder than anyone else.

Who would make the next attempt? Who else might prefer the safe, though thoroughly unhealthy, life of the main encampment?

Assassinations of unpopular officers rarely, if ever, occurred in camp. There were just too many witnesses about. Such attempts were more likely to happen during the heat of battle, where a murder could easily be lost in the confusion and mayhem of combat.

Stiger rubbed the stubble on his chin, irritated by the thought of another of his men attempting such a vile act. If it came, he would have to make a real example the men would be unlikely to forget.

"Hog tonight," Lieutenant Ikely announced as he cheerfully approached. The farmhouse had become the captain's command post and quarters.

"Seems that way," Stiger said softly. The lieutenant, though green, had worked alongside the men over the last two days, as the captain had. He had done everything Stiger had expected and more. Sparing the lieutenant a quick glance, he decided that it was likely the lieutenant was a good man, whom he would probably one day name a friend.

"I am told there is a lake a few miles from here," the lieutenant offered. "Some of the men hail from fishing villages along the eastern coast…"

Stiger nodded in agreement at the unspoken suggestion. There was no guarantee that once the march began, there would be time to hunt and cook game. Freshly caught fish could easily be salted and dried for the coming march. It would help stretch their durable food supply and also provide some variety beyond salted pork, which, unfortunately, they had in plenty.

"Put a couple of men on it," Stiger said. "Anything they manage to catch, get them drying."

The two officers were silent for a few moments, both watching the men. Stiger, after a second hard day's work on the camp, was thoroughly blown, though he was careful not to let it show. He was really looking forward to turning in for the night. Sleep beckoned strongly, and he stifled a yawn.

"The cook…" Stiger asked abruptly. "What's the man's name again?"

"Cross," the lieutenant answered. "Miles Cross."

"Thank you," Stiger responded neutrally. "I would like to have a word with him after the men are fed this evening."

"I will see to it, sir," Ikely said.

Eli separated himself from the scouts and walked over.

"A successful hunt," Stiger said by way of greeting.

"It was." Eli sat down on another stump a few feet away. Stiger had set a fire between the two stumps. It crackled happily. The elf freed a canteen from his travel pack, placing the pack carefully at his feet before taking a sip. Having spent a night and a day out with his scouts, he seemed refreshed and at ease.

"How are the scouts working out?" Ikely asked.

"They are coming along nicely," Eli answered. "A few more days, and some of them will be able to operate fairly effectively without my direct oversight."

"What I want—" Stiger began with a frown.

"What you want is the best," Eli interrupted.

"Exactly," Stiger growled softly. "I want the best scouts."

"The best scouts," Eli continued with a sardonic look, "to find the enemy before the enemy finds us. They must also be the best hunters, because if they are good at hunting animals, they will be good at hunting their fellow man."

"Correct," Stiger responded.

Lieutenant Ikely's eyes widened at this.

"A month with me, and they will be the finest scouts in the South," Eli asserted. "Though I must admit, they don't need to learn too much to do that. Competence does not seem to be a strength highly valued here in the South."

"Eli," Stiger breathed heavily, patience drawing thin, "drop it."

"It will take my scouts at least a month before they get their wind," Eli continued, moving away from the sensitive topic.

"Their ... wind?" Lieutenant Ikely asked.

"He means that each scout will need to build the endurance to run long distances without tiring," Stiger explained. "Having sufficient wind is essential."

"I instruct them as I would an apprentice striving to become a ranger. A good ranger should be able to run ten miles without tiring or stopping for a break," Eli explained. "A ranger should also be able to flow through the forest, silent, undetected, and at a quicker pace than we marched to this camp." Eli paused. "Much of what I teach my scouts, besides simple conditioning, is how to move silently and rapidly. They learn to read the signs and listen to the voice of the forest."

"Voice of the forest?" the lieutenant asked with a curious frown. "What is that?"

"Birds, animals," Stiger answered with a deep sigh. "If you don't hear any birds ... something or someone has disturbed them."

"Ah ..." The lieutenant nodded. "I understand."

"Scouting is arduous work," Eli explained further. "Over time, a scout must become one with his environment ... he must feel the very life of the forest."

"Now, that I just don't understand," the lieutenant admitted. "How can you feel the forest?"

"It is an elf thing," Stiger said, waving a hand in his friend's direction. "Trust me."

"The captain makes a passable scout, but a ranger he will never make," Eli said, flashing a close-mouthed smile at his friend.

Stiger frowned, declining the opportunity to reply to the dig, as he knew he was more than "passable" in Eli's eyes. However, the ranger comment was true. Very few ever became true rangers—masters of the forest—like Eli.

"So you don't feel the forest, then?" Lieutenant Ikely asked, noticing the captain's frown.

"I've tried...believe me," Stiger said wryly, scratching at his stubble again, which itched. He felt the urge to shave. "To frustration's end...I have tried."

"Will any of our scouts learn to feel the forest?" the lieutenant asked, looking back over at Eli.

"Doubtful," Stiger admitted. "Eli has only ever been able to teach one human to feel the forest, and he was an odd one. Bren was one very odd man."

"A fine scout he was," Eli nodded soberly, the merriment leaving his face.

"Was?" Ikely looked between the two. "What happened to him?"

Stiger said nothing. Instead, he pulled out his pipe and tapped it clean.

"His life force ended in the forests of Abath," Eli finally answered, breaking the uncomfortable silence, a look of profound sadness marring his perfect face.

"Life force?" Ikely asked, looking over at the captain. "He was killed, then?"

"Yes," Stiger said softly. "An arrow took him in the neck."

The three became silent for a time.

"Captain," Lieutenant Ikely began hesitantly. "The men have been asking about your back. What should I tell them?"

"Tell them whatever you flaming wish," Stiger snapped, jabbing the pipe in Ikely's direction. The captain glared at the lieutenant for a moment before standing abruptly. He turned and, without another word, stomped off in the direction of the stream.

"I did not aim to offend," Lieutenant Ikely said, concerned, watching the captain disappear into the darkness. "The men want to know more about the man commanding them..."

"You did not offend." Eli breathed a heavy sigh, looking into the fire.

"What did he do to deserve such a flogging?" Ikely asked, deciding to be blunt.

"Deserve? He did absolutely nothing," Eli responded, looking up from the fire and meeting the lieutenant's eyes levelly. "Nothing."

"Then why was he flogged?" the lieutenant asked.

Eli sighed deeply, looking again into the captain's fire, which was beginning to die down. He stood, grabbed a log from a nearby pile, and tossed it onto the fire, which crackled enthusiastically. He then resumed his seat. He remained silent, staring into the fire. Ikely was beginning to think Eli would not answer. He turned to go.

"He willingly took the place of a convicted man," the elf finally said, looking back up at Ikely with sadness in his eyes.

"He what?" Ikely exclaimed, shocked. "Why? Why would he do such a thing?"

"You must understand. The captain is a complicated human. I have known him for many years, and there are times when even I do not understand his motivations. Those under his command mean a great deal to him," Eli explained. "He takes his duty to the empire very seriously... almost, you could say, as a sacred trust. What he considers his personal honor is bound up in it."

"I guess I can understand that," Ikely said. Personal honor was something imperial families took very seriously. "But taking the place of a convicted man... Why would he do such a thing?"

"One of his men was accused, by General Lears, of theft and sentenced to four hundred lashes," Eli continued. "The captain felt that the man was a good man... a fine soldier and innocent. The punishment, shall we say, was overly harsh even for a guilty man. When the captain appealed the sentence, General Lears offended and impugned the captain's honor and that of the company he commanded. On the day of punishment, the entire legion was assembled to witness justice being administered. The captain publically insisted upon taking the man's place."

"And General Lears accepted the substitution?" Lieutenant Ikely asked, aghast at such ungentlemanly treatment of a fellow gentleman.

"Yes," Eli answered.

"Four hundred lashes should have killed him!"

"Yes," Eli answered with a small nod, "our captain is a tough man."

"Astonishing," the lieutenant breathed. "All for an innocent man..."

Eli looked up at Ikely with a surprised look. "I never claimed he was innocent, only that the captain believed him innocent."

"He was guilty then?"

"Very," the elf replied with a sad chuckle.

"What happened to him?" the lieutenant asked after a moment. "What happened to the thief?"

"His life force ended in the same battle that Bren's passed this plane of existence," Eli explained, a look of sadness once again gracing his face. "The man gave up his life saving the captain's."

"Again," Stiger shouted to the men. He could feel his voice beginning to grow hoarse. It had been a long while since he had personally led a drill. "Begin!"

The men locked their wooden training shields together with a mighty crash and stepped forward. "HAAAH," resounded from close to a hundred thunderous voices.

"No, no, no!" Stiger shouted, frustration boiling over. The captain moved up to the shield line and the men relaxed their stances, practice shields thudding heavily to the ground. "What is your most dangerous weapon?" Stiger thundered at the line of men. No one answered. He selected one man. "You, tell me. What is your most dangerous weapon?"

"My sword," the man ventured cautiously, raising his wooden practice sword and shaking it slightly.

"Wrong," Stiger thundered back, pointing at the man's head. "Your mind is your most dangerous weapon. It is time to use it."

He pushed his way through the line of men so that he was behind the formation.

"Lock shields right!" the captain shouted.

The shields snapped up and thunked together loudly.

"That is NOT how you lock shields," Stiger roared. "In a real battle it will get you planted in a shallow grave, providing fodder for the worms."

He began manually adjusting the men, moving their shields into proper alignment. Sergeant Blake stood passively a few feet away, watching the captain work the men. Stiger could only guess the sergeant's thoughts, as it was not every day he got to see an officer act like an average sergeant. Usually officers, as proper gentlemen, declined such close contact with the rank and file. It was almost unheard of for officers to participate in regular drills. Most, only ever caring to understand company and regimental maneuvers, would not have been able to spot an improper shield alignment.

"I want every one of you to look at how these five men have their shields—properly interlocked," Stiger told the rest of the men in the line, who stepped back to look. "These five can push at this point here, with the force of five men. You five ... push forward!"

The five men took the prescribed half step forward.

"Now unlock shields and jab," Stiger ordered.

The shields scraped apart a few inches and, lightning fast, five short swords jabbed out and back before the shields thunked back into the original interlocking position.

"Excellent. Let's try that again with the whole line. Reform!"

The men quickly reformed their line.

"Lock shields right!" Stiger snapped. "Push!"

The men pushed a half step forward and the shields unlocked in unison. The swords jabbed out and back, and then the shields locked back into place as the men shifted their weight to the opposite side, pushing the imaginary enemy line again.

"Push!"

The men took another half step forward. Shields unlocked, swords jabbed out, shields relocked.

"Push!"

Stiger continued for another five revolutions.

"Stand easy," Stiger ordered.

The shield line set their heavy practice shields down on the ground with a solid thud. Real shields and swords were never used for practice. Those, being the personal property of each legionary, were saved for the real thing, and only tested in battle.

"This movement must be performed with precision and speed." Stiger paced back and forth along the line. "There can be no errors … there is simply no margin for mistakes. Lapses in the tiniest detail will get you or your comrade stone dead. Against rabble, the line push can be devastating. Against a formidable foe, like the Rivan, who I fought in the North, the line and the ability to perform the line push seamlessly *is* life!"

Stiger allowed that to sink in.

"Discipline! Remember your discipline! Whichever side has better discipline will live to fight another day. Make no mistake, the real killing on the field begins only when a line comes apart and one side breaks. Those who break, die. Our line will not be the one that comes apart. We of the Eighty-Fifth will hold, no matter what happens. We will hold to protect our brothers and our honor. Holding the line means life! What does holding the line mean?"

"Life!" the men thundered back.

"We will practice again and again until you get it right!"

"Dispatch rider coming in," Lieutenant Ikely announced, gesturing toward the camp entrance, where a rider had galloped up and was speaking with the sentries.

"Take over," Stiger ordered the lieutenant and moved off to meet the dispatch rider, who rapidly dismounted upon clearing the sentries. His eyes were wide as he took in the camp and the men doing their drill. The dispatch rider saw Stiger coming, drew up to attention, and saluted with fist to chest. He then drew a dispatch from his saddle pouch.

"With General Mammot's compliments, sir," he said, handing over the dispatch. He was clearly nervous at being in the presence of a Stiger.

Stiger broke open the seal and quickly read the contents. The supply train had been delayed another week, perhaps two, the general informed him, which suited Stiger just fine. Under different circumstances, the dispatch might have been considered bad news. But the delay bought him time—time to get his company in order. Stiger took out his dispatch pad and charcoal pencil. He rapidly wrote out a reply and confirmation of receipt while the dispatch rider waited. He signed and sealed the dispatch, then handed it back to the rider.

"Deliver my response to the general," Stiger ordered.

The dispatch rider saluted, mounted back up, and rode out of the encampment. Stiger stopped himself to study the dispatch rider as he departed. The man's armor was dirty and poorly maintained. His legs were muddy from having to walk through the muck and filth of the main encampment. He had also smelled awful. Stiger looked over at his own men, who just days ago had appeared shabby and undisciplined. They now looked vastly different.

He let slip a small smile of satisfaction. His men were now clean and shaven, with hair trimmed short. Their tunics had been thoroughly laundered and their armor painstakingly maintained. The rust and grime had been removed, and the armor polished and waxed. His company had been here a mere five days and the change suddenly seemed very apparent.

With extra time, his men would be much better conditioned and disciplined. They looked, at least to his critical eye, inept. Stiger intended for his men not to simply pick up the basic drill, but to master it. Once the basics had been mastered, they could work on more advanced maneuvers.

Forgetting the dispatch rider, Stiger turned and walked back to where his men were drilling. He watched, silent for a time, as Lieutenant Ikely and Sergeant Blake ran the men through the practice exercises—shouting orders, calling attention to mistakes, and providing advice. The men were, in essence, relearning what they had already been taught, but had not practiced in a good long while.

Stiger had placed the company on a training schedule. The schedule was built around a daily rotation, with half his men drilling while the other half went out on forced practice route marches, complete with full kit. The goal was not simple conditioning, but to make his men capable of marching twenty miles in under five hours. The legions prided themselves on the ability to march hard and cover great distances rapidly. The ability to outmarch the enemy was critical.

Having rotted away in the South, Stiger's company had lost the ability to march effectively. That would rapidly change. Once his men accomplished twenty miles in five hours, they would be permitted a short break before immediately marching another twenty. A good company could easily cover forty miles in a day, usually in ten to twelve hours.

For those who were not participating in the daily practice march, the morning focus was on formation drill, and midday was devoted to weapons and kit maintenance. This was followed up by camp upkeep and improvement. The men's late afternoons would involve weapons and hand-to-hand drill. Each day one half of the company would march and the other half would train. Both groups would have the evenings off to recover and relax.

Stepping forward, Stiger began making the rounds—observing, providing instruction, and offering criticism or advice where he thought it appropriate. The morning wore on and the temperature climbed. The men began to perspire heavily as they worked at drill. The wooden practice shields and short swords grew heavier the longer they worked. Both practice implements were made weightier than the real thing with the intention of strengthening the men's arms. They were hated with a passion.

Stiger eventually called a stop to the drilling and sent the men to eat. He motioned for Ikely and Blake to walk with him as he went back to the farmhouse. "Have you had an eye out for any suitable corporals?" The company's previous corporals had been removed from the unit prior to Stiger taking command.

"We have discussed it," the lieutenant admitted with a slight hesitation. "The sergeants would like to get to know the men better before they select candidates for your approval, sir."

"A wise move." Stiger nodded, wiping sweat from the back of his neck. The corporals would provide the glue that held not only a file of twenty men together, but more importantly, a portion of line under the stress of combat. It was essential to not only select a respected man, but one who was reliable and capable. In a typical company, which Stiger's current command was not, retirement, death, or disability were the usual reasons behind promotion. Decisions concerning whom to promote were given serious thought, and the men selected had proven themselves to the company over a number of years of service.

Stiger was under the time constraints set by the supply train and his mission. He needed to select his corporals sooner rather than later so that they could get comfortable with their new rank and roles prior to departing for Vrell. Without the sergeants really knowing the men, any candidates they selected could potentially create problems that might not be apparent until the company was in battle.

"Will a week be sufficient?" the captain asked, mentally wincing. He knew it was an unfair thing to ask, but there was simply no choice.

Sergeant Blake hesitated. "Should be, sir."

"Good," Stiger said, and then decided to change the subject. "I want the trees and brush pushed back another three hundred yards around the encampment. This will deprive anyone wishing us ill the opportunity of close cover."

"Yes, sir." Lieutenant Ikely nodded. "Clearing that land should yield plenty of firewood and kindling. Sir, I meant to ask about the scouts and drill—"

"Lieutenant Eli'Far will handle the training of the scouts," Stiger answered, cutting off the lieutenant. "Those men are essentially detached and will not be subject to drill or marching practice."

"We have a few who are good with their hands," Sergeant Blake spoke up. "I would like to form a detail to work on the barn. It leaks, and if we intend to stay here much longer or use this site again in the future, some repairs are needed."

"Excellent suggestion, Sergeant. Detail a party," Stiger said. He should have thought of that sooner. There had just been too much to get done in the basic setup of the camp. "Put them to work on the farmhouse as well. I need a few chairs and also a table for work."

The farmhouse was a two-room affair. One room the captain intended to reserve for his personal quarters, and the other for company work. Once cleaned out and patched up, it should work nicely.

When the company returned from Vrell, if he could swing it, this site would become the company's permanent home. The captain understood that if he kept his unit combat effective, it was likely they would be assigned real work more often than the other companies, keeping them out of the main encampment and safe from the risk of disease being bred there.

The wind shifted suddenly, bringing the smell of fresh bread and drawing his thoughts away. He turned to look in the direction of the two new ovens, which had been built the day before.

"Cook's working on the first batch of fresh bread," Ikely remarked.

"Make sure he has sufficient help in preparing meals," Stiger ordered, gesturing at the cook, who was checking on the bread. "Have the squads rotate, providing some assistance each day. I think that it would not be a bad idea to also assign him a permanent assistant. Someone properly suited to learn his job."

"It has already been done, sir," Sergeant Blake admitted. "A few years back, we was on campaign when our cook went and died. No one else in the company knew how to prepare a meal proper-like. It was not a fond experience."

"Suffered a bit of intestinal disorder, did we?" Stiger chuckled.

"A bit, sir," Blake said. "Just a bit."

SEVEN

The camp was settling in for the night. The men had drilled and trained heavily over the past few days, showing vast improvement under the instruction of the officers and sergeants. The camp was coming together as well, now clearly resembling a fairly typical temporary company camp. The barn and farmhouse were fully habitable, having been cleaned out and thoroughly patched. The tree and brush line around the camp was also in the process of being cut back, receding farther with each passing day. This provided plenty of firewood and kindling.

The scouts under Eli's supervision had become very skilled in both hunting and trapping, not to mention more proficient at scouting. Their catch had included hog, deer, hare, pheasant, partridge, goose, duck, and a number of other game. The men were eating well and it showed in both their physical activity and morale.

The fishermen had turned out to be quite capable as well. Their catch, large-bellied trout, was drying on several hastily built stands near the far side of the barn. The fish would help supplement the regimen of salt pork, mush, and hard bread for the march.

Stiger had made it a habit to move about the camp in the evening, stopping to speak and visit with his men. He had found that after a long, hard day's work, they were more relaxed and willing to open up, if ever so slightly, to their commanding officer. It allowed him to sample their temper and needs. He felt that making such rounds also allowed his men to become better acquainted with him. A few had even ventured to offer ideas—some good and some poorly thought out—on improving the encampment.

A good officer listens to his men, General Treim had told him. Stiger made a point of implementing the good ideas and making sure that those with the ideas got the credit for them.

Stiger had always been very perceptive when it came to reading others. Though no one else had dared ask about his back, he noticed that the men had been acting a tad more respectful. Yes, he had done a great deal to improve their lot since taking command, and yet... there was something more to it than that. He rather suspected that Eli had shared the story of his flogging with Ikely, who had then passed it along. The lieutenant had also been acting a bit differently, too. Sighing, he knew it mattered little. No one spoke of it, at least within his hearing, which he appreciated. The flogging was more of a personal embarrassment—a stinging slap to his pride and honor. One day, he fully intended to address the matter to his satisfaction. Until then, he would not speak of it. It was good that the men knew the story. If it earned him a bit of respect, he would take it.

Deep down, he felt they were all good men. In reality, he chose to believe each was a good man, though many were likely not. He would give them all the benefit of the doubt, until one or another proved otherwise, like Bennet. Likely, a number had been convicted of petty crimes and sentenced to a term with the legions. Some had more than likely joined for adventure or glory. Others had signed up to escape the crushing poverty, debt, and city slums.

The legions promised a hard life in return for a pension and a plot of land upon retirement after twenty years. One acre was awarded for each year of service. Those veterans who signed up for an additional five years and completed twenty-five would receive fifty acres and a bonus to their pensions upon retirement. Whatever the reason for joining, all that really mattered to Stiger was what each man made of himself. Who they had been before was of no consequence.

They were legionaries now, members of his company, and it was as simple as that.

Returning to the farmhouse, Stiger took a seat on his customary tree stump by the fire. Someone had thoughtfully kept the fire fed, and it crackled comfortably. The smoke kept away the bugs, which were few on this chill night. He pulled out his pipe and tapped it clean before filling it. Taking a small twig from a pile he had set aside for such a purpose, he lit the pipe. He puffed up the burn and took a moment to enjoy the rich, relaxing flavor of good old Eastern tobacco as he stared into the depths of the fire.

Riding south on his way to his new post with the southern legions, he and Eli had spent many a night before their campfire. It had been the first time in a long while that he had not had any real responsibility. It had almost seemed carefree, and he had enjoyed it. He glanced up at the night sky and sighed softly. He missed his evening conversations with his good friend. Without Eli, the evening fire was a lonely one.

Alone with his thoughts, Stiger found himself dwelling on his past. He had been an officer in the legions for nearly a decade, and in that time he had seen more than his share of fighting. A number of good men had died under his command, for the battlefield was not a perfect place, and tough decisions often translated into blood. Even when he had done everything right, he had still lost men.

He preferred to think that in the scale of life, on balance, he had saved more than he had lost. It was not much, but it was some form of comfort. Ultimately, on nights like this, when there was no one to talk to, he was haunted by those whom he had lost.

Stiger pulled out his dispatch pad and put pencil to paper. He wrote out a brief update to both General Kromen and Colonel Karol on his progress with the company. Stiger had long since learned the value in keeping his commanders informed. Regular updates helped to minimize misunderstandings. Finished, he sealed the dispatch and tucked it, along with the pencil and pad, back into his tunic pocket. A messenger would deliver it in the morning.

Rising, Stiger threw two more logs onto the fire and then cleaned out his pipe, putting it away carefully. He could have slept in the farmhouse, but the night was cool and the ground thankfully dry. Though the farmhouse had a serviceable fireplace, tonight he preferred to sleep under the stars, next to the fire where it was warm. Retrieving his field blanket from the farmhouse, he arranged it on the ground and sat down. He removed his boots and made sure they were upright so that unwanted critters would have a more difficult time of crawling in. He rolled up a spare tunic to use as a pillow, then placed his dagger underneath it. He kept his sword within easy reach. With the fire crackling merrily, he lay down and closed his eyes.

"Sir."

Stiger's eyes snapped open, hand shooting for his sword before he realized that it was his lieutenant. Alarmed, Ikely stood up and took a step back.

It was still dark. The moon had traveled farther down the sky, though Stiger felt as if he had just closed his eyes a few moments ago. A quick glance at the embers glowing in the remains of his fire told him a significant amount of time had passed. The large rocks placed around the edges of the fire still radiated heat. Sitting up, the captain rubbed at his eyes, driving the sleep away.

"Sorry to wake you, sir," Ikely apologized, sounding grave.

"What is it?" Stiger asked bluntly, throwing a log on the fire and using a smaller one to stir the embers up. With luck, the log would catch and not require additional effort.

"Sergeant Ranl discovered one of the sentries asleep," the lieutenant stated.

"Damn it," Stiger cursed, angrily throwing the smaller log into the fire. He wasted no time in pulling his boots on. "He has the offender in custody?"

"Yes, sir," Ikely responded. "He placed the man under arrest and put another at his post."

"All right," Stiger growled, standing up. Catching a sentry asleep on post was bound to happen sometime. It was what Stiger would be forced to do to keep it from happening again that really bothered him. Sighing deeply, he slipped on his sword. Better to set an example now than have it occur in the field. "Let's go see the man."

Lieutenant Ikely led the captain toward the other side of the camp, where the latrines were located, behind the farmhouse. Most of the tents had been erected on the other side of the house, the front side of the camp. Since they did not have a proper stockade, they found the man sitting on the ground, between the two sergeants, who were verbally berating him. He looked miserable and afraid, especially when he saw Stiger. The sergeants stepped back. The legionary stood and came to a shaky attention. A bruise was forming around his left eye. One of the sergeants had clearly made a point with a fist.

"You fell asleep on watch," Stiger said. It was not a question.

"Yes, sir," the legionary responded, voice trembling a little. The man was young. If Stiger had to guess, he would bet that the man had not been under arms for more than a year.

"What is your name?" Stiger asked coldly.

"Legionary Teg, sir," the frightened man answered.

"The watch are the eyes and ears of the company. You realize that by falling asleep, you jeopardized not only your life, but the lives of the entire company?"

"Yes, sir," Teg said more firmly. A look of resolution crossed his youthful face. This impressed the captain. Teg might be worth something. "Sorry, sir," Teg stated firmly. "It won't happen again, sir."

"Damn right it will not happen again," Stiger growled, getting in the legionary's personal space. He could sentence a man to death for such an infraction. Teg and the sergeants knew this as well. All stood still, holding their breath and wondering if the Stigers were as terrible as everyone said they were. The captain, however, was not in the habit of executing his men for petty infractions. Deep in enemy territory, it would not be so trivial. Regardless, such lapses could not be tolerated. "Five lashes, to be administered first thing in the morning, followed by punishment detail."

Legionary Teg said nothing, but his shoulders sagged slightly in relief. The sergeants' eyes also reflected relief. They had clearly expected worse.

Stiger spared his legionary a last cold, hard look that said *I expected better of you*, before turning on his heel and stalking off. As Stiger made his way back to the farmhouse, he knew there would be no more sleep for him tonight. In the morning, he would have to watch someone flogged. Damn...damn...damn! How he hated the lash. Yet deep down he understood it was a necessary part of the legionary's life. Without it, there would be no order.

As soon as the sun was up and before breakfast, Stiger had the company drawn up to witness the administration of punishment. The prisoner, without a tunic, was led to a tree in the center of the encampment. The tree was a lovely old oak that contrasted harshly with the ugliness that was about to happen. The tree had been spared by Eli, who for some unknown reason insisted it not be chopped down like all of the others that had once stood around it. Stiger supposed Eli had felt some type of primal connection with the tree.

Unfortunately, the lovely oak would now forever be known by the company as the punishment tree. Legionary Teg was bound to the tree with rope.

"This man fell asleep on watch," Stiger said, loud enough for all to hear. "He has admitted his guilt. His breach put all of us at risk. In a few days' time, we march. Where matters little. What you need to know is that we are marching into hostile territory. Should a sentry fall asleep at the wrong moment, we will all be in dire peril. Such lapses will not be tolerated! I have ordered five lashes, followed by punishment detail. Sergeant Ranl?"

"Sir," the sergeant responded, turning to face the captain. He was standing a couple of feet behind the judged man, holding the implement of punishment, a short yet vicious judicial whip. Sergeant Blake stood off to the side. He had just given Teg a small piece of wood to bite down on.

"Sergeant Blake?" Stiger asked harshly.

"I stand ready, sir," Blake replied with a grim look.

"You may administer punishment," the captain ordered harshly, hating himself even as he spoke the words.

"One!" Blake thundered, and Ranl let the wicked-looking judicial whip fly.

Crack! The whip sounded loudly across the near-silent camp. Teg said nothing, but tensed as the strike landed, trying with all his might to keep from crying out. The whip drew a thin red line of blood across the legionary's bare back.

"Two!"

Another vicious crack, followed by a second red line across the man's back. Stiger kept his gaze unwavering, fixed on the legionary. He mentally recoiled with each crack of the whip, recalling his own punishment as if it had occurred yesterday. He could almost feel the searing pain that accompanied each crack, until there was only numbness.

"Three!"

The legionary issued a groan, but did not cry out.

"Four!"

Another groan. Legionary Teg embraced the tree tightly, knuckles turning white.

"Five!"

Teg let out an anguished groan followed by a short sob.

"Punishment has been administered, sir," Ranl said, turning to face the captain. Some blood had spattered across his face.

"Cut him down and see to his wounds," Stiger ordered, thoroughly sick to his stomach. "Lieutenant Ikely, dismiss the company."

"Company dismissed!" Ikely shouted as the sergeants cut Teg down. The company was too small to rate a surgeon, but they had a surgeon's mate. Teg was helped to lie down on his stomach as his wounds were attended to.

Stiger watched for a moment more, then turned and walked back to the farmhouse, where he wanted to be alone with his thoughts.

"A pleasure to see you again," Captain Handi said pleasantly, flashing a radiant smile filled with teeth that seemed a little too perfect. Handi's eyes betrayed his true feelings, though. The man dismounted, handing his reins to Sergeant Ranl as though the sergeant were a mere stable boy and beneath notice.

Stiger said nothing as he took the captain's offered hand. The handshake was weak. Stiger had encountered men like Handi before, foppish, phony, and filled with ambition. He disliked such men intensely, as they tended to use and abuse their power with little regard for the consequences other than in relation to themselves. In Stiger's experience, such men typically thrived under weak or ineffectual commanding officers.

"So nice to get away from the dreary day-to-day life in the encampment," Handi exclaimed, taking a deep breath of fresh air while making an exaggerated show of glancing around the camp. "I just love occasionally getting out into the country."

Handi turned back to face Stiger, flashing another very false smile. Stiger had already tired of the man's game, though he was careful not to let it show. He had little interest in useless people. Still, he had to permit this charade to play out. There was a reason Captain Handi had come out, and it was not for pleasure.

"Captain Stiger, I must say I am deeply impressed," Handi said, gesturing around expansively at the camp. "You have been busy, haven't you?"

"The men have worked hard," Stiger responded neutrally.

"Well…if you must play at war," Captain Handi responded, "then I don't see why your men should not bend their backs and make it look good for you."

"I can assure you, sir," Stiger bristled, taking umbrage at Handi's implication, "I do not play at war."

"A jest poorly delivered," Captain Handi soothed, laying a calming hand briefly on Stiger's shoulder. "I offer apology for any perceived insult."

Stiger frowned. He fairly itched to rearrange those perfect teeth. The supposed jest was only cover, for which Captain Handi had not actually apologized. He had only offered apology on a perceived insult, not the actual insult that had been delivered.

Technically Stiger could seek satisfaction. Though dueling was rare among legionary officers, it was not an unknown occurrence. The problem with dueling was that the commanding generals typically frowned very aggressively upon the practice. Stiger suspected that Captain Handi was counting on this to effectively tie Stiger's hands. Frustrated, Stiger looked beyond Handi, who turned to see where Stiger was looking.

Handi had brought a troop of cavalry as a personal escort, which was clattering across the makeshift bridge and into the camp. Stiger recognized the cavalry lieutenant as the one who had been escorting the wagon train out of the main legionary encampment on the day of his arrival.

Captain Handi was his enemy, of that Stiger was confident. What he wasn't sure of was the cavalry lieutenant. Was he an ally of Handi's? Or had he had been brought along as a simple escort for the pompous fool? The lieutenant dismounted and handed his reins to one of his men, who remained mounted. Stiger noticed the lieutenant was looking around with ill-feigned interest at the camp. Though fairly young, he carried himself erect and proud. He did not seem the type of man to lick anyone's boots to curry favor. But how one looked did not determine how one behaved, Stiger knew.

"Lieutenant," Stiger directed himself toward the cavalry officer, stepping around Handi. Stiger's intention was to provoke a response from the staff captain. What would Handi do when he was no longer the center of attention? He extended a hand. "Lieutenant Lan, isn't it?"

"Why yes, sir." The lieutenant shook Stiger's hand. Stiger found it a firmer grip than that of the man Lan had been sent to escort. Lan seemed surprised that Stiger had remembered him. "Yes, sir, that's correct. We met outside of the encampment."

"Lieutenant," Handi interjected himself. He shot an irritated look at Lan. "Please see to your men. Captain Stiger and I have important matters to discuss."

"Yes, sir," Lan said stiffly. He turned away from Stiger with a slight frown of irritation. It seemed the lieutenant was no friend of the staff captain's.

"Sergeant," Stiger directed to Ranl, who was still holding the reins of Handi's horse. "After you attend to the captain's horse, please see that the lieutenant and his men get some grub. It seems Captain Handi and I have pressing matters to attend to."

"Yes, sir," Ranl said sharply, saluting with fist clenched to chest.

"Captain." Stiger gestured toward the farmhouse. "This way, if you please."

Both walked quickly toward the farmhouse. The men had constructed a roughhewn table and two chairs. Removing his riding gloves slowly, Handi glanced around the interior of the farmhouse with ill-disguised disgust. Stiger took a chair and offered Handi the other. Tucking his riding gloves into his sash, Handi sat. The table separated the two.

"A bit rustic," Handi commented.

"We are in the field, after all. Though there is no reason we cannot be a bit civilized. Would you care for some refreshment?" Stiger asked, pouring himself a mug of wine from a pitcher on the table. Without waiting for an answer, he poured Handi one as well.

"Thank you," Handi replied, accepting the mug and offering a silent toast to his host. "I agree … a little civilization can go a long way."

"Poor Southern stuff," Stiger apologized. "I am afraid it is all we have."

"I think I might be able to help you there," Handi said with a false smile. "I'll have a small barrel of Orkland sent over. We received a supply a few months back."

"Orkland?" Stiger asked with a raised eyebrow. Orkland was from the heart of the empire and a staple for the common nobility.

"Just because we are on campaign does not mean we have to live like savages," Handi replied, taking a sip, which elicited a sour look. "You were not kidding about this being poor. Though poor or not, riding builds up thirst." Handi took another pull.

"How can I help you, Captain?" Stiger asked pleasantly after several moments of silence.

The staff captain carefully placed his mug on the table, having drained it. "General Mammot requested that I inform you of a certain situation," Handi said theatrically, leaning back in his chair, which creaked.

"Oh?" Stiger asked, without displaying any emotion. General Mammot had likely asked nothing of the staff captain, but had instead given an order. Mammot did not seem the type to ask.

"General Kromen has taken a turn for the worse," Captain Handi explained, a look of exaggerated sadness crossing his face. "You know the dear man was like a father to me."

"Was?" Stiger asked, wondering if it was wishful thinking on Handi's part, or perhaps General Kromen was already dead. He poured the man another mug of wine.

"I misspoke," Handi admitted hastily, with an annoyed frown. "He has been like a father to me."

"I am relieved to hear that the general has not passed from the realm of the living," Stiger said carefully. "I can only imagine how upsetting this must be for you."

"The physicians feel there is a chance he will recover," Handi said. "I can only pray he does."

"I will offer a prayer to the High Father," Stiger said, playing along, though he was tiring rapidly of this game. He wished Handi would get to the point.

"I assure you, such prayers are more than welcome," Handi said softly, with an embellished sigh. The staff captain took another long pull of his wine and then set the mug down on the table. He locked eyes with Stiger. "With the fighting season nearly upon us, General Mammot felt that keeping General Kromen's illness from the men was of critical importance."

Stiger said nothing, but offered a nod in agreement. He had no idea whether General Kromen was popular with the men or not. If he was, Kromen's death could seriously affect morale, what little of it was left. Mammot could simply be exercising prudence by keeping this information confidential.

"General Mammot has assumed command, then?" Stiger asked simply, though the more he thought about it, the more alarmed he became. There was no possible way that Mammot could keep such news from the men. Gossip traveled fast in legionary encampments. There was much more to this visit than was readily apparent.

"With General Kromen being incapacitated due to illness and unable to maintain his...shall we say, responsibilities," Handi oozed, "General Mammot felt it the only reasonable course of action."

"Of course," Stiger responded neutrally. Mammot was working to consolidate his powerbase. It was clear now that Handi had come to see if Stiger would follow General Mammot. Stiger had no doubt that if he responded negatively to the news, Handi would likely produce an order relieving him of command. That was the last thing Stiger wanted to happen at the moment.

Perhaps Kromen had indeed taken a true turn for the worse, and Mammot was simply filling in, as was proper for a second-in-command. However, the presence of Captain Handi seemed to indicate something far more sinister was at play. It was possible General Mammot had decided to advance himself to commander of the army.

When Kromen crossed over the great river, Mammot would undoubtedly be terribly saddened at the general's demise. His duty and honor would require him to assume command, which he would hope to be ultimately confirmed by the senate and emperor. Such things were nothing new to imperial politics.

Though Stiger could use more time training his men, he itched to be on the road and well away from these political games.

"General Mammot felt it important that a personal envoy accompany such news," Handi said, flashing a smile, which rapidly slid from his face as he waited to hear what Stiger had to say.

"I stand to serve the empire," Stiger said simply, repeating part of the legionary motto. "What does General Mammot require of me?"

Handi smiled so thinly, it was almost a frown. Stiger realized the bastard had been hoping to relieve him. Having recently arrived, Stiger had no personal loyalty to either Kromen or Mammot.

"As is to be expected," Handi responded, recovering from his disappointment quickly. "General Mammot expects only that you continue to follow your orders, as issued by General Kromen."

"Of course," Stiger responded gravely. Something was afoot. Stiger rapidly thought it through. On one hand, had he been removed from command, he could have been shipped home, where he would spend several months traveling, effectively out of the way while Mammot consolidated his hold and bought loyalties in the senate to secure his confirmation. On the other hand, sending Stiger to Vrell achieved nearly the same result. It was more likely that the path Mammot wished him to follow was the one that led to Vrell. Though Stiger was no spy, marching into hostile territory would keep a potential spy for the senate isolated, unable to communicate with his masters. The plan had been to isolate him from the moment he arrived.

Stiger suppressed a sigh of resignation. "I will follow General Mammot's orders as if they were General Kromen's."

"The general expects nothing less from one of your, ah ... venerated lineage," Captain Handi said.

Stiger could not decide if he meant this as a calculated insult. After a moment, he decided it had been intended as one. The urge to reach over the table and throttle the pampered fool before him was nearly overpowering. With great effort, he restrained himself, vowing that one day he would make the man pay for such ungentlemanly insults. On that day, Handi would know with whom he was toying.

"Duty," Stiger said by way of reply, forcing a smile. "Duty to the empire is our responsibility."

"I could not agree more with such honest sentiments," Captain Handi breathed rather dramatically. He pulled an envelope out of a cloak pocket and handed it over to Stiger. "Confirmation of your orders...from General Mammot."

Stiger took several minutes to read through his orders while Captain Handi waited patiently. The staff captain pulled out a pipe and filled it with tobacco, then went to the fireplace to light it.

Stiger found the orders nearly identical to the set he had previously been given. It was very clear Mammot wanted him on his way to Vrell. He set the orders down on the table after he had read them twice over. Handi, seeing that Stiger had finished, returned to the table and sat, taking a deep pull and puff of his pipe.

"Do you have any questions concerning your orders?" the staff captain asked.

"None," Stiger responded firmly.

"Excellent," Handi replied. "General Mammot will be pleased to hear that."

"Has there been an update on the supply train?" Stiger asked. He had heard nothing for several days on its progress. He had been using the extra time to push his men hard.

"As a matter of fact, there has been news," Captain Handi said. "The supply convoy from Aeda will arrive within the next five days."

"That is encouraging news," Stiger responded, thinking that the sooner it arrived, the quicker he would be on his way. Mammot might be the type to use assassins to cement his control. It was quite possible that it would be healthier for Stiger to be on the road and away until the dust settled.

"Yes it is, isn't it," Handi said, standing with his pipe tightly clamped between his teeth. He gave Stiger an odd look before he pulled on his riding gloves. "It will be good to reopen communications with Castle Vrell."

The two officers left the farmhouse, Stiger following slightly behind Handi. They found the cavalry escort sitting on the ground, with their backs against the barricade wall near the entrance. They were downing a fresh bowl of stew. The men looked to be enjoying themselves. Handi gave them a sour look and called for his horse.

Lan jumped up, setting his bowl aside. He called his men to their feet. Their mounts were easily at hand, having been tethered along the inside of the barricade. They stood, while at the same time shoveling the rest of the stew into their mouths as fast as they could. Cook, with an assistant, took the wooden bowls from the cavalrymen. Stiger was pleased to see the lieutenant's men thank Cook before turning to their horses. It wasn't every day a cook received thanks from a group of young noblemen, even if they were only unimportant second and third sons.

"A pleasure seeing you once again, Captain," Handi said, not bothering to offer Stiger a handshake. It was yet another intentional insult. Stiger felt dirty enough from the man's visit and was far from disappointed at not having to take the man's hand.

Sergeant Ranl led Captain Handi's horse forward and Handi mounted up.

"Likewise," Stiger responded, struggling to keep the distaste from his voice. "Please inform General Mammot I am at his convenience."

"I will," Handi said, wheeling his mount around and nudging it forward out through the gate. His cavalry escort scrambled to mount and catch up.

"Captain," Lan said to Stiger as he pulled himself up onto his horse. His charge was rapidly getting away. The cavalry lieutenant remained a moment to offer a salute, with a lopsided, youthful grin. "Thank you for your hospitality and the quick meal. I am confident I speak for my men in that it is greatly appreciated."

"You are more than welcome to visit for a longer stay," Stiger responded with a return salute, "and break bread with us once again."

"I believe I might take you up on your offer, sir," Lan said. "We are scheduled for perimeter patrol tomorrow. Would it be convenient if we called toward the end of our circuit?"

"It would," Stiger agreed. "I will speak with Cook and make sure we have something fresh."

"Thank you, Captain," Lan said with a genuine smile. He wheeled his horse around and started her forward out of the camp. Once beyond the gate, he sent his horse into a gallop to catch up with his men and charge.

Stiger watched for a moment, thinking about Mammot, Kromen, and Vrell. He wondered where Colonel Karol stood with the change of command and power struggle that appeared to be well underway. The colonel had seemed like an honorable man. Stiger found it interesting that Handi had not mentioned him.

"Seems like a right good officer, that cavalryman," Sergeant Ranl commented. Stiger nodded in agreement, hoping the sergeant's instincts were right, for though in general he disliked the cavalry, he felt the same way.

EIGHT

"Begin again," Stiger barked harshly. The rain, driven by a goodly wind, was coming down in near sheets.

"Lock shields right!" Sergeant Ranl thundered, standing behind one file, which was facing another in the downpour.

"Lock shield left!" Sergeant Blake roared. He was standing behind the opposite file of men.

Shields snapped and thunked solidly together as the two files of men prepared to clash with each other yet again.

"Push!" Sergeant Blake roared.

"Push 'em, boys!" Sergeant Ranl thundered. The two files slammed together with a resounding crash. The sergeants shouted orders as each file attempted to break the other's line by using their shields and brute strength. It was an old, time-tested drill that was good practice, and fun, despite the driving rain. Not only did such contests boost morale, it prepared the men for the real thing. The competition made a tremendous clamor as practice shields hammered violently and repeatedly against each other. The ground on the practice field outside the main gate had been churned up. The mud was ankle deep, making the contest that much more difficult. Stiger believed in training his men under all types of weather conditions, for sometimes battles were fought when conditions were far from ideal.

The captain watched closely as each file fought the other for dominance. The contest was rough, brutal, and aggressive. That evening, there would be plenty of nursing lumps and bruises.

Sergeant Blake's file abruptly and without warning broke into two parts as a man slipped and fell into the churned-up mud. The winners let loose a terrific cheer, followed closely by the rest of the company that had been watching the contest.

These two files had bested all of the others, and the winners were champions for the day. There was no prize. They were simply the best, and in that they took pride. There were good-natured back slaps and ribbing from both sides.

"Lieutenant," Stiger called over the rain, after the cheering and celebration had died down. Dusk was fast approaching, and with the help of the rain clouds, the day was darkening rapidly. "Dismiss the men for the evening."

"Yes, sir," the drenched lieutenant said.

Stiger turned and walked back through the camp's gate as Ikely dismissed the company. The sentry on duty snapped to attention and saluted as he passed. Returning the salute with a nod, Stiger walked rapidly to the farmhouse. The rain was chilly. Stiger wanted nothing more than to dry off and warm up.

The warmth of the house washed over him as he entered. He had left a fire blazing in the fireplace. It had burned low, but was still crackling at the remains of two logs. The fireplace provided the only light in the dusk-darkened house, made blacker by the rain. The captain threw on another two logs, which caused the fire to spit and flare in a shower of sparks. Stiger removed his boots and placed them by the fireplace to dry, then stripped off his drenched tunic. Unlike his men, he had not been wearing his armor. He pulled on a dry one before dragging a chair over to the fireplace to hang his wet clothing. He lit two thick tallow candles, which he placed on the table. An oil lantern hung from above. He lit that as well. The room brightened considerably.

On the table, a map was stretched out, corners held down by small river rocks. The map was old. It had not been a quick reproduction made by some camp scribe. Reproductions could be unreliable, as camp scribes were few in number and overworked. They were usually rushed, and known to omit details. Having an original map depicting the accurate lay of the land was a rare treasure.

The map had arrived by courier that morning, courtesy of General Mammot. Stiger leaned over the table and traced the road to Castle Vrell with his finger. Someone had penciled in the location of the legionary encampment. There were a couple of villages marked along the road. Based upon his meeting with Generals Kromen and Mammot, Stiger doubted he would find any villagers; it was likely both villages had been thoroughly sacked. Ashes and shallow graves were all that likely remained. Coming south, Stiger had passed a number of small villages and towns, pillaged and burned, devoid of life. The empire punished rebellion harshly.

Stiger sighed and took a seat, studying the map. The silence from Castle Vrell was telling. Either the rebels were besieging the castle, which would mean they had a substantial force operating in the area, or they had simply cut the road. The latter was the more likely scenario. According to the map, there were no roads leading from Castle Vrell farther south into rebel territory.

Stiger returned his gaze to the castle, which seemed to be in the middle of nowhere, built astride a mountain pass leading into the valley. He supposed, prior to the empire swallowing up much of the South, a local lord had built the castle for his own protection. The castle then would be old, likely very old. If the walls were poorly maintained, he considered the possibility that a small rebel force might have stormed and overcome the garrison. Having seen the legionaries of the main encampment, the captain could only imagine what condition the garrison was in.

The Vrell Valley boasted a few towns and villages. Oakheart, the largest town, was notated on the map. A few other settlements were named, but the only other feature that caught Stiger's eye was not in the valley itself, but on one of the mountains on the north end of the valley: Thanedom Mountain. It was an odd name. After considering it for a bit, the captain supposed one of the long-dead lords of the valley had named the mountain as his own or some such nonsense.

Stiger sighed deeply and took a seat. His chair creaked alarmingly as he leaned back. Could the rebels have taken the castle? Was it simply that the road had been cut? The questions were maddening.

In the North, Stiger had relied heavily on Eli's detailed knowledge of the ground. But in all of the elf's long years, his friend had never been this far south. Eli knew nothing about the ground. Stiger had asked for someone who was familiar with the lay of the land and Vrell. General Mammot had provided the map, but had not yet produced anyone who had been to Vrell, which was troubling. Was he setting Stiger up for failure? It certainly felt that way.

An entire legion had once disappeared in this area. Every legionary knew of the Thirteenth, subsequently known as the Vanished. The Thirteenth had been led by a great man, General Delvaris. It had occurred when the empire had first decided to expand into the wild, untamed lands of the South. There were, of course, rumors, speculations, and legends, yet no one knew for sure what had happened. The legion had been the first to march south, and had simply disappeared into the vast Southern forests, as if by magic. Many had gone in search of the Thirteenth's eagle, the symbol of the empire, but none had ever found it. Over three hundred years later, the mystery of the Vanished was no closer to being solved, and had since become legend.

With the loss of the Thirteenth, the Delvaris family reputation, prestige, and influence had subsequently been ruined. Unfortunately, Stiger had a personal connection to the story—he was a direct descendent, on his mother's side, of General Delvaris. Though Delvaris was a distant relative, the entire affair was also a black mark on the Stiger family history.

Stiger rubbed his eyes, tired. There was a hard knock on the doorframe, jarring him from his contemplations. Despite the cold, Stiger had left the door open. He enjoyed hearing the sound of the rain. He found it relaxing.

"Yes?" Stiger asked, looking up.

"Sorry to bother you, sir. I thought you would like to know Lieutenant Lan's patrol is coming in," Corporal Kennet reported. Stiger had recently approved ten men for promotion to corporal. A week later, it appeared that his sergeants had made good recommendations. Yet the true test of their worth would ultimately come with battle.

"Thank you. Have their horses put up in the barn," Stiger ordered. "See that his men get fed and are allowed to dry out somewhere. When the lieutenant is ready, please escort him over."

"Yes, sir," the corporal responded, and left.

Stiger leaned back in his chair, contemplating the lieutenant. This was Lan's fifth visit to their camp in as many weeks. Each visit had only lasted a few hours as the troop took a break from their patrolling. Lan was from a good, though moderately prosperous, family from the province of Venney. The family was known for their exquisite wines, which they produced and shipped throughout the empire.

There was another knock at the door. Stiger looked up to find the lieutenant. The man was dripping wet and looking a tad bit miserable, but proud.

"Lieutenant," Stiger greeted, without getting up. "Nice to see you again. I trust that, despite the rain, you had a quiet patrol?"

"Lieutenant Lan," the lieutenant said formally, stepping into the room. He drew himself up to attention and saluted. "Reporting for duty as ordered, sir." Dripping water on the roughhewn wood floor, the lieutenant reached inside his overcoat and withdrew a set of orders. He handed them over for Stiger to examine.

"I see," Stiger said, retrieving the orders, which were slightly damp. He glanced them over. The lieutenant and his troop of cavalry had been detached from their current patrol assignments and attached to Stiger's command for the duration of the supply run to Vrell.

"I understand that you requested us personally," the lieutenant stated.

"That's right," Stiger said, grabbing a mug on the table. He poured himself some tea from a pot that had long since cooled. At the time, Stiger had doubted that General Mammot would approve his request. Perhaps the general suspected that Stiger was reporting his activities to the senate. That might also explain the delivery of an original map instead of a camp copy. Mammot might be giving Stiger everything he requested to avoid any type of bad report. It was an intriguing line of thought. If true, Stiger wondered what else he might request.

"May I ask why? There are other cavalry troops in the encampment."

"I know you," Stiger said simply, taking a slow sip. "I do not know the other troop commanders. Your men respect you, which, in my experience, speaks well. I also think you show promise."

"I see, sir," the lieutenant said, without betraying any emotion.

"Did the general inform you of our mission?" Stiger asked.

"No, sir," the lieutenant answered. "I did not actually speak with the general himself. Captain Handi delivered my orders."

Stiger simply nodded, satisfied that the mission was still a secret. If the rebels found out what they were up to, things might get ugly.

"However, sir," the lieutenant added after a moment, "I must admit…word around the encampment is that your company has been tasked with escorting the next supply train to Castle Vrell and opening the road."

Stiger slammed a fist down on the table in irritation and the lieutenant jumped slightly. If word had gotten around the encampment, then it was likely the rebels knew as well. Damn!

"That is correct," Stiger said after a moment, getting himself under control. "What do you know of the road to Vrell?"

"A solid road," the lieutenant reported. "It was repaired a few years ago by imperial engineers. A wagon train should have no real problem, but…"

"But what?" Stiger asked as the lieutenant trailed off.

"It is not a particularly safe road. It is heavily forested, with plenty of places to hide," the lieutenant explained. "I was on the last supply run about six months ago. We took an entire company of cavalry to ensure the train made it."

"Did you?" Stiger asked, leaning forward. Here was his man with direct personal experience of the road to Vrell and the castle. Stiger had requested an interview with someone who knew the land. General Mammot had delivered once again.

"Yes, though at the cost of ninety men," the lieutenant said with some anger heating his voice.

"How many rebels were killed in exchange?" Stiger asked.

"That we know of," Lan answered, hesitating slightly, "we were only able to locate two bodies."

"Two?" Stiger asked with some surprise.

"Yes," the lieutenant answered. "The rebels hid like cowards, ambushing the column with archers and then melting back into the trees."

Stiger's eyes narrowed. "So, there were no standup fights? Only ambushes?"

"Correct," the lieutenant answered grimly, with a worried look. "To be frank, I do not relish the idea of making the journey back to Vrell."

Stiger pushed himself back from the table, stood, and began pacing the room, thinking furiously. The road was mostly forested. A handful of good men could have made life hell for a slow-moving supply train escorted exclusively by cavalry. Stiger had seen it done in the forests of Abath. He looked back at the map. A small force. It had to be a small force. He was more convinced of that than ever. Had the rebels had a substantial force, they would've easily taken the train after having whittled down the escort.

Stiger stopped pacing and glanced over at the lieutenant as a thought occurred to him. The lieutenant's troop had been one of the few noticeably active units he had seen in the south. Studying the young man, who shifted uncomfortably under his gaze, Stiger suddenly knew with certainty that the lieutenant was out of favor. Mammot had not given him this troop from the goodness of his heart. The lieutenant's troop was active because they had been pulling all of the shit assignments. Mammot had probably jumped at the opportunity to rid himself of another trouble officer.

"Lieutenant," Stiger said abruptly. "I've noticed your men and animals are always clean. Why is that the case when everyone else in the encampment appears to be covered in mud and shit?"

"I insist my men care for themselves and their mounts," the lieutenant stated firmly, and then added, "It also helps that we are stationed at a small village two miles from the encampment."

"Exiled?" Stiger asked, knowing the answer even before the lieutenant confirmed with a curt nod. They had thought to isolate Lan from camp society as punishment, but in doing so had inadvertently spared him and his men from the rot and disease.

"The condition of the men in the main encampment offends me," the lieutenant admitted after a moment's silence. "I said as much. It was—"

"No matter," Stiger waved a hand dismissively, cutting the lieutenant off.

"You don't care what I—"

"It only speaks well of you," Stiger said. He went to the door and looked out into the rain. "Corporal Kennet?" Stiger called across the rain-drenched farmyard.

"Yes, sir?" Kennet hustled over. The rain was coming down even more heavily, if that was possible.

"When Lieutenant Eli'Far returns, I would like to see him. He is due sometime this evening. Also send for Lieutenant Ikely."

The corporal saluted and left.

"Make sure your men are settled," Stiger addressed Lan, returning to the table. He sat. "Get yourself dry, fed, and rested. We will have an officer's council tonight. You will tell me everything you know about the road to Vrell, what you noticed and experienced. Anything and everything."

"Of course, sir." The lieutenant nodded, eyes troubled. The captain knew what the man was thinking. The thought of riding that road again scared him badly.

"Lieutenant," Stiger said. "I cut my teeth in the forests of Abath. We have good scouts and an elven ranger, giving us a huge advantage. It will not be an easy task, but I am confident that we can teach these rebels a lesson they will not soon forget." Stiger looked back down at the map. He had not just survived the forests of Abath, he had made them his own. He doubted that there was a better commander in the South suited for their current mission. Forest fighting was Stiger's specialty, and besides, he had Eli.

"Yes, sir," the lieutenant said, still looking concerned.

"Now, go see to your men," Stiger ordered without looking up. "And make sure you get something hot to eat."

The lieutenant stood, saluted, and left.

"Sir?" Ikely asked, stepping inside a few moments later. He was moderately dry, having made the run from his tent to the farmhouse.

"Lieutenant Lan and his troop have been assigned to us. Help them get settled and make sure they have everything they require. This evening, after Eli returns, we will have an officer's council."

The lieutenant nodded.

"Also, pass the word on to Cook. Have him prepare one week's cooked rations for the scouts," Stiger ordered. "They will be going out in the morning, along with Eli."

"Yes, sir," the lieutenant said, clearly surprised at the news.

"It was a difficult time," a somber Lan finished up. Stiger, like his lieutenants, stood at the table, a fire crackling in the hearth. The rain continued unabated, drumming steadily on the roof. The fire provided the room with abundant warmth.

As the cavalry officer had talked through the nightmare that had been the last supply train to Castle Vrell, both Stiger and Eli had questioned everything, from the road to the density of the forest to the variety of trees and ground cover. They also asked about the types of arrows and bows the enemy used, how they fought, how the cavalry responded, and on and on. The lieutenant seemed exhausted from both the telling and the detailed questioning.

"Supposing most of the forest is old hardwood," Eli spoke up after a brief silence, "then I believe we can expect the rebels to ambush us at points where there are younger trees and an abundance of undergrowth. I would assume these sites specifically to be located around the remains of any human settlements."

"Agreed," Stiger said, feeling somewhat relieved after having heard the lieutenant out. He looked over at Eli, rubbing his jaw thoughtfully. "I would think you should not have too much difficulty locating the rebel camps."

"Sir," Lieutenant Lan spoke up, confused. "How can one company and a troop of cavalry hope to deal with the rebels in that forest?"

"I believe that the last train encountered only a handful of rebels," Stiger answered matter-of-factly.

"That simply cannot be," the lieutenant protested, appalled at the thought. "A handful of men … do you really think so? I just can't believe that …"

"In the forests of Abath, ten to twenty men armed with bows would seem like an army," Stiger said and then gestured to the map. "Look at the terrain. There are mountains between the forest and rebel strongholds to the south. Simply put, the rebels are too far from their supply base, and the physical obstacles are just too great to field more than a few men. They are living off the land. I would bet my pension on it."

"A handful of men caused us that much grief?" Lan breathed, shaking his head in disbelief.

"Eli and I have done the same," Stiger explained. "I would be surprised if they have more than thirty or forty men operating along the entire road. Supply trains are slow by nature. They could easily have taken advantage of the pace, ambushing the column at carefully selected points."

"It cannot be so," Lan insisted, shaking his head.

"Look," Stiger said, "had the force been large, don't you think they would have whittled you down and then taken the train by force? They didn't, so it stands to reason they did not have the strength to do so."

"As you say, there should be no difficulty in locating their camps," Eli said, bringing the conversation back on track. He was looking thoughtfully at the map spread out on the table. "I suppose they would have to be camped quite close to the road to keep it effectively cut."

"My thoughts exactly," Stiger agreed, turning back to the map. "If we are lucky, we may be able to catch them by surprise, eliminating one camp at a time."

"And if we are unlucky?" Ikely asked, looking up from the map.

"Then the captain is wrong, and we run into a large number of rebels," Eli said, cocking his head to one side. "We may also find Castle Vrell in their hands."

"Eli." Stiger looked meaningfully at his friend. "I received word today that the wagon train has arrived at the main encampment and should be ready to depart in two days. Tonight, I want you and your scouts to deal with our rebel friends. I would prefer to deliver a 'live' rebel to General Mammot for interrogation."

"It will be as you ask," Eli said.

"What are you talking about?" Lan asked, eyebrows raised. "There is not a rebel within twenty miles."

"We have identified several rebel observation posts in the hills around the main encampment," Stiger answered with a gesture toward Eli. "Once removed, with a little luck, we can be on the road before the rebels realize we have departed or discover that they have lost their eyes."

Lieutenant Lan said nothing, though he blushed furiously, most likely at the thought that he and his men had missed something this important. They had been patrolling for months now, and had seen no signs of the enemy.

"Eli," Stiger continued, "I have ordered a week's worth of rations cooked for you and your scouts. Once the observation posts have been dealt with, set out. I want the rebel camps located long before the company arrives. Stay in contact with our main body. You know what I expect."

Eli nodded in understanding, but said nothing. It was an old dance between them, and he indeed knew what the captain expected of him and his men.

"Once we discover the locations of the enemy camps," Stiger growled, "we will eliminate them as we come upon them, taking care to let no one escape. I trust we will make the journey with a lot less grief than the previous supply train encountered."

"Should we discontinue training?" Ikely asked. "Have the men begin preparing for the road?"

"Yes," Stiger responded after a moment's thought. "I want all gear inspected and ready. Anything that needs to be replaced, from sandals to cookware, must get done before we depart."

There was a knock at the open door. Everyone turned at the interruption.

"Sir," Kennet ventured tentatively from the door, "rider coming in, sir."

Stiger glanced over at Eli, who looked back. They were both thinking the same thing: trouble. For only trouble could bring a messenger out into the black of night with the heavens pouring out sheets of cold rain.

"Thank you," Stiger said. Corporal Kennet left as the captain turned back to Ikely. "I want three days' cooked rations prepared for the men. Make it extremely clear that eating their rations straight off will not be tolerated. I have known legionaries who felt that rations were more easily carried in their stomachs than on their shoulders."

"Yes, sir." Ikely chuckled at the comment. "I will impress it upon them."

"Most of the company," Stiger said, looking around at those gathered, "are going to be marching hard and ahead of the train."

"We are going to leave the train lightly guarded?" Ikely asked, astonished at the thought.

"Not completely," Stiger admitted. "I will leave two files and the cavalry to guard the wagons. The bulk of the company, however, will push ahead to deal with the rebel camps.

The plan is simple. Our scouts will locate the enemy camps and each will be dealt with as the main body comes up. Speed and surprise will be our main weapons. With luck, the rebels should never get close to the train."

"Sir," Lan protested. "I would like to request the honor of joining the main body."

"I know how you feel," Stiger said with a trace of a frown. He wanted to give the lieutenant his wish; however, he could not. Lan's men were still an unknown factor, whereas Stiger's men were not, having been worked hard these past few weeks. "The terrain where the enemy will have camped will be more suited to infantry. Besides...I don't want to risk losing a few of your men or your horses needlessly. We may need your troop at a later time."

"I understand, sir," Lan said, clearly disappointed. He accepted his commanding officer's wishes without complaint. Stiger was impressed at this display of control.

"If we are unlucky," Eli interjected with a mischievous smile filled with little needle-like teeth, "your cavalry troop might get some action."

Stiger frowned at Eli.

There was a knock on the doorframe.

"Father Thomas," Corporal Kennet announced solemnly. Everyone turned in surprise.

A large man wearing brown, priestly, cloak-like robes, with the hood pulled up against the rain, stepped through the door. The man threw his hood back, revealing a shock of red hair and a bushy red beard. His eyes were kindly and seemed to twinkle with a child's delight.

Father Thomas took in the four officers. He cocked an eyebrow at the sight of Eli. As he placed his hands on his hips, his robes parted slightly to reveal a heavy chainmail shirt emblazoned with the High Father's sigil. The hilt of a large sabre emerged, hanging low and to his left side, the tip nearly dragging on the floor.

"I see that I finally found Captain Stiger and the Eighty-Fifth Imperial Foot!" The large man's voice boomed in the small room. "Do you know how difficult it was to find your camp? In the dark? In the rain? However did you manage to select such an isolated place to camp?"

"Holy Father, it is an honor to be in your presence," Eli said with reverence, for here before him was the direct representative of one of the gods that his race honored. He offered a respectful bow.

"The High Father's will drew me here," Father Thomas responded jovially, smiling at the elf before looking back at Stiger. "You must be Captain Stiger. I understand you are traveling to Vrell, sir. General Mammot was quite kind enough to provide me a pass to accompany you. Do you wish to see it?"

"Oh shit!" Stiger breathed, blood draining from his face. His hand suddenly trembled, then clenched as he glared at Father Thomas.

"What's wrong?" Lan asked, confused, looking between Father Thomas and Stiger. "He is the High Father's representative. We should be honored to have been blessed with a warrior priest. Should we not?"

"He is no simple warrior priest," Stiger growled angrily, pointing an accusatory finger in the direction of Father Thomas, who frowned in reply. "We are in the presence of a great, big, bloody holy warrior of the High Father."

There was shock from Ikely and Lan as the words sank in. They both turned to look at Father Thomas in awe. Eli simply stood there, saying nothing and betraying no emotion.

"A paladin?" Ikely asked after a moment. "He is a paladin? A real paladin? Is that what you are saying?"

"Yes," Stiger snapped in mounting rage, jabbing another accusatory finger in Father Thomas's direction. "A great, big, bloody, red-headed paladin sent to us by the blessed High Father!"

"That's me," Father Thomas said with a cheerful wink.

"Mark my words," Stiger continued, "where paladins go, there is always trouble, and not the little kind either."

"I thought paladins were good?" Ikely breathed, shocked at his captain's harsh words.

"Well, Lan," Stiger snapped irately, never taking his angry gaze away from Father Thomas, "you may get your wish after all. It looks as if we are unlucky enough to warrant a paladin on quest. Now, gentlemen, if you will excuse me, I am going to go for a piss before bed." With that, Stiger tipped his head slightly to Father Thomas and stepped around the man and out into the pouring rain, without bothering to grab his cloak.

⚜ ⚜ ⚜

"That seemed to go so well," Father Thomas said, watching the captain disappear into the rain-lashed night. "I do so try with first impressions…"

"Pardon him, Father," Eli said softly, stepping near. "I can say that he is the best of men, but…"

"But," Father Thomas finished, glancing back in the direction of the door, "he has encountered another paladin on quest, I presume?"

"Father Griggs joined us for the campaign in Abath," Eli answered.

"Poor Griggs." Father Thomas breathed a heavy sigh. "His loss and sacrifice was a great blow to our order."

"Are you really a paladin?" Ikely asked, still awed.

"I am a simple warrior in the service of the High Father," the paladin said, his joviality returning along with his booming voice.

"He is a holy warrior called by the High Father to serve," Eli confirmed for the lieutenant. "He is, indeed, what you humans would name a paladin."

"It is an honor to meet you, sir." Ikely bowed reverently. "Will you bless our company with a morning service?"

"I think a simple service can be arranged," Father Thomas said. "As long as it does not upset our good captain too much."

"Thank you, Father," Ikely said. "The men will be greatly encouraged by your presence on our march to Castle Vrell."

"Is it true, then?" Lan asked, eying the paladin carefully. He appeared deeply troubled by the captain's reaction to Father Thomas.

"Is what true?" Father Thomas asked, raising an eyebrow at the cavalry lieutenant.

"Is what the captain says true?" Lan asked plainly. "Does your presence represent trouble on our way to Vrell?"

"The High Father called me here," Father Thomas said with a simple shrug, never losing his smile. "The call could be in service to something related or unrelated. I will not know until I recognize it."

"I see," Lan said thoughtfully. "So it could be as bad as the captain suggests?"

"It is possible," Father Thomas conceded with a slight frown. "There could be great danger for all, and that could be the High Father's purpose in calling me here. My assistance in defeating it may be necessary."

"What of this Father Griggs?" Lan asked of Eli. "Was the danger grave?"

"It was," Eli admitted.

"A priestess of Avaya, if I understand correctly," Father Thomas said. "The High Father called Griggs to deal with her."

"Great gods!" Lan breathed, aghast. "I pray we never come across such evil!"

"My son, I pray that be so as well," Father Thomas agreed, making the holy sign of the High Father.

"Lieutenant Ikely," Eli said. "Father Thomas will need a place to stay and dry off."

"It will be my honor to arrange it," Ikely said. "Father, have you eaten?"

"Why, I thought you would never ask!" Father Thomas's stomach rumbled, at which he laughed deeply.

"I think we can find you something," Ikely said, grabbing his cloak from by the fire. The lieutenant led Father Thomas out into the rain. Eli followed a moment later, leaving Lan alone in the room. Lan looked down upon the map, wondering just what was waiting for them on their journey to Castle Vrell. He had a growing feeling that, whatever it was, he would not like it.

NINE

Sometime during the early morning hours, the rain had passed. Shortly after sunrise, Eli and a couple of his scouts marched in with a battered, but very live, prisoner.

The rebel was a small, wiry man. His clothing was threadbare and tattered. He looked very unimpressive, especially to the men of the company, who had gathered 'round for a look. Most had never seen a live rebel. It was an eye-opening experience. Seeing the stares, Stiger decided to take advantage of the situation.

He pushed through the throng and approached the prisoner. The man was wet and shivering, though probably more from fright than cold. His hands were tied securely behind his back. The rebel collapsed to his knees at the captain's feet, babbling in what passed for one of the many guttural Southern languages, which Stiger did not know. The captain looked down at the groveling man for a moment, feeling nothing but disgust. The prisoner, no matter his reasoning, had rebelled against his empire. There was no excuse. His life was forfeit.

"This is your enemy," Stiger said flatly, gesturing at the blubbering prisoner. "At the moment, he looks pathetic, weak, and frightened. Why shouldn't he? This wretch is our helpless prisoner.

"Make no mistake, when armed and in his element, he can kill. He will end your life if you give him the chance. If you let your guard down, he will happily stick a knife or sword between your ribs in a heartbeat."

Stiger paused to allow that to sink in. The men were all ears, hanging onto his words. "This one was caught observing the main legionary encampment. The rebels have been watching it for a long time. Lieutenant Eli'Far even witnessed a rebel sneaking around our camp."

The men looked startled at that revelation. Eli's scouts, under orders, had not breathed a word to the men. He was confident the rebels had spies and sympathizers in the main encampment, most likely either slaves or camp attendants. The captain had kept the knowledge from his men for fear that a loose word to a dispatch rider or some other visitor from the main encampment would alert the rebels.

Stiger specifically sought out Legionary Teg from the crowd and intentionally locked eyes with the man, sending a silent message. Teg held the captain's gaze for a moment, before bowing his head slightly and nodding, as if to say that he would not fail at his duty again.

"This is your enemy." Stiger's voice rose in tone. "In the forests of Abath, I have seen a wretch like him take down a veteran of twenty years. They will move about in the darkness or under the cover of the brush, looking for an opportunity to get close ... to catch you with your guard down. Do not fear this wretch. Instead, respect what he is capable of doing. Properly respected, the rebel is less dangerous. They are not to be feared, but respected. Trust in me to lead you. Trust in me to respect our enemy ... for when properly respected and dealt with, they are nothing but rabble."

Stiger paused again, allowing his words sink in. "We march soon. Keep a watchful eye. Stay vigilant. Do not let your guard down, for if you do, it could cost you your life and that of your fellows. Trust in me, and we will teach these curs to fear us!"

The men gave a hearty cheer at that.

"Sergeant Blake." Stiger turned to his sergeant. "Have the prisoner secured. The men may view him, but they are not in any way to molest him. He is to be delivered to General Mammot for questioning."

"Yes, sir," Blake replied, then turned to two of the armed sentries who had just come off watch. "Boatman and Feld, you two guard the prisoner. Make sure no harm comes to him."

Both saluted and then stepped up to the prisoner, relieving the scouts. Stiger spared one more look at the prisoner, made a motion for Eli to follow, and they walked off toward the farmhouse. The men parted to let them pass. Stiger hoped his speech had made an impression. Perhaps it would save lives in the coming days.

"Did you get anything from him or the others?" Stiger asked once they were inside. The fire had died down. He threw on another log to drive away the damp, chill morning air.

"Yes," Eli answered, removing his cloak and hanging it by the fire. "There is a rebel force to the south, somewhere around the city of Teml. It seems to be no more than forty miles away, which is rather close, don't you think? I could not get an exact number, but it appears to be a significant force of many thousands."

"What about toward Vrell?" Stiger asked. "Did he know anything important to us?"

"Nothing. He came from one of the rebel lands to the far south," Eli stated. "He seemed exclusively concerned with the main encampment. I don't think he knows anything of Vrell, which seems rather odd if the rebels have a force operating along the road."

Stiger agreed. It seemed damned odd that those sent to observe would know nothing of rebel activity along the road from the encampment to Vrell. Though it was certainly possible they had been kept in the dark. It did not make sense. There should have been some level of contact among rebel forces operating in the area.

"Were you able to recover any documents?" Stiger asked.

"No," Eli said. "The one we captured is illiterate, along with the others I interrogated. It appears someone personally comes around to collect verbal reports on what they have seen. If we had more time, we could lay a trap for this person."

"No time for that," Stiger sighed regretfully. "General Mammot will have to arrange for it. I will write up a report for the general to make him aware of this enemy force and the intelligence you gathered. I will also forward the prisoner on to him for further questioning."

"I would prefer you be more respectful of Father Thomas," Eli said, abruptly changing the subject. Though they respected the other gods, the elves worshiped the High Father almost exclusively. A direct representative of the High Father was to be treated with honor and utter respect.

"When are you planning on departing?" Stiger asked, not wishing to engage in such a discussion. Stiger had prayed never to see another paladin again. Where paladins went, death usually traveled as a close companion.

"When we are finished here." Eli let out a heavy sigh. "I have most of my scouts on the road already."

"Eli," Stiger said, hesitating. "I do not like this mission we have been given. With a paladin showing up...well, it bodes ill. I want you to—"

"Ben," Eli said, a look of sadness passing across his face. "Consider that we have been blessed by the High Father. Whatever evil lurks ahead..."

"The last one he sent us did not work out too well," Stiger interrupted. "Or have you forgotten?"

"I never forget," the elf said softly, but with steel in his voice. "Father Griggs failed us not. We fought great evil in the name of what is good. It would have been worse for us had the High Father not sent us his warrior cleric."

Stiger grunted, turning to the fire. Eli sighed softly. He retrieved his cloak and turned to leave, then stopped.

"I will leave signs and messages," Eli said, one hand on the doorframe, looking back. Eli would also have his scouts guide the company to suitable campsites along the march.

"Take care, my friend," Stiger said, turning back from the fire. He would not see Eli for several days. Eli gave a simple nod in reply and then left.

Stiger sat down at the table. He remained silent for a while, thinking about the ghosts of the past that visited him whenever he was alone. After a bit, he shook himself free, sending the ghosts on their way. He pulled out his dispatch pad and charcoal pencil. He wrote out a report to General Mammot, concerning the prisoner and the elimination of the observation posts. Once complete, he sealed the dispatch and sent for Sergeant Ranl.

It would be interesting to see how General Mammot took the news. Would Stiger be praised for initiative or reprimanded for not sharing the information sooner? Since the visit from Captain Handi, Stiger had heard nothing about General Kromen's condition or the power struggle undoubtedly underway. He had also heard nothing in reply to his dispatches to Colonel Karol, which did not bode well.

Stiger fairly itched to be on the road and away from what was transpiring in the main encampment.

"Have this dispatch delivered to General Mammot with my compliments, along with the prisoner," Stiger ordered when Ranl arrived, handing over the dispatch. "Provide sufficient escort and make sure he arrives alive and in good condition. General Mammot may wish to have him questioned."

"Yes, sir," Sergeant Ranl acknowledged, taking the message. "I will have one of the corporals lead the escort."

Stiger stood and walked to the front door as the sergeant left. He discovered Father Thomas sitting on the front porch, gazing at the prisoner across the camp. The paladin looked up at Stiger briefly before returning his gaze to the prisoner. The captain wondered how long the paladin had been there. Had he overheard Stiger's and Eli's conversation some minutes ago? In the end, Stiger decided, he didn't care if the man had heard or not.

The paladin got to his feet, gaze still on the prisoner. A number of legionaries were studying the wretch. "An ugly business," was all the paladin said before walking off.

Stiger watched as the escort detail was organized. Within minutes, the prisoner was led away and out of the camp. Stiger came to the conclusion that he could not disagree with the paladin's statement. War and rebellion...all of it was an ugly business.

The escort detailed for the supply train marched out of the camp to the rendezvous point that Eli had selected. The march had begun a little over an hour after sunrise. It was rapid and well-executed. There were none of the sullen looks and foot dragging that had been in evidence when the company had first marched from the main encampment. The practice marches had paid off handsomely. They looked like a completely different company than when Stiger had first taken command. The men were fit, conditioned, and ready.

The main body of the company, around one hundred sixty men, under the command of Lieutenant Ikely, had marched out a couple of hours prior to daybreak. They were already on the road to Vrell and marching hard. A normal movement, under full kit, consisted of thirty minutes of marching, followed by a fifteen-minute break, to be repeated continuously. The captain had instructed the main body to spend forty-five minutes of every hour on the move, followed by a fifteen-minute break.

Speed and surprise were the keys to success. In the event the rebels managed to get word of the train's movement, they would assume the pace would be a slow one. Such assumptions created an opportunity for surprise, which Stiger intended to fully capitalize on. He was also relying heavily on Eli and his newly trained scouts to give him a further edge. In this respect, Stiger had complete confidence in his friend, a trained ranger. There was no one better at this kind of work than Eli.

It was all rather simple, really...at least in theory. Once the enemy camps were identified and located, Stiger intended to fall on them before they even knew they were in mortal danger. In this way, he hoped to clear the road of the enemy. The captain hoped theory would translate into reality, though he knew from experience the unexpected frequently threw the best plans awry.

Kromen's orders had anticipated around four weeks' travel time to Vrell. If possible, the captain intended to arrive at Vrell within two weeks. The gods only knew what he would find on the way or what delays he might encounter. Worse ... he had no idea what he might discover at Vrell itself. One way or another, he was sure he would find out.

Stiger had elected to initially remain with the escort as the main body pushed ahead. The escort was some forty strong. Lieutenant Lan's mounted troop would bring the total strength of the escort to seventy men, thirty of them mounted. This force would guard the supply train and the four company wagons.

The captain's purpose in remaining with the escort was to meet the sergeant in charge of the supply train. Though the man was essentially the lead teamster, he would also be a legionary. Therefore, the sergeant would be subject to Stiger's orders, whether he agreed with them or not. Having this man's cooperation, or at the very least obedience, was critical.

The escort had been carefully selected with consideration of those who had experience in handling wagons. With the main bulk of the company ranging far ahead, the supply train would need to cover more ground on a daily basis than the teamsters were likely accustomed to. When the teamsters tired, Stiger intended for his men to take over. He expected some level of friction with this last point.

The rendezvous was a crossroads, with one fork leading to Vrell. There were no signs, just the two roads intersecting amidst abandoned fields separated by stone walls. A scattering of trees grew close to the edges of the roads.

The empire's initial interest in the South had been the vast hardwood forests. Many of the trees were old and tall, perfect for ship masts. Prior to the rebellion, there had once been a massive logging operation in this area. As the forest was cleared one acre at a time, settlers moved in to work the land. The result had seen the roads heavy with traffic and the surrounding fields well-tended. The people who had lived and worked here had long since either fled or, worse, taken up arms against the empire.

Having arrived at the rendezvous point, Stiger and the escort began their wait for the train to arrive. Though fall was fast approaching, the day was rapidly turning hot and humid. Perspiring under the sun, the men had fallen out and sought cover in the shade amongst the trees along the roadside. Some napped, while others played cards or threw dice.

Waiting seemed to be a requirement for the legionary. It was the same old tale of hurry up and wait. The last several weeks of whipping his company into shape had not only been physically demanding, but exhausting for Stiger. When the opportunity presented itself, he had learned to take sleep where he could find it. Moving to the shade of a large oak, the captain sat down with his back against the hard trunk. He shut his eyes and almost immediately fell asleep.

The men traded amused looks. Captain Stiger was an incredibly active and intense man. Napping was the last thing they expected him to do. Perhaps order additional training, but take a nap? No.

As the men waited, lounging about and talking, gaming, or sleeping, the sun climbed higher in the sky. The air grew warmer, more humid, and more uncomfortable. Insects buzzed about. The sergeants and all of the other corporals had gone with the main body. Only Corporal Beni had remained, though he would have preferred not to. He was new to his rank and responsibilities. Beni was more than a little nervous to be under the direct supervision of the captain, without a sergeant in sight to run cover.

To make matters worse, the paladin, Father Thomas, had also decided to join the escort. He was praying in the shade a few feet away from the captain. The two had spoken little. Beni had the feeling the captain disliked the paladin.

Superstitious, but not particularly a religious man himself, Beni had always felt uncomfortable around holy men. At least Father Thomas did not seem to be the kind to ask for money along with faith. The paladin was a powerful cleric with a strange mystical power that was to be feared. Corporal Beni had accordingly steered clear of him at every opportunity.

The corporal turned his thoughts to the orders Sergeant Blake had given him. He was to keep his men disciplined, under control, and make sure that they maintained their kit and provided an effective watch during camp. He was to check on the guard regularly as the train moved toward Vrell. In addition, as ordered, the corporal had also reinforced in stark terms to the men not to eat the extra rations they had been issued. He had been afraid that while the men waited, idly passing the time, they would become bored and pick through their rations. To prevent such an occurrence, he had threatened to thrash any man who violated this order. A thrashing by the corporal, one of the largest and strongest men in the company, was a serious threat. It also helped that Beni excelled in unarmed fighting. When the sergeants had begun instruction, a natural brawler, he had taken to it like a fish to water. As he stood along the road, waiting impatiently, the corporal smiled at the thought of what he could now do with his hands.

Beni glanced in the direction the supply train would come. The road was deserted. Lieutenant Lan and his troop had ridden before sunrise to meet and escort the supply train to the rendezvous. That had been hours ago. After weeks of constant activity and training, it felt odd to be doing nothing other than waiting alongside an abandoned crossroads. He wondered for the thousandth time about the holdup.

In irritation, the corporal kicked a stone. The stone rolled several feet before coming to a rest in the grass to the side of the dirt road. The bulk of the company was by now miles ahead, while the escort stood waiting and wasting time.

Beni glanced over at the captain, who was snoozing quietly against the tree. The corporal chuckled softly at his stupidity, as it suddenly occurred to him that if the captain was unconcerned, perhaps he should be as well. He had been with the legions long enough to know that waiting for someone else to do their job was perfectly normal.

It was his new rank and responsibilities that were getting to him. He had never thought to make corporal. He was profoundly grateful to the sergeants for recommending him and the captain for approving the promotion, which also meant more pay and an increased retirement pension. He was determined to live up to their expectations and exceed them.

Taking the captain's example to heart, the corporal selected a tree, sat down, and leaned back. He doubted he could sleep, though he could at least make it look like he was unconcerned, like the captain, if only for the men to see. Taking a deep breath, he closed his eyes and forced himself to relax.

The corporal awoke with a start. He blinked several times and glanced up through the leaves. The sun was well up in the sky, meaning it was sometime around noon. He was surprised to have actually fallen asleep.

Frowning, he was not sure what had woken him. Looking around, he realized it was the sound of hooves approaching. A rider was galloping up. He stood to see better, stretching as he did so. It was one of Lieutenant Lan's troopers. Beni approached as the rider pulled his mount to a stop. Half the company also stood up in anticipation. The corporal glanced over at the captain, who had not moved. He was still sleeping.

"The supply train is about ten minutes out," the trooper reported to the corporal.

"I will inform the captain," Beni responded.

The trooper nodded and dismounted to wait, leading his horse over to the grass and shade.

The corporal approached his commanding officer.

"Captain," he said tentatively.

"Yeah?" Stiger asked, cracking an eye and squinting at the corporal.

"The wagon train is ten minutes out, sir." Corporal Beni struggled to keep his voice under control. Beni had seen serious action during the first few years of the rebellion, though not much in the last few. Very little frightened him, but he was man enough to admit to himself that the captain unnerved him plenty.

"Is it now?" Stiger said tiredly. "They sure took their sweet time. In twenty minutes, have the men fall in then."

"Yes, sir," Corporal Beni said as the captain leaned his head back against the tree and promptly went back to sleep. Beni breathed a quiet sigh of relief as he stepped away.

It took fifteen minutes for the lead wagons to arrive. The train, comprising fifty heavy covered wagons, was strung out in a line that stretched out for more than a half mile. The lead teamster, Arnold, was a grizzled old legionary sergeant from supply. With difficulty, he climbed down from the lead wagon. Limping very badly, the sergeant hobbled over to the captain, who was standing with Beni. It was clear he had been wounded at some point in his career. Unable to march, he had likely been transferred to supply rather than being discharged as a disabled man. Either he had performed some impressive feat, or an officer had taken pity on him by securing him the position.

The sergeant frowned sourly at the legionaries drawn up alongside the road. Hobbling up to the captain, he saluted sloppily and introduced himself as Sergeant Arnold. Without introducing himself, Stiger briefly outlined his expectations for Arnold.

"My men only travel six hours per day, sir!" Sergeant Arnold protested in a wheezy voice that cracked with irritation. "You can't ask more than that."

"I can and am," Stiger said firmly. "Your wagons will roll from sunup 'til sundown."

"The mules won't last," Sergeant Arnold protested again.

"They will be fine," Stiger said, glancing at the team pulling the sergeant's own wagon. Beni looked too and judged them as well-fed and capable, though on the heavyset side. They appeared more accustomed to a sedate lifestyle than pulling a wagon. Had they been on a near-starvation diet, it might have been a different matter. In this case, he concluded, the extra exercise would not harm them.

"You can take a twenty-minute break every three hours," Stiger said.

"Twenty min—" the sergeant sputtered.

"Lieutenant Lan," Stiger called, cutting off the sergeant.

The cavalry officer cantered up and saluted. Beni noticed he looked rather put-out and irritated. He guessed the source of the irritation was Arnold and his slow-moving train.

"Sir?" the lieutenant asked calmly, carefully keeping the irritation from his voice.

"I have informed Sergeant Arnold I expect the wagons to roll from sunup to sundown, with a twenty-minute break every three hours. If his men tire, we have men in the escort who have experience handling wagons."

"Yes, sir," the lieutenant responded as Stiger called for his horse. The sergeant made to protest, which Stiger pointedly ignored.

"Keep in touch and send a rider forward with any issues you may encounter," Stiger ordered as Legionary Teg led over his horse.

"A few files of men and his troop for the trip to Vrell!" Sergeant Arnold exploded, turning red. "I was told we would have a full company! Where are the rest of your men? We will be cut to ribbons!"

"I am leaving you forty capable men and your troop," Stiger continued, addressing Lan, though the statement was clearly for Arnold's benefit. "You are in direct command of the train. See that you make good time."

"Forty men?" the sergeant asked again, aghast. "You are condemning all of us to death!"

"I will deal with the rebels," Stiger growled as he grabbed the reins of his horse and mounted up in a smooth, practiced motion. The captain pointedly ignored the sergeant's insubordination and disrespect. "I am taking the bulk of the company well ahead. We will strike at the rebels and take them apart before you even get close to their camps."

Stiger kicked his horse forward, leaving the sputtering old sergeant behind. He motioned for Lan to join him as he guided his horse onto the road to Vrell.

The irritated sergeant looked over at Beni, who smiled thinly at him. Then they both turned to watch the captain and lieutenant ride up the road a ways before coming to a stop.

"Who is that officer?" the irate sergeant asked the big corporal.

"That," corporal Beni responded with a wider smile, "is Captain Stiger."

The sergeant looked sharply at the corporal. Beni nodded in silent reply.

"A Stiger in the South?" Sergeant Arnold spat on the ground. "May the gods help us."

Farther up the road, having stopped his horse, Stiger turned to look back at the train of large, heavily laden covered wagons. The captain felt the full weight of responsibility, as if it had suddenly landed upon his shoulders. His orders were to resupply the garrison at Vrell. Not only were his own men relying upon him, so were the teamsters, and though they didn't know it, the entire garrison at Vrell. Should he fail, he wondered, how many would suffer? He would not fail, he swore silently.

"If the sergeant causes trouble, relieve him," Stiger ordered after a few moments. "Send word immediately and I will dispatch additional men to help manage the wagons, especially if the teamsters protest."

"Don't worry, sir," the lieutenant said confidently. "I believe I can handle Sergeant Arnold without having to relieve him or his men. I should think the threat of losing their pensions will prove a sufficient motivation. We may be a little slower than you are expecting, but I will get the train to Vrell."

"Your orders." Stiger pulled a sealed envelope from a pocket and handed it over. "Nothing we have not previously discussed."

"Yes, sir," Lan said, pocketing the orders.

"Very good, Lieutenant." Stiger leaned over and offered his hand, which Lan took. "I will see you at Castle Vrell in a few days."

"You can rely on me, sir," Lan replied confidently. "Have no doubt."

"I know I can," Stiger said, and with that he kicked his horse forward into a fast trot, leaving the supply train behind. It was time to catch up to the main body.

TEN

"**A**re the men ill?" Stiger asked Sergeant Blake as a man broke ranks, darting into the dense, man-high brush that lined both sides of the road. The captain was walking his horse at the end of the column, the sergeant walking alongside him. Dusk was fast approaching and, with it, the heat of the day was thankfully beginning to abate. The company had not yet entered the Sentinel Forest. The road to Vrell cut straight through its heart.

The company was marching past abandoned farmland as it approached the forest. The countryside on both sides of the road was littered with burned-out farmsteads. The once cultivated lands had grown wild with grass and brush. The region at one time had been rich and prosperous—a breadbasket, shipping grains back to the empire. Now devoid of inhabitants, it was an abandoned wasteland.

The captain watched as another man, farther ahead than the last, darted off the road to disappear into the brush. Bad food? The men had been eating well the past few weeks, but perhaps something in their game-rich diet was causing stomach disorder.

"Berry picking, sir," Sergeant Blake admitted sourly, after a slight pause. "Seems it is berry season, and many of these farms grew berries."

"Berry picking?" Stiger snarled with a deepening frown. The captain's blood boiled at this lapse in discipline. Sure enough, one of the men emerged from the bushes carrying a handful of what appeared to be end-of-summer jayberries. The man was smiling happily at his rich bounty.

"This is a march into hostile territory," Stiger snapped at Blake, beside himself with irritation. "I will not lose men because they are berry picking!"

"Yes, sir," Sergeant Blake said, casting his captain a careful look. "I will put a stop to it immediately, sir."

"Make sure they know not to wander off by themselves," Stiger ordered. "Once we are in the forest, if they need to step off, they are to do so in pairs and notify their corporal. We need to hammer this habit into them now. Should the rebels prove competent, they will know this forest. We will not."

"Yes, sir," Blake acknowledged.

"In the forest, it will be extremely easy to become turned around. Losing a man or two because he gets himself lost is the same as losing one to the enemy. We will not be able to stop to look. Do you understand me, Sergeant?"

"I understand, sir," the sergeant said seriously. "I will make it so the men understand, too."

Sergeant Blake hurried forward, calling for the corporals and sending a runner up to the front of the column to fetch Sergeant Ranl. The captain watched the sergeant for a moment, thinking furiously. If he wasn't careful, he would lose men he would be unable to replace to such thoughtlessness.

In short order, there were no more forays into the brush in search of berries. The sky was slowly beginning to darken with the arrival of dusk. Continuing to lead his horse, Stiger was left alone with his thoughts. The road climbed a gentle rise. Once at the summit, the Sentinel Forest came into view. Like a veil drawn across the land, the boundary of the forest stretched out to the left and right as far as the eye could see. In the gathering dusk, the tree line looked more like a foreboding wall of impenetrable darkness.

Stiger stopped. Nomad nuzzled his shoulder as he stared at the tree line. The Sentinel Forest reminded him very much of Abath. The captain's gut clenched as he felt his nerves wavering ever so slightly. Clamping down on the fear, Stiger started forward once more, leading his horse down the hill and toward the forest line. *This time it will be different,* the captain vowed silently, eying the forest.

This time he would conquer it.

One of Eli's scouts, Legionary Marcus, met the company at the tree line. The road cut a path right into the forest. Stiger had since moved to the head of the column, more out of an effort to control his fears and memories than by setting an example.

"Sir, the lieutenant sent me to guide you to a campsite he selected," Marcus reported, saluting. "It has plenty of open space and a fresh stream with water, and even a few crawfish."

"Is the lieutenant waiting at the campsite?" Stiger asked.

"Uh … no, sir," Marcus replied. "He is scouting ahead."

"Lead on, then," Stiger directed. He nodded for Ikely, who had just ridden up, to follow the scout. Stiger waited impatiently for the end of the column to come up. Once it did, he joined Sergeant Blake, who had once again stationed himself at the rear. As the column moved off into the outer edge of the forest, the sergeant made sure there were no stragglers.

Stiger said nothing as he walked his horse into the forest. The forest smelled deeply of pine, moss, and wet earth, dredging up memories the captain wished would remain buried. With each inevitable step forward, the canopy of leaves became thicker and made the early evening hours seem that much later.

The campsite was a short fifteen-minute march from the tree line, ten minutes along the road and five following a narrow game trail. A stand of much older trees had created a leaf-covered floor, bereft of brush and undergrowth. It was a pleasant enough spot, Stiger decided, studying the large clearing with a good-sized stream bubbling through.

Worn out from the heat of the day, the men fell out, some simply sitting down where they had stopped. Others made for the stream to refill their canteens. The men were allowed a few minutes of rest before beginning work on the camp.

Stiger hoped that it would not rain. The forest air was chilly, and with every passing hour would grow colder still. With the wagon train several miles behind, the men would be sleeping on their arms, without tents. Stiger looked around at his men. Those serving in the empire's legions were accustomed to such hardship.

"Marcus," Stiger called to the scout, seeing him across the camp.

The scout jogged over.

Stiger expected Lan to send a messenger updating him as to the train's progress. The campsite was pretty secluded, and it would prove difficult for the trooper to locate.

"Would you find the wagon train and lead one of Lieutenant Lan's troopers back to our camp, so they know where we are?"

"Yes, sir, I will," the scout said cheerfully, saluting. Grabbing his kit where it rested against the base of a nearby tree, the scout jogged off in the direction of the road. Several legionaries offered the scout a wave or backslap as he headed out. Stiger watched Marcus leave. Eli had reported good things about the man. He was perhaps Eli's best. Should he continue to develop, Stiger anticipated a time when the optimistic and good-natured scout would be promoted to scout corporal.

After a short break, work on the camp began. Had an entire legion been making the march, camp setup would have been very different. A legion would have carried their fortifications with them, each night constructing a temporary encampment, complete with dug trenches and fortified walls. There would be none of that for a simple company march, especially without the wagons on hand.

Stiger was taking a risk by not fortifying his camp. He needed to move fast to catch the rebels unaware. Setting up a minimally fortified camp would take at least two hours each evening and another two in the morning to break it down, limiting the amount of time his men marched. Stiger would rather spend that time on the move. He was relying heavily on Eli and the scouts to be his eyes and to keep the company from danger. In this, Stiger had complete confidence in his friend. Once Eli found evidence of enemy activity, Stiger would order more vigilant measures. Until then, a simple sentry and a picket system would do.

The men worked rapidly to clear the camp of sticks and brush. Wood was gathered and a fire was started, pushing back the deepening darkness. Additional fires were built throughout the camp. Having brought along a couple of mules with supplies, Cook set about preparing an evening tea while the men were ordered to clean up and maintain their equipment. Their precooked rations would serve as the evening meal.

Stiger spent time caring for Nomad, removing the saddle and carefully brushing him down. He made sure

Nomad had some time watering at the stream and left the horse securely tethered to a tree, happily munching on a bag of oats. A couple of handfuls of hay, hauled in by the mules, had been tossed at the horse's feet.

The captain cleaned up at the stream, washing off the sweat and dust of the road. He rinsed his hair and face in the ice-cold water, changed his tunic, and carefully washed the one he had worn. Once clean, he hung it from a low-hanging tree limb near the spot where he had decided to bed down for the night. One of the sergeants had made sure the captain had his own fire, which crackled. Stiger set out his bedroll and stifled a yawn. They had traveled far today, and he was ready for sleep. However, there was still camp business to attend to.

When the general camp work had been completed, Stiger ordered the men to gather around the large central fire.

"The forest we have entered is dense." Stiger gestured around at the dark woods. "Not only are there rebels, but there are also man-eating cats that roam these woods. It is a dangerous place, and should be respected. If you wander off the road…trust me on this, it is extremely easy to get turned around. You will become lost. By the time anyone thinks to look for you, the company will be miles away. Worse, nobody will be coming back for you. We move and we move fast. It is that simple. Nothing can be allowed to slow us down."

Stiger paused to gather his thoughts, pacing a little as he did so. "Our scouts are out looking for the enemy. Consider also that it is possible, though unlikely, that rebels could be watching us, hoping for the chance to jump one of us. If they catch you alone…well, let's just say that you don't want them to catch you. Never go off by yourself. Understood?"

"Yes, sir," the men shouted.

Stiger looked at his men. The heat from the fire was hot enough to almost singe, but he paid it no mind. He said nothing for a minute. It was known that the rebels did terrible things to captured legionaries before they allowed their prisoners to die. The rebellion in the South was a fight without mercy or kindness.

"Good work today," he continued, softening his tone a bit. "You marched well. Tomorrow we rise early and do it all over again. The enemy has no idea we are coming. Speed will bring us victory."

"Company dismissed," Sergeant Ranl hollered, taking his cue from the captain, who had nodded to him.

Stiger stood for a moment, watching as his men moved off. Sergeant Blake approached with a slight trace of a grin.

"Very inspiring, sir," Sergeant Blake said drolly as the men departed. "It nearly brought a tear to me eye."

"Let us hope it saves a life or two," Stiger replied, feeling every ounce of the responsibility that rested upon his shoulders.

"It might at that, sir," Blake added, the grin slipping from his face. "There is always one who thinks he knows better, though."

Stiger frowned but said nothing in reply. The sergeant was right, of course. He glanced toward the trail that led to the road. Lan's update had not yet arrived. It had only been two hours since he had dispatched Marcus. The slow-moving train was miles back. Stiger knew there was nothing to be worried about...yet.

Bidding the sergeant a good night, Stiger made his way to the tree, where he had set out his gear. His fire had burned low. He threw on two more logs and poked at it with a large stick to flare it up. He unbuckled his sword and placed it within easy reach. He sat down on his bedroll and leaned back against the tree. He could see Ikely with sergeant Ranl and the corporals across the camp, setting pickets and checking on the sentries.

The lieutenant's bedroll rested only a few feet away. The sergeants had ensured that the men had given the officers a little privacy. The nearest man was about twenty feet away. Stiger pulled his cloak out of his saddlebag and draped it across his legs. It promised to be a cold night. Looking up at the sky through the dense canopy of leaves, he hoped once again that the rain would hold off. Sleeping in the rain was a miserable experience, even if you had some tree cover. He closed his eyes and listened to the sounds of the camp. It felt good to be on the march again, he decided, even if he was in a forest much like those in Abath. The captain was asleep within moments.

The sergeants woke the camp before sunup. Cook had prepared a hot meal of mush, a tasteless oatmeal that the legionaries had become accustomed to. The company mules had carried in some basic cooking implements and supplies for him to use. After a chilly night spent sleeping on their arms, the hot meal, though plain, was more than welcome.

The men were allotted thirty minutes to eat, clean up, and pack for the march. The sergeants eventually called for fall in, after which a quick count began. Stiger had ordered that at least four times a day roll call be taken. He was doing all he could to keep from losing his men to the forest.

"Third File all present and accounted for, Sergeant," Corporal Durggen reported to Sergeant Blake after concluding his own count.

The sergeant nodded and moved on to the next file. Stiger was standing off to the side, near Third File, patiently waiting for roll call to be completed.

"You sorry sums of bitches better stay on that poor excuse for a road," Durggen barked at his men. "Any of you need to wander off to pass water or the like had best check with me first. You then take a friend with you to hold it as you piss and then git right back. Only bears shit in the woods. You make me have to explain why you got lost and you will be plenty sorry. You got that?"

"Yes, Corporal," the men of Third File answered in unison.

"Know that the gods gave me patience...but only so much," the corporal added.

A chuckle ran through Third File. Stiger could tell the men liked and respected their corporal. It was a good sign for the future.

"Now, how 'bout that inspection," the corporal continued. He moved forward to look each man over. There was a little grumbling. That was also a good sign; legionaries always grumbled about something.

The captain watched for a moment more before he turned away and walked over to his horse. He had saddled Nomad and packed his gear earlier. He gave Nomad a friendly pat on the neck as he untethered the horse and led him back.

"Sir," Ikely said as he approached, leading his own horse. "All being present and accounted for, the company is ready to begin the march on your word."

"Very well, Lieutenant," Stiger responded. "You may begin the march."

"Company," the lieutenant shouted, turning to face the men. The company was drawn up in a line of two abreast in the clearing, where they had spent the night. Several of the files were stacked up behind each other, as the clearing was not large enough for one complete line. "Right face!"

The company as a whole pivoted to the right.

Gods, Stiger thought, *they look good.* Was this the same company he inherited a few weeks back?

"Fooorwaaard!" the lieutenant shouted. "Maaarch!"

The column stepped off, with Marcus in the lead. The cheerful scout had returned late into the night with one of Lan's troopers, bearing a report on the train's progress. Lan had reported that there had been no problems so far with Arnold and his teamsters.

Leading the men back to the road, Stiger saw Marcus disappear into the trees. Eli had trained his scouts well. They were exceptionally conditioned and motivated, seemingly tireless. Once back on the road, the scout slipped into a slow jog and disappeared up ahead, around a bend in the road. Marcus would be miles ahead of the column before midday.

Stiger waited patiently for the column to move by. Sandals crunched rhythmically in the soft forest bed. Blake once again had elected to bring up the rear. Ranl was somewhere near the front with Ikely. Blake nodded to his captain, who began walking with him once the last file passed them by. Stiger walked his horse, working out the stiffness, a result of spending the night on the hard ground.

"Lovely morning for a march, sir," Blake offered cheerily as the two stepped from the woods onto the road.

The morning had brightened considerably, though the sun had not risen high enough to break through the canopy of leaves. It was still chilly, which was a relief from the ever-present heat, rain, and humidity that had plagued the region for the past few weeks.

"Lovely morning for a march," the sergeant repeated.

Stiger spared the sergeant a glance, frowning. He was beginning to like the sergeant. The man was efficient, knew his business, and showed good judgment. He was also fair and a good hand with the men. Stiger said nothing by way of reply and the two walked in silence together.

The road could not be described as much more than a simple dirt track that cut through the forest. If the captain had not known better, he would have decided it was a long-abandoned logging path. The road sometimes ran straight for a stretch, while other times meandered madly like a stream. It was just wide enough for a single wagon to pass. The trees that crowded in on the road were young and much smaller than those farther back in the woods. A good amount of underbrush grew on both sides of the road, making it impossible to see farther than a few feet into the woods. It looked as if within the last twenty years or so someone had cut back the tree line, only to have it once again begin encroaching closely on the road. He suspected that another cutting in the coming years would be required to keep the road open.

As the march continued through the morning, with the rhythmic crunch of more than a hundred fifty sandals, the underbrush slowly receded and grew thinner as the trees became harder, taller, and older. The canopy of leaves moved higher and became thicker with the change in the trees.

Stiger understood the pace was a hard one, made more so because the men were wearing their armor and carrying their shields and full kit. When on the march, legionaries always wore their armor. In hostile territory, a surprise attack could come at any moment. It was better to be prepared to meet an attack than not. It was a practical solution, which, when needed in those rare instances, proved beyond a shadow of a doubt the sound reasoning behind the practice.

The men's shields were secured in canvas weatherproof bags, which they had strapped to their backs. The shields would only be removed from their protective covers in the event of a battle or for maintenance purposes. The men purchased their own armor and kit, with the shields being their most expensive and valuable possession. Sources of personal pride, they were lovingly cared for.

While marching, helmets were typically not worn, unless it was raining. In a rain shower, though heavy and uncomfortable, a helmet kept water off the head and out of the eyes. Under fair weather conditions, the helmet hung on the chest from the neck by a simple leather strap. This was much easier than wearing the heavy metal helmet day in and day out, which, on the march, was literally a pain in the neck.

At the fourth stop of the day, the company reached a small stream that intersected the road. Ikely had called a stop early so that the men would have an opportunity to refill their canteens. Marching was thirsty work. There had, at one time, been a small bridge over the stream. It had long since been washed away, leaving only the remains of the rotten, termite-infested wooden supports.

Taking a look at the small stream, Stiger could see that the men and mules would have no problem crossing. The flood-lined banks indicated that, had there been more rain, the crossing might have proved difficult. At this low level, only their calves would get wet. The supply train, however, would have to lay planking to pass, which they carried for such a purpose. It should take Lan no more than a half hour to lay a makeshift bridge.

Having satisfied himself with the knowledge that neither the company nor the supply train would have any difficulty crossing, he decided that this would be a good spot for the men to take an extended break for lunch. He passed the orders to Ikely, who then promptly passed them down the line. They would remain here for thirty minutes to rest and eat their precooked rations.

Stiger secured Nomad, then selected a tree next to the stream and sat down against it. He quietly munched on his ration of hard bread and salt pork. The men gave him a respectful space, which allowed Stiger to think and watch them.

Though tired, the men chatted amiably. He noted laughter. Morale was good and spirits were high. They were responding well to the challenging march.

"Sir." Ikely approached. "Time to march, sir."

"Very well." Stiger put his mess kit and the remainder of his rations away in a small canvas travel bag. "Have the men fall in."

"Yes, sir," Lieutenant Ikely responded, passing the order to the sergeants and corporals, who began barking out orders.

The men fell in, and roll call was taken. All were found to be present and accounted for. Within minutes, the march began again. Stiger could have easily ridden, instead of sharing the miles on foot. Most officers would have taken the easier path. The captain, on the other hand, felt that marching was good exercise. Besides, he was an infantry officer and, as he saw it, an infantry officer belonged afoot with his men.

Shortly after their next break, a rider galloped up from behind the column. Stiger, still walking his horse, turned and watched the rider approach. It was one of Lan's troopers. The man was road-dusty.

"Sir, Lieutenant Lan's respects," the trooper said, dismounting. Once his feet touched the ground, he offered the captain a smart salute and handed over a dispatch. "He wishes you to know that all is well with the wagon train."

"How far back are they?" Stiger asked. He had been marching along the center of the column. As he stood speaking with the trooper, his men continued to tromp by.

"Around twenty-five miles, sir," the trooper answered with a gesture back down the road.

"Very good," Stiger said, pleased. His men were marching hard indeed. The wagon train seemed to be making good time as well. "Please convey my compliments back to the lieutenant and tell him to continue to proceed as ordered."

"Yes, sir," the trooper said. He offered another snappy salute and then mounted back up. Stiger watched the young man as he rode off, turning at a bend in the road and disappearing from view. Everything seemed to be proceeding well. Coldly, Stiger wondered how long it would be before something went wrong. Sighing, he turned back toward Vrell and began marching. They had a long way to go.

That evening the company once again found Marcus waiting patiently along the roadside. The scout looked chipper and cheerful as always.

"I hope you have a nice spot picked out for us," Stiger said from his horse. He had mounted up several hours ago, deciding Nomad needed exercise. Expecting to find one of Eli's scouts waiting, he had ridden to the head of the column.

"A wonderful place, sir," Marcus responded. "There is a natural spring-fed lake just a couple of miles off the road. We found the remains of a farmstead alongside the lake with ground that is mostly open space on one side. It is a perfect place for a camp."

"Lead on," Stiger ordered, dismounting to better lead his horse. The scout led Stiger, followed by the column, off the road and down a small path. The men were forced to walk single file. When they emerged into a large clearing, another scout, Davis, was waiting. He was tending to several deer being roasted over open fires. Stiger actually smiled at the sight. Marcus grinned, clearly enjoying his captain's reaction. The men gave a hearty cheer, many hustling forward and eagerly slapping Davis on the back. Two days of nothing but precooked rations were at an end.

"Lieutenant Eli'Far felt the men would appreciate a hot meal, sir," Marcus said.

"The lieutenant is one smart elf," Stiger responded, taking a look over the lake's placid surface and then at the campsite. The men would bathe, clean their clothing, and eat well tonight. The scouts had even gathered a meager supply of firewood, which the men would soon expand upon.

"That he is, sir," Marcus agreed with a nod.

"Do you know where the lieutenant is?" Stiger asked, turning to the scout.

"Last I heard, way up the road," Marcus said, a frown briefly crossing his face. "He apparently found something interesting and went to investigate. None of us know what he found."

"I would not worry too much about it," Stiger said with a slight sigh. "If it was important or led to potential danger, he would have passed word back."

"You think so, sir?" Marcus asked, a hopeful look on his face.

"I've seen the lieutenant become overly excited about a rare flower," Stiger said with a chuckle, in an attempt to keep the scout from worrying. Though to be perfectly honest, he was more than a little concerned over what his friend had found interesting.

"I am sure you are right, sir," Marcus said, seeming relieved. "He does love to point out the exotic plants."

"No point in worrying," Stiger said, and led his horse farther into the clearing. The evening rays of sun glinted like orange fire on the placid surface of the lake. Stiger actually found himself smiling. Though the lake was no substitute for an imperial bathhouse, he was looking forward to taking a plunge and scrubbing off the accumulated dust and grime of the march. *First things first,* he thought, and set about looking after Nomad.

ELEVEN

It was the fourth day of the march and the company had covered a great deal of ground. He had pushed them very hard. Stiger figured that they were likely two to three days ahead of where they should have been. Shortly after the noon break, the lead elements of the column found four of Eli's scouts waiting along the roadside. Stiger had been walking his horse when the column abruptly stopped and word was passed back for the captain to come forward. He mounted and cantered up past the men, who, weary from the hard pace, had dropped to the ground and were enjoying the unexpected break.

The captain found scouts Marcus, Davis, Todd, and Bryant waiting, along with Ikely, who had halted the column. Having parted with four of his ten scouts, Stiger understood immediately that Eli had found the enemy. He had been expecting something like this for the last day or so. They were approaching one of the villages marked on the map provided by General Mammot. The scouts saluted with clenched fist to chest.

"You have located the enemy?" Stiger asked as he dismounted from his horse. He handed the reins to a nearby legionary, who scrambled hastily to his feet.

"Yes, sir," Marcus replied, gesturing in the direction of the company's march. "They have lookouts on the road two miles up and are encamped near the remains of a small village, about six miles away from this spot."

"What are their numbers?" Stiger asked. He had been slightly concerned that the enemy might outnumber them, but he knew from experience that providing for a large force so deep in a forest, far away from a supply source, was extremely difficult.

"They number about forty," Marcus answered matter-of-factly. Stiger breathed a small sigh of relief as the scout bent to pick up a stick lying in the road. He scratched out a crude map in the dirt. "Near as we can tell, we feel they have an ambush point…about here, just beyond the ruins of the village, say about five miles away. The village has been completely razed. There is not a single building standing."

"What type of village was it?" Stiger asked, wondering what the ground was like. If it was farming-based, there should be a patchwork of neglected fields. If the village had been hunting- and trapping-based, there would be much less cover.

"It seems to have been a small farming community, cut right into the forest. The fields are completely overgrown with brush and run on both sides of the road for nearly a mile here. The brush is so thick that it is a perfect spot for an ambush. The enemy camp is here." Marcus pointed with the stick. "Off the road and south of the village, at an old farmstead. Much of the farmstead seems to have escaped the destruction that ravaged the village. The enemy uses a footpath to get to and from the farmstead. It is a pretty secluded spot."

"Have you seen them personally?" Stiger asked.

"We all have, sir," Marcus responded. The other scouts nodded. "A pretty ragged lot, if you ask me. I don't think they will be much trouble. They look half-starved."

"How are they armed?" Stiger asked.

"Poorly, sir," Davis spoke up. "Some bows, old swords of various kinds, and no armor."

"Do they watch the road at night?"

"Not that we were able to determine," Marcus answered, "but they have it watched from dawn 'til dusk. They do not seem terribly disciplined. Lieutenant Eli'Far told me to tell you he will have a complete report for you."

Stiger nodded. Eli's report would be more thorough. Rubbing the stubble on his jaw thoughtfully, Stiger studied the map that Marcus had drawn in the dirt. Forty ragged, half-starved men did not seem like enough to wreak havoc on the previous supply train. There must be more about, perhaps another group up the road.

"Did you find any evidence of additional enemy forces?" Stiger asked, looking up from the map.

"No, sir," Marcus answered without hesitation. "We took a looksee a ways up the road and found nothing."

"How far?" Stiger asked, eyeing the scout.

"About twenty miles, sir," Davis answered.

"No other signs of anybody about," Marcus added, "but this sorry bunch of scum."

"I see." Stiger spared Davis and Marcus a quick glance before looking down once again at the crude map drawn in the dirt. He committed it to memory before kicking the map to dust.

"I expect we will strike before dawn," Stiger announced, looking over at Marcus. "Do you have another spot for us to camp? Preferably near their camp?"

"Another wonderful spot, sir!" Marcus suddenly smiled. "Though I must admit, there will be no venison this evening."

Stiger flashed a rare smile at the hard-working scout. Marcus seemed like a natural leader. After they reached

Vrell, he would speak to Eli about having him promoted to scout corporal.

"The lieutenant suggested no fires tonight, sir," Davis added. "Our camp will be close enough to theirs that they might get a whiff of our campfires."

Stiger had suspected as much. Eli would put them within easy striking distance, and, knowing his friend, that would likely be rather close indeed. Stiger glanced back at his men. Those nearest had been listening. They hastily glanced away.

Well, this is it, Stiger thought. All of his work and training would be put to the test.

"The lieutenant also asked me to inform you he will join you in a couple of hours," Marcus added, drawing the captain's attention back.

Stiger nodded in reply as the sergeants came up. Marcus gave a repeat of the report.

Once they were done, Stiger turned to Ikely and the sergeants. "We will hold an officers' and sergeants' council when Lieutenant Eli'Far joins us and plan our assault. Now... let's get the men moving to the campsite."

⚜ ⚜ ⚜

Moonlight filtered through the tree canopy as the men quietly worked their way up to the enemy camp. Their bulky shields had been left behind. This was one of those rare occasions when legionary infantry would go into action without them. Keeping their swords sheathed lest someone get accidently stuck, the men still wore their segmented armor. Stiger had considered ordering personal armor left behind, but in the end had opted for the protection it offered over any gains through stealth.

The captain had his hand on Marcus, who guided a long string of fifty men toward the enemy camp. Another man behind Stiger had his shoulder, and so on. The line shuffling through the forest sounded alarmingly loud. Though moonlight filtered through the leafy canopy, it was not nearly enough to clearly see by. There was the occasional muffled crash, followed by a curse, as someone tripped or a branch, pushed aside, smacked the face of the man behind. The need for silence was critical for the element of surprise to be achieved. As the line moved into position, it sounded to Stiger as if the entire company were crashing through the forest, though in reality they were being very quiet. With effort, he forced himself to calm down. He knew from experience noise in the forest became muffled and would not carry very far. The brush around the enemy camp was quite thick, which helped to muffle and conceal their approach.

As they neared the enemy camp, Stiger could smell smoke from fires drifting through the brush. It became stronger with each step. A general flickering glow soon began to show on the surrounding trees, brush, and canopy above. They were close ... extremely close.

They crept to within a few feet of the enemy camp. Stiger could see one main fire going, which meant at this early hour someone was actively feeding it. A watch-stander, perhaps? Through the brush, he could see other fire pits, which had been reduced to glowing embers.

Stiger took a moment to rapidly scan the enemy camp. There was not much left of the old farmstead. The barn had long since collapsed in on itself. The farmhouse was in little better shape, but still stood, barely, leaning slightly to one side. It had a tired, old look that Stiger had come to expect from the South. It had likely been abandoned long before the legions had razed the village, which was probably why it was still standing. There had been no need to burn or pull it down. There were a few tents and a handful of small huts that had been hastily constructed around the decaying building. Everything had a ramshackle look to it.

Eli had explained that a stream flowed through the clearing. In the gloom, Stiger could not see it.

He turned to look back. Marcus, having stopped, used hand motions to direct those who followed to spread out in a line both to the left and right of the captain. Two other groups, one under Eli and the other under Ikely, were doing the same on the other sides of the encampment in the form of a triangle. As they moved into their final positions, the men seemed to make even more noise. Stiger knew that in his mind it was louder than it actually was. Once in position, the noise ceased almost immediately. Stiger strained to hear any hint of alarm from the enemy camp. Nothing stirred.

In the gloom of the early pre-morning, Stiger tried to study the camp further. Despite the fire burning brightly, no sentry or watch-stander could be seen. Perhaps the man was on the other side of the camp. Sloppy and careless, Stiger thought. It was about to cost this nest of rebels dearly.

Nothing about going into a fight was normal. He could feel the tension building. In Stiger's experience, most men dreaded the day when it finally arrived, though some bragged they were eager for it. In reality, a legionary's life was generally pretty regimented and boring, only punctuated once in a great while by the occasional skirmish or battle. No sane individual ever looked forward to the opportunity to be potentially skewered or carved up. A normal person longed to run and find some safe place to hide at such times, which is what made legionaries so unique. They were known for standing and fighting, despite the terror. Discipline, drill, and duty were what kept the legions moving on such days.

Stiger mentally repeated the oft-used mantra, *Battles are just additional drill with more blood.*

The captain, as was his custom, bowed his head. He offered a brief prayer to the High Father asking for a blessing of success and a personal request to spare as many of his men as possible. He then made sure to commend his spirit into the hands of the High Father.

Prayer complete, he looked back up and resolved to do his duty to the end. The enemy camp slept, unaware that the emperor's hammer was about to fall heavily upon them. Stiger reached for his sword hilt in anticipation and gripped the rough handhold tight. He sensed it was almost time.

Stiger had directed that Eli's force begin the assault, whereupon the other two groups would move into the camp and attack. Eli, on the other side of the enemy encampment, had the benefit of superior vision at night, a blessing of his race that humans could only envy. In the early morning gloom, the elf would be able to easily observe the two other groups moving into position, which was why Stiger had tasked him with beginning the assault. Not for the first time, Stiger felt thankful that his friend was on their side.

Marcus silently moved up and down the line, checking each man to make sure everyone had been accounted for. Night actions were particularly dangerous, as accidents and blunders were commonplace. It was almost an unwritten rule that night actions were never undertaken unless under specific and desperate circumstances. The average commander avoided conducting any and all night actions. Stiger, having Eli, felt this was the exception. He was willing to risk a little to gain a lot.

The suspense was beginning to weigh heavily on Stiger as the minutes wore on. Nothing was assured by even the best-laid plans, and the what-ifs were running through his mind. The tension and anxiety he felt were not over his own safety. He worried that they would be discovered before the assault began. He worried that he would make a mistake in leading them in and he would lose men as a result. He worried that once the men went in, in the heat of the fight, they might panic and forget their training, costing lives. What if he'd missed something critical? He worried...

Despite this, he had not once reconsidered carrying the assault home. It was natural for a commander to worry. He was careful to project a sense of calm and resolve to the men around him, and not betray fear. He had trained and worked his men hard. He felt they were ready for this. The enemy was before him, and he meant to destroy them. It was as simple as that.

Stiger drew his sword with a soft hiss. The man next to him did the same, and like a spring up and down the line, his men drew their swords one after another. From what he could see in the gloom, the men were grim and determined. This was what they had trained for, and they knew the butcher's bill had come due.

There was a sudden shout from across the camp, which ripped shockingly across the quiet night, followed by a massed battle cry as Eli's men pushed forward out of the brush and into the enemy camp.

"Advance!" Stiger shouted, standing up. Something similar happened from Ikely's side, which was drowned out as Stiger's line stood, roaring a battle cry of their own, and began to push through the last layers of brush.

Stiger only had time to observe how unimpressive the camp was before the enemy began stumbling out of their tents and ramshackle huts.

One suddenly appeared before the captain, half dressed, unarmed, and wide eyed. Stiger's sword flashed out, stabbing the man through the gut. The man let out an anguished cry as the sword went home, grating terribly against bone. The captain gave a savage twist of his sword. He shoved the man roughly back with a stiff arm, pulling the sword out in the process and spilling the man's guts on the ground. The man, crying out in agony, crashed to the ground and flailed about.

Stiger's arm and hand were covered in the man's blood. The rough cord grip on the hilt of his sword prevented him from losing his hold, despite the slickness. He gave it no thought as he left the disemboweled man to die, looking for his next opponent.

He stepped forward and chopped another who had just emerged from the same tent, catching this one in the side of the neck as he was starting to stand up. The man fell heavily with a massive spray of blood, neck almost completely severed from the vicious strike. A sword fell from limp fingers as the man died.

Someone crashed violently into Stiger's right side, pushing him roughly to the left. An errant sword scraped along his armor, making a screeching sound as it went. Stiger turned and saw the man to his right grappling with a rebel, who was naked and unarmed. The rebel had thrown himself on the back of the legionary and was trying to strangle him. It had been the legionary's sword that had scraped along the captain's armor.

Recovering himself, Stiger stabbed the rebel in the back as the legionary spun around, attempting to dislodge his assailant. Stiger gave the sword a powerful twist, severing the rebel's spine with an ugly crunch that he felt communicated through the hilt of his sword. Both the legionary and the rebel collapsed to the ground in a heap, the rebel suddenly dead weight. Stiger stabbed the rebel again for good measure and then kicked him off of his fallen man.

Stiger quickly glanced around as he offered his man a hand up. The legionary was young and had a wide-eyed look as he regained his feet. He stood for a moment, looking down at the dead man who had just tried to strangle him. The legionary spat angrily on the corpse and bent down to retrieve his own sword, which he had dropped in the scuffle.

"Thank you, sir," he said through the noise, looking back up at the captain.

"No time for that now. Come on, son." Stiger used his free hand to push him toward the action. "Let's get back in the fight."

Stiger advanced, looking for another rebel. All across the camp, men were shouting wildly, with cries of pain and screams of fear mixed in. Above it was the metallic clash of swords. Put all together, it was a sound all too familiar to the captain.

It was the ring of battle.

Stiger's heart beat rapidly with the excitement of the moment. Turning, he saw a desperate rebel not five feet from him, trading sword strokes with one of his legionaries. Before he could move to assist, another legionary stepped up behind the rebel and stabbed him cleanly in the back, then tossed the stricken man to the ground like a ragdoll. Just beyond, another rebel was cut down by three of his legionaries, and yet another went down under a flurry of stabbing swords just feet away.

Stiger started to step toward a rebel, who had emerged from a hut twenty feet away, and then forced himself to stop to take stock of the situation. There were plenty of his men about. It was easy to lose oneself in the moment and chaos of the fight. Yet he understood that battles frequently needed direction.

"Deal with that man!" Stiger shouted, pointing at the rebel. Six legionaries turned and began advancing. Satisfied, Stiger took a studied moment to look around the camp to see what else needed doing. In the dim morning light, he could see his men everywhere, and only a few rebels resisting.

Stiger rubbed sweat and blood off of his face with his free forearm. Realization hit home, and along with it came a deep sense of satisfaction. He had achieved what he had wanted most: not just surprise, but complete surprise. So much so that the assault had become a slaughter.

In mere moments, before he could give any further orders, the fighting petered out. The surviving rebels began throwing down their weapons. Two rebels attempting to surrender were cut down by legionaries. Sergeants and officers began shouting orders at the men to take prisoners. It wasn't an act of compassion; there was little place for mercy in the emperor's legions. Stiger had a great need for intelligence. He had given specific orders that, if at all possible, prisoners were to be taken.

Tents and huts were checked and several additional rebels who had been hiding were roughly dragged out or forced out by sword point. None were handled gently. They were herded to the center of the camp, where they were forced to sit by the fire. Stiger looked around to find Eli and Ikely directing the securing of the camp. With the sergeants and corporals also working so efficiently, there was not much for Stiger to do at the moment. Everything seemed well in hand.

Stiger was tempted to interfere, but in the end, he let them work. He began walking through the camp, taking it all in. In the growing light, it was becoming clearer that the camp was in a truly deplorable state. He could not believe that these were the men who had harassed the last supply train so effectively. The more Stiger looked over the camp, the more disgusted he became.

Were these the rebels that had so frightened General Kromen?

Sergeant Ranl came up with a big grin. The large sergeant drew himself up and saluted his captain, fist to chest. "Sir, congratulations."

"How many wounded?" Stiger asked, fearing the answer. "How many dead do we have?" They had won the fight, but he was now thinking about the cost. How expensive was the butcher's bill?

"A couple of minor cuts, sir," Ranl answered, the grin spreading further across his face. "Nothing more."

"No one killed?" Stiger asked with an incredulous look. "Are you sure?"

"Yes, sir," Ranl affirmed, teeth flashing in the dim light. "A brilliant victory, sir."

Stiger shook his head in disbelief, astounded. He had never been in a fight this size where a man had not been lost or grievously wounded. "How many prisoners have we taken?"

"Twelve, with twenty-seven killed."

"I want the twelve interrogated," Stiger ordered. "Find out what they know."

"Yes, sir." Sergeant Ranl saluted again and turned to leave. Stiger stopped him, catching the sergeant's arm.

"Are you absolutely certain none of our men were seriously injured or lost?" Stiger asked once more.

"The High Father found our cause righteous this day," Sergeant Ranl answered. "It is a rare thing to lead men into battle, sir. It is even rarer to have them all come out mostly whole. I declare we were blessed this day."

Stiger nodded in agreement. He would offer his heart-felt thanks to the High Father later.

"Have the camp searched," the captain ordered. "I want anything we can possibly use."

"Yes, sir." The sergeant started off.

"A fine victory for a fine morning," Father Thomas said cheerfully. Stiger turned, astonished to find the paladin standing behind him. Father Thomas had been with the wagon train yesterday. The man must have ridden hard to catch up. He was also not bloodied, the captain noted, which meant that he had not participated in the fighting. It was not unexpected, so Stiger did not hold it against the man. Paladins chose when and where to fight. No one gave them orders.

"A lucky victory," Stiger breathed, looking back around at the camp. A number of enemy bodies lay about haphazardly where they had fallen. "We simply caught them by surprise."

"Perhaps." Father Thomas shrugged. "Perhaps not…we both know some men are more blessed than others."

"Perhaps some men make their own luck, Father," Stiger took a seat on a tree stump, setting his sword down point-first into the ground, leaning the hilt against his thigh. He suddenly found himself bone weary. The excitement of the fight had begun to drain away. He had not slept at all, which made the exhaustion worse.

"I suppose that is true also," Father Thomas replied, looking down on the weary captain with some amusement. "Though I rather suspect you agree with me to some degree."

"I do plan to thank the High Father properly," Stiger added after a slight hesitation.

Father Thomas nodded, but said nothing more.

The men had performed well. There were smiles all around. His men had been bloodied under his command and, more importantly, they had won. Granted, it had been an easy victory and very one-sided, yet he and the men had needed the victory badly. Weeks ago, Stiger had started the process, and this battle had sealed it. They once again saw themselves as true legionaries, the most professional group of trained killers the world had ever known.

When his company finally returned to the main legionary encampment, his men would see the stark difference between themselves and their fellows. At that moment, they would truly appreciate just how far he had brought them.

"What do you suppose lies up the road?" Father Thomas asked, breaking in on the captain's thoughts.

"I figured you would know better than I," Stiger responded mildly, which was followed up by an involuntary yawn. Having been up all night planning and preparing for the assault, he was dead tired. He wanted nothing more than a nap.

"The High Father may call me to some place, but he does not tell me what evil I must confront."

"Would that evil be with my legionaries?" Stiger asked, looking directly up at the paladin.

Father Thomas returned the look. After a moment, he closed his eyes, appearing to be looking within himself.

"No," Father Thomas replied after a long pause. He gave a very heavy sigh. "The evil is not within your company. The High Father's call is pulling me toward Vrell."

"Vrell?" Stiger growled as Father Thomas's eyes opened and refocused on the world around him, blinking as he did so. "That is what I was afraid of."

"Captain," Father Thomas said gently, looking off in the direction of the road to Vrell. "There is something ahead, on both our paths ... perhaps on the path of the company as well ... all of us. I can feel it. I fear you will need my services before long."

"You are just full of good news and cheer," Stiger replied sourly.

"Ben," Eli said, interrupting both of them as he approached. Eli bowed politely to the paladin. "Father ... it is good to see both of you well."

"You too, my friend," Stiger said with a tired smile, his scar tugging at his cheek slightly.

"I do not believe any of the rebels escaped," Eli reported. "I posted several of my scouts to prevent such an occurrence. They will check for fresh tracks, though I do not expect to find any. I have also dispatched two scouts in the direction of Vrell."

"Good job," Stiger said.

"Thank you," Eli replied.

"Marcus seems to be a good scout," Stiger said, changing the subject.

"He shows promise," Eli replied with a casual shrug.

"High praise," Father Thomas commented, "coming from a ranger."

Eli glanced at Father Thomas without saying anything, only blinking his perfectly formed almond-shaped eyes once, as if to say, *I have no idea what you are talking about.*

"I assume you will be heading out immediately, then," Stiger said.

"I do not intend to leave as of yet." Eli hesitated before continuing. "I have found something ... well, something interesting, that I believe you need to see personally."

"Found something?" Stiger asked, perking up. "I heard that you had. What, exactly?"

"It is better you see it for yourself," Eli answered with a slight frown. "I feel it would be better explained that way."

"Where is it?" Stiger asked, starting to stand.

"Half a day from here," Eli said, pointing into the woods away from the road.

Stiger sat back down heavily, looking up at his friend in surprise. Eli wanted him to leave the company to look at some unknown thing. It wasn't the first time his friend had made such a request. Elves could be incredibly difficult.

Stiger had spent an entire year with Eli learning about the forest and the ways of the ranger. Eli had gone out of his way to show him some extremely rare flowers, which had, in some cases, taken days to find.

"It isn't a flower this time, is it?" Stiger asked wryly.

"We can travel there and meet back up with the company on the march," Eli said, refusing to take the bait. "I think it important I show you personally."

Stiger just looked at Eli for a moment. He wanted to argue and order his friend to tell him what he had found. Then he saw it, that stubborn elven look hidden under the placid youthful countenance. Stiger had known Eli long enough to know the elf had found something important. There would be no budging him. If Eli wanted Stiger to see something for himself, then there was a very important reason behind it. Even though he was irritated at not knowing what it was, Stiger knew he would go with his friend, no questions asked.

"Very well," Stiger conceded. "We will do it your way."

"Thank you," Eli replied. He nodded politely to the paladin and turned to leave.

"I think it will prove interesting to see what he has discovered," Father Thomas said softly, watching Eli walk off.

Stiger glanced over sharply at the paladin with a sinking feeling. Father Thomas would be coming. Did he feel the call to go? Stiger was almost tempted to ask, then decided against it. He would rather not know.

"A good one, that elf," Father Thomas stated firmly. "A little frustrating... but a good soul."

"The best," Stiger agreed tiredly. He decided that he needed a little nap. Putting thoughts of the paladin and Eli aside, he shifted to sit on the ground with his back against the stump, laying his sword down next to him within easy reach. It was streaked with dried blood, and he would need to clean it before he returned it to the sheath. At least there was a nearby stream to help. He spared one last look around and determined that Ikely and his sergeants had everything well in order. Gods, he was tired. Stiger closed his eyes and was asleep in moments.

Father Thomas, who had been watching Eli round up his scouts, turned at hearing the quiet snores from the captain. A smile briefly lit his face and he shook his head in wonder. Less than thirty minutes had passed since the assault on the rebel camp had ended, and the captain was already taking a nap.

"You too are a very interesting and blessed man," the paladin whispered to himself as he walked off, shaking his head in amusement.

TWELVE

"Three passable tents, parts of six others not considered serviceable and will be cut up for bandages. Twelve blankets that, surprisingly enough, can be used; the rest are worthless. Ten flints of fair quality. Four quarter-barrels of flour. Two quarter-barrels of oats." Sergeant Ranl read the list of captured items off a pad to the captain. He had been reading for several minutes.

They were sitting before a fire in what had been the enemy camp. Ikely had joined them and was listening to the report. It was now late evening and the company had brought up their supplies and mules. The camp had been cleaned and organized. The bodies removed and buried.

Ranl was using the firelight to read by, which required him to tilt the pad in the direction of the fire, squinting as he did so. "Fifty-two swords, most of which are useless to us, though there are nine legionary short swords and three cavalry sabers, seven knives and daggers, six mules, one horse—"

"Those weapons are legion make?" Stiger interrupted, looking up. He had been reclining against a stump in front of the fire, quietly smoking his pipe while listening to the sergeant.

"Yes, sir." Sergeant Ranl looked up from his pad, a serious look in his eyes. "The horse and mules are also branded with the legion's mark."

"Do we know how they got them?" Stiger asked, suspecting that they had captured them. However, it was not unknown for corrupt supply officers to sell equipment, animals, and supplies to the other side. From the looks of the camp and the prisoners, Stiger seriously doubted these people were behind the attack on the last supply train.

"We are still questioning the prisoners," Ranl replied evenly, which was punctuated by a scream of agony from the other side of the camp. The sergeant, like everyone else around the fire, did not even flinch at the agonized scream. "At this point, if I had to guess, it looks like they ambushed imperial messengers and patrols."

"I see," Stiger said with a sigh. "Please continue."

"The horse appears to be a cavalry mount," Sergeant Ranl reported. "She is a bit underfed, but I expect that Lieutenant Lan will be pleased to have a spare mount for his troop."

"No doubt," Ikely said. The lieutenant was whittling down a piece of wood. It was something he did in the evenings to pass the time. He made little figurines of the gods. Oddly, he never took them with him, instead leaving them behind where he had spent the night. The figurines were highly prized by the men, and in the morning someone was always lurking, ready to scoop them up.

All legionaries were superstitious, particularly considering their vocation. It was simply the nature of the business. One just could not afford to ignore the gods, which could prove unhealthy, as some of the gods were known to be spiteful. Stiger suspected that each man would have at least one figurine by the time the company returned from Vrell.

"Three imperial-issued saddles," the sergeant continued, "and a variety of coinage, estimated to be worth around sixteen gold imperial talons. The rest of what we seized is garbage. These animals did not take care of much. That concludes my report, sir."

"Sergeant, make sure that the coinage remains under the guard of a corporal 'til the supply train arrives," Stiger ordered. "Set aside the customary amount for the general legion fund. Half of the remainder will be applied to the men's pensions; the other half will be distributed according to custom amongst the sergeants and officers. It is all to be deposited into the strong box."

"I will, sir," Ranl said, making a note in his pad.

Stiger had known officers who would have simply kept the money for themselves. All legionaries took their pensions very seriously. The men would be pleased when they discovered he had contributed to their pensions.

"Lieutenant," Stiger turned to Ikely, "I want you to choose five reliable men to remain here with the captured supplies until the train arrives."

"I will make sure to stress that they keep a close watch," the lieutenant replied, "in case this band have friends nearby."

"Good," Stiger responded with a satisfied nod. It was unlikely these rebels had any friends about. Eli would have found evidence if there were. "Let the men sleep in and rest a little tomorrow morning. They deserve it. The company will march out around noon. Eli, myself, and Father Thomas will depart at first light. We will meet up with you at some point during the next day."

"Are you sure, sir?" Ikely asked. He obviously did not like the idea of the captain leaving the column.

"We will only be gone one night," Stiger reassured him. "I will have written orders for you in the morning."

"Messenger coming in, sir!" Corporal Kennet shouted from across the camp. Stiger looked over and saw one of

Lan's troopers being escorted in. The messenger spotted the captain by the fire. He dismounted, secured his horse to a tree, and then walked a little stiffly over to the captain. The man was dusty and weary. He had ridden hard to get here, and in the dark that was a dangerous thing. He saluted fist to chest. Stiger remained seated, taking another pull on his pipe as he nodded in reply.

"Lieutenant Lan's compliments, sir," the messenger reported. "He would like to congratulate you on your victory over the rebels. He also reports the wagon train has made camp for the evening about six hours' hard ride back."

Stiger nodded, pleased. That meant the train was about a day and a half behind them, maybe slightly more. The train was making excellent time.

The trooper drew out a dispatch from the lieutenant and handed it over. Stiger pocketed it. He would read it later.

"Any trouble?" Stiger asked, looking up at the trooper.

"It has been a tad boring, sir … though there was one little incident," the trooper reported with a chuckle. "Sergeant Arnold protested a bit too much at the pace and threatened to go no farther until a break was called. The lieutenant proposed taking his wagons and leaving the sergeant to walk back."

Those around the fire chuckled, amused at the thought.

"I take it the sergeant became much more manageable after that?"

"Very, sir," the trooper responded. "He decided it was safer to be escorted than alone in a rebel-infested forest. He said as much, he did."

"Very sensible of him," Ikely remarked wryly. "No more complaints after that?"

"No, sir," the trooper reported.

"I have written out a report of the fight here and our progress," Stiger said, reaching into a pocket. He pulled out the sealed dispatch and handed it over to the trooper. "Have Lieutenant Lan send a messenger back to General Kromen with this."

"Yes, sir," the trooper said, accepting the dispatch.

"See Cook. Get yourself something to eat and bed down for the night," Stiger added. The trooper looked about ready to drop. "You can ride out in the morning."

"Thank you, sir," the trooper said, appearing greatly relieved that he would not have to ride back immediately. He saluted before stepping away for some grub.

Stiger took a slow pull and puff on his pipe. He stared off into the fire, lost in his thoughts.

"If you will excuse me, sir," Ranl said, standing. "It is getting late and I need to check on the men."

The captain gave a curt nod to the sergeant. Both officers watched the sergeant leave. Once he was out of earshot, the lieutenant looked over at his captain.

"I would feel more comfortable if you took a few men with you tomorrow," Ikely said cautiously.

"You would," Stiger said, letting a puff of smoke escape and casting a glance at his lieutenant.

"I would," Ikely said firmly. He had resolved himself to insist upon this.

The captain returned his gaze to the fire and was silent for several moments as he considered. Stiger noted the resolved look. His lieutenant was right. He should take more men . . . although, he would be in the presence of an elven ranger and a paladin of the High Father.

"I will take four men with me," Stiger finally said, giving in. "Make sure they are good men. If I know Eli, we will be moving fast through the forest, and they will need to keep up."

"I will, sir."

Stiger clamped his pipe in his teeth and stood, stretching his sore muscles. Ikely stood as well.

"I think we should see what Cook has rustled up for dinner," Stiger suggested, hoping it was something better than warmed up salt pork.

"So, they are not rebels?" Stiger asked with obvious irritation. Cook had prepared some coffee, a rare treat, for the men this morning. Stiger took a sip from the cup he held, savoring the taste. It was a nice break from the tea that was more easily prepared and served.

"They are not," Ranl stated.

Blake nodded in agreement. He looked tired. He and several corporals had spent a long night aggressively interrogating the prisoners.

Ikely stood by Stiger, receiving the report at the captain's fire. The sun would be up in less than an hour, and the morning air was clear and crisp. Stiger threw a couple of logs on the fire and stirred it up with a thick branch.

Father Thomas had also joined them, looking surprisingly fresh, as if he had just climbed out of a comfortable bed. He was having coffee too, and seemed to be enjoying the treat.

"This group were bandits," Blake added tiredly, "but it seems they did have some contact with the rebels."

Stiger raised an eyebrow at this and took a sip of his coffee, which steamed in the cool morning air. He wished they had sugar, but in the field that was a luxury they could not afford. He took another sip. After a night of sleeping on the cold, hard ground, the warmth of the coffee felt good.

"It appears a small force of rebels came over the mountains to the south a few months back," Blake explained, "probably around the time of the last supply train. A deal was struck with the leader of this band. As long as they ambushed any imperials on the road, the rebels would leave them alone."

"And if they messed with the rebels?" Ikely asked.

"The rebels made it clear that would not have been a wise move," Ranl said. "A few examples were made in advance to ward off any trouble. The rebels had some type of holy man with them. He was the one who made the examples. Apparently, it was not pretty."

"What kind of holy man?" Father Thomas asked.

Stiger looked over at the paladin, wondering the same.

"This bunch is more ignorant than our average recruit. They did not know, and the rebels did not say," Blake explained. "They were pretty impressed. Apparently he was fond of a ceremonial knife."

"A black priest of some kind, then," Father Thomas said, looking over at the captain. "Sacrifices, I would hazard."

Stiger said nothing at that, but instead looked down at his feet. The memories of what they had run into with Father Griggs were still too fresh ... too raw.

"The rebels left them some arms and supplies," Blake added, wanting to change the direction of the conversation as well. The last thing any legionary wished to discuss were the dark gods. "They then left."

"Where to?" Stiger asked, hopeful, but knowing the bandits in all probability had no idea as to where the rebels went.

"It is hard to tell for sure," Blake admitted, scratching his stubbly jaw. "They seem to think the rebels went back over the mountains to the south. The bandits were left with the impression that the rebels would soon return with a much larger force to take Vrell, but they didn't know when."

Stiger did not like the sound of that either. Having to potentially confront a black priest was bad enough. Although perhaps that was why Father Thomas had been called?

"The bandit leader … did he survive?" Ikely asked.

"He did not," Blake answered. "He was killed in the assault."

"Any word on what to expect at Vrell?" Stiger asked, changing the subject.

"This band did not wander too far from this area," Sergeant Blake said. "They seem pretty ignorant of Vrell itself. None we interrogated had ever been there. They did intercept several messengers from the castle."

"Is it too much to hope that the dispatches survived?" Stiger scowled, suspecting the answer.

"I am afraid so, sir," Ranl said. "The dispatches were used to start fires or wipe asses. They didn't bother to question the messengers. Anyone who came along was ambushed and immediately killed for their valuables."

Stiger frowned unhappily.

"Oh, and we did get the name of the leader of the rebel band," Sergeant Blake spoke up. "A Captain Myeld."

The name meant nothing to Stiger. It seemed probable the rebels had pushed a company over the mountains. Perhaps they were still in the area, perhaps not. It had likely been this band that had harassed the last supply train and then returned back over the mountains. With the legions blocking the main rebel army, it was probable the bandits were simply led to believe the rebels were returning in the hopes of encouraging the band to continue to harass any imperials they came across. With any luck, they took their dark priest with them and went south, back to rebel territory.

"Another thing, sir," Blake said. "One of the fools mentioned another group of cutthroats staking out a territory up the road in the direction of Vrell. They had regular contact and occasionally traded. A few weeks back, this other group disappeared, as if they just up and walked off. Strangely, they left all of their stuff, though."

"Perhaps the rebels took care of them for us," Ikely postulated.

"It is possible, sir," Blake admitted, though he sounded skeptical.

"Nothing but a bandit camp." Stiger spat in disgust, glancing around.

The camp was in the process of being broken down. The spoils would be moved to the road for the supply train to better pick up when it arrived. The rest would be burned or abandoned. It mattered little to him what happened to the other band. They were one less problem he would have to contend with. In the end, all that mattered was getting the supply train to Vrell. If the rebels were still about... well then, Eli and the scouts would find them.

"What of the prisoners?" Blake asked.

Stiger thought about it for a moment, looking over at the prisoners across the camp, who were under armed guard. There were twelve of them, sitting down, with their arms tied securely behind their backs. They were dirty and dressed in near rags. Stiger figured most had been local farmers at one time, at least until the legions had arrived to put down the rebellion. He had seen this cycle before. Men driven from their homes, wives raped and killed, farms burned... With nothing left, they had turned to banditry. If he took them along, he would have to feed and provide a guard for them.

The prisoners knew the penalty for banditry, which would mean he could reasonably expect an escape attempt.

Such an attempt might put his legionaries at risk. Under these circumstances, taking them along to Vrell was not really an option. The prisoners were dead men and they knew it.

"Execute them," he ordered, his voice sounding harsh in his own ears. "Organize a detail and get it done immediately."

Ikely glanced uncomfortably at Father Thomas. The paladin said nothing, but looked on impassively. After a moment, he let out a soft breath that was part sigh.

"Do you have anything to add, Father Thomas?" Stiger asked, having caught the lieutenant's look.

"No, Captain," Father Thomas said sadly. "The High Father allows all men free will. No matter who they were previously, the prisoners willingly chose a life of banditry."

"These men killed legionaries and conspired with the enemy," Stiger growled, addressing the sergeants and lieutenant. Stiger felt it was important that he was clear with them. "How we suspect they were driven to this life is irrelevant. They are bandits. There is one penalty for banditry, and that penalty is death. They either die here or at Vrell. They know this, and that makes them desperate. I will not risk any of my men to these animals, who will be looking for any chance to grab a weapon in a careless moment and escape their punishment. They die now and quick, which is better than the scum deserve."

"Yes, sir," Ranl said, having heard enough. He stood, as did Blake. He saluted sharply. "I will see to the detail myself."

Sergeant Ranl turned and, with Blake following, walked off in the direction of the prisoners, leaving Stiger alone with Ikely and Father Thomas. Stiger watched them go. He hated having to order executions. But it was something that had to be done. There were no regrets. Their shades would not be visiting him during lonely moments. The prisoners meant nothing to him. These men had more than earned their fate, and he hoped they burned for it.

"Would you mind if I hear their sins and provide last rites to the condemned?" Father Thomas asked after a moment's silence.

"If you wish to ease their transition to the next world," Stiger said quietly, with a shrug, "I have no objection."

"Thank you, Captain," Father Thomas said, clapping a comforting hand on Stiger's shoulder as he stood. "I suspect, at heart, that you are a good man."

Stiger frowned, watching the paladin walk away in the direction of the prisoners. He looked over at Ikely.

"Shouldn't you be seeing to the captured supplies and equipment?" Stiger growled.

"Uh…yes, sir." Ikely strode away.

Stiger was left alone with his thoughts. His duty was not always pleasant. As a legionary captain and a Stiger, he had a responsibility to the empire. Sentiment was rarely a consideration. Turning away from the prisoners, the captain looked in the direction of the road and wondered what exactly was waiting for them at Castle Vrell.

THIRTEEN

"Believe it or not, at one time a road ran through here," Eli announced, having abruptly stopped.

They had left the camp almost five hours before, heading deep into the forest. The trees were old, nearly all hardwoods that grew extremely tall, aspiring ever skyward to catch as much sunlight as possible. The canopy of leaves far above their heads was so thick, very little direct sunlight ever reached the forest floor, which was covered with the previous season's leaves and a thick carpet of green moss.

Stiger stopped and looked up. They had been following the elf up a very steep hill and had been moving at a good pace. In fact, for the past hour the elf had been leading them from one hill to another, each one seemingly higher than the last. Eli had set a punishing pace and they were all winded. Like Father Thomas, the captain had left his horse behind.

"Really?" Father Thomas asked, having also stopped, with hands on his hips as he caught his breath. The paladin looked about, turning in a complete circle. "I don't see it."

Stiger studied the surrounding terrain carefully. He too could find nothing that suggested a road. It must have been a very old one, judging by how there was no longer any ready evidence. The four legionaries accompanying them—James, Todd, Beck, and Starnes—seemed just as baffled.

"This tree." Eli patted it affectionately as if it were an old friend. "This tree is much younger than any of the others eight feet that way. Imagine for a moment that where I am standing was once the roadside. If you look in the direction we are traveling, all of the trees in a direct line leading that way," Eli pointed up the hill, "are younger and somewhat slimmer than the others farther out into the forest. Look back and you will notice the same. The younger trees snake through the older ones."

Stiger frowned, studying the trees carefully. Eyes widening, he realized the trees Eli indicated were indeed slightly slimmer. The bark also had a different hue and appearance than the older trees just a few feet away. It was so obvious he was surprised he had missed it. Then again, they had been moving hard and fast.

"I believe these were intentionally planted," Eli continued. "In another thirty or forty years, it would have been much more difficult to spot the telltale signs. The roadside embankments were also leveled. They did not do such a good job at that. If you look closely in some places, you can see remains of the embankments."

"You are saying someone intentionally destroyed the road?" Father Thomas asked, intrigued.

"I am." Eli flashed a quick smile full of needle-sharp teeth. "Someone went to a lot of trouble to remove any evidence this road ever existed."

"How did you manage to find this, sir?" Legionary Starnes ventured to ask, amazed.

"I have spent many years in the forests of my homeland," Eli explained, as if it should be common knowledge. "We are an old people, and reading the history of the land becomes second nature—almost instinctual, if you will."

"Reading the history of the land?" Starnes asked, clearly confused. "I can't read none, sir, and I don't see any of them symbols on the ground people use to read."

"Eli," Stiger interrupted. His friend was never shy about explaining the abilities of his people when given the opportunity. The last of the elder races, elves considered themselves superior in every way and never hesitated to say so. "Where did the road go?"

Eli pointed in the direction they had just come. "It travels right back to the road to Vrell, surprisingly running through the destroyed village and bandit camp."

"Who would destroy a road?" Stiger asked, baffled.

"That's a very good question," Father Thomas said with genuine interest. "I am pleased I came along. I find such mysteries fascinating."

"Judging by the height of these trees," Stiger said, looking up at the canopy, "the destruction of the road must have been completed...what...over a hundred years ago?"

"More like one hundred fifty," Eli supplied, flashing another one of his clever smiles as he affectionately patted the tree again. "These are old fellows, but the others are much older. This forest is ancient. If I had time, I would welcome the opportunity to listen to its voice."

"There is no time for that," Stiger asserted, knowing what was involved with such a communion. Elves were tied to the land in ways a human could never fully appreciate. The captain could ill afford to lose Eli for a week or two.

"I know," Eli sighed deeply. "She has been calling to me..."

"Why go to all that effort?" Stiger asked, looking back at Eli. "What are they trying to hide?"

"Climb to the top of the hill with me and have a look on the other side," Eli said with another self-satisfied smirk. He pointed to the top of the hill. Stiger frowned. His friend was really enjoying himself.

Father Thomas and the legionaries looked at Stiger for a moment and then scrambled forward up the steep rise of the hill. The captain followed, just as eager to see what Eli had found. The crest of the hill was, in reality, a ridge overlooking a small tree-choked valley, which dropped out steeply beneath them.

A road abruptly emerged before them and traveled down into the heart of the valley. Whoever had destroyed the road had stopped at the crest.

But that wasn't the most amazing thing that greeted the small party. A massive white marble building dominated the center of the valley. It reached toward the sky, almost stretching up to the height of the surrounding ridges. The structure spoke of magnificence and power. Stiger felt it looked very similar to one of the grand temples in Mal'Zeel, the capital of the empire. Oddly, the building had a very imperial look to it, but at the same time, something spoke of a different origin.

"Very unexpected," Father Thomas breathed in awe as the sun broke free of a cloud and illuminated the building in all of its magnificence. "I say, this is terribly unexpected."

"I thought so as well," Eli admitted. Stiger felt that was an understatement. To build something so majestic in such a remote location was an impressive feat.

"Is anyone down there?" Stiger asked, looking for any signs of life in the tree-choked valley. Through the canopy of leaves, he could see no other buildings or smoke that would indicate someone had a fire going.

"The valley is not settled," Eli stated firmly. "As far as I can tell, no one lives here."

"Someone," Stiger said, marveling at what Eli had discovered, "went to a lot of work to hide this valley. What is so important that they would build this here?"

"Allow me show you," Eli said, leading them quickly down the ridge and stepping onto the road. The others followed him. The clay-based road was in surprisingly good shape for its age, and in a few minutes brought the small party down into the heart of the valley.

"Who built this?" Stiger asked in awe as they approached the massive structure, which seemed to grow taller and more imposing the closer they got.

"Dwarves," Eli answered lightly, flashing another one of his devious smiles. "And I think perhaps humans helped."

"Dwarves?" Stiger stopped in his tracks, shocked by the statement. Had he heard his friend right? Dwarves were mythical creatures—a race of legend and tale. Like gnomes, they simply did not exist.

"I assure you, dwarves are very real," Eli replied, stopping also, a twinkle in his eye as he winked at Stiger.

"They are?" Legionary James asked in astonishment. "My mother used to tell us stories..."

"Of course," Eli responded and started walking again.

"How do you know?" James asked, brow furrowed as he followed. Stiger started moving as well.

"Many years ago, I saw several," Eli offered, leaving Stiger and Father Thomas to share a startled glance. The legionaries looked to Stiger for confirmation. Stiger shrugged.

As they neared the building, the forest fell back, revealing a series of gardens composed of wild plants, which ran around the building. The gardens looked maintained and not overgrown, as would have been expected. The road led through the gardens to the building. Hundreds of marble steps led upward to a grand set of double doors. Everything about the structure was imposing, impressive, and magnificent. The party stood, looking up in awe, feeling very small.

"This looks like the Temple of Hirya in the capital," Father Thomas said in a hushed tone. Hirya was the daughter of the God of War, and dedicated to healing.

"It does," Stiger agreed. As a child he had gone to the temple to make regular devotions with his father. The building was very similar. Many thousands of workers would have been required to erect this, he realized. Where had they come from? Where had they gone? Stiger knew he was missing something important. Then a thought occurred to him.

"Eli, I thought you said there was no one in the valley?"

"As far as I can determine, there is no one about," Eli confirmed.

"Then," Stiger asked, pointing about, "who maintains these gardens?"

"That is an interesting question," Eli responded. "Who indeed?"

"What lies inside?" Father Thomas asked, looking up the great row of steps leading up to the sealed doors.

"That is what the captain must see," Eli stated firmly. The elf stepped forward and placed a foot on the first step. He looked over meaningfully at Stiger, as if daring him to follow, and then turned, beginning the steep climb. Stiger watched his enigmatic friend for a moment before Father Thomas caught his eye. The paladin followed Eli. Sighing, Stiger began the long climb, his legionaries following a few steps behind.

The doors to the entrance were massive. There were no hinges on the outside, which meant that they opened inward. They were constructed of a heavy, steel-plated shod that had a dull, ancient look. There was writing on the door in a script that Stiger had never seen before.

"Dwarvish," Eli announced, noticing the captain's look. "And yes, I am sure."

"I don't suppose you can read it?" the paladin asked hopefully.

"I can," Eli admitted with a slight trace of smugness.

"However did you learn Dwarvish?" Father Thomas asked curiously.

"He likely found himself bored to tears one day and decided it was time to learn something new," Stiger said before Eli could manage an answer. "Elves have a lot of time on their hands. Am I incorrect?"

"Close enough," Eli admitted.

"Well?" Stiger asked, a little impatiently, when Eli said nothing further. "What does it say?"

"Unity, honor, and friendship," Eli read rather dramatically.

"That is a little cryptic," Stiger growled, frowning. "Don't you think?"

Eli offered another of his devious little smiles. He leaned forward and pushed on one of the doors. Silently, as if freshly oiled, the door swung inward. A dark corridor, seemingly cut right into the stone, greeted them. Sconces lined the walls every few feet and disappeared into the darkness of the building. Eli stepped forward, and with a startling suddenness, the sconces flared to life, bathing the corridor in light.

"Magic," one of the legionaries breathed, taking a step backward and making the holy sign of the High Father.

"Indeed," Father Thomas agreed, looking rather impressed. Magic was rare. It was extremely unusual to find a wizard who was willing to use his craft for something as mundane as providing magical lighting.

"This way," Eli said, turning back to them briefly before starting off down the corridor. Eli turned, beckoning the party forward. Stiger followed, knowing that if there had been anything to fear, Eli would have said something. Father Thomas moved forward next, with the legionaries bringing up the rear, muttering prayers to their various gods.

Eli led them through the corridor, which looked completely dust-free to Stiger, though the building had an old feel to it. The party emerged into a grand, rectangular-shaped room typical of the important temples in the capital, designed to shock and amaze at the same time. Two massive rows of majestic white marble columns, at least six feet wide at the base, reached upward to the ceiling sixty feet above. Between the two rows of columns lay a rich blue carpet that stretched outward, running the length of the incredible room. Great, intricate metal chandeliers hung from the ceiling. These blazed with a whitish magical light that bathed the interior and accentuated the polished white marble columns and stone walls. The magic lighting drove back all shadows. Stiger was even startled to see that his shadow and those of his men were gone.

The group stood for a few moments, staring in awe at the grandeur of the room before them. The blue carpet led down to some kind of an altar at the far end of the room. Eli started down the carpet without a word or a look back. Stiger and the others followed.

"Is that what I think it is?" Stiger asked when they were within a few feet of the altar, which he realized was actually a sarcophagus. Lying on the sarcophagus was a wooden pole with a golden eagle attached to the end of it. Next to the eagle was an imperial legionary sword sheathed in an ornate blue casing covered over in strange runes. The sword and golden eagle lay on top of a folded rich blue cloak. Blue cloaks were typically worn by legionary generals.

The captain could not take his eyes off the eagle.

"This is most unexpected," Father Thomas said, eying the captain carefully.

"An imperial eagle!" Legionary Starnes exclaimed excitedly. "There is a *13* stamped on it!"

"The Vanished!" Legionary Beck breathed in awe. "Sir…you have found the Thirteenth Legion!"

Stiger shook his head in disbelief. He could not believe what was before him. In his wildest dreams he would never have imagined finding the lost legion's eagle.

"Here lies the honorable General Delvaris," Eli read from the strange Dwarvish writing etched into the side of the sarcophagus. Stiger had not noticed it until Eli began reading. There was an etching of legionaries fighting alongside a group of short, squat people with long braided beards. "This tomb stands in memorial, as a place of honor to the legionaries of Thirteenth Legion, who fought alongside the Clans. The Ironbound Clan holds this imperial eagle in sacred trust, until such time as it can be returned. Only one of sufficient blood may retrieve and return the legion's honor."

"I must admit this little trip to Vrell has really gotten interesting," Father Thomas said as he began walking around the sarcophagus.

"Interesting is not what I would call it." Stiger was having trouble catching his breath. His heart was pounding so hard it felt like it would burst from his chest.

"There is some type of trunk back here," Father Thomas announced. Stiger forced himself to look away from the eagle and walked around to join the paladin on the other side of the sarcophagus. Sure enough, a large oak chest was nestled against the base. From the other side, it had been hidden from view.

Stiger stepped forward and bent, sliding the latch slowly back on the trunk. As he did so, he felt a funny tingle run up his arms. It happened so quickly, Stiger was unsure it had occurred at all. He opened the trunk, revealing an engraved set of armor inside. The armor gleamed as if it had been freshly polished that very morning. It had an archaic look to it, which Stiger had seen before. Every imperial family of standing had a room in their house completely dedicated to honoring their ancestors. Such rooms told the history and prestige of the family. Many included wax death masks and personal items such as swords or sets of armor that important ancestors had once used. Stiger stood and backed up, looking down at the armor in the chest. He had no doubt to whom the armor belonged.

His own family's ancestor room held nothing for General Delvaris. Stiger had the distinct feeling that was about to change.

Legionary Beck moved forward for a look. There was suddenly a deep hum that reverberated angrily through the air. The legionary got a strained look on his face, began to sweat, and rapidly backed away, breathing heavily. The hum immediately ceased.

"I would not attempt that again," Father Thomas offered casually. "It would seem that the chest and the items on the sarcophagus are magically warded."

"Gods, that hurt," Legionary Beck breathed in relief. "I had a feeling that if I went farther it would have killed me."

"I suspect that it would have," Father Thomas said matter-of-factly. "There is a very good chance that had you taken another step or two…"

"Then how did the captain get close enough to touch it?" the legionary asked. He was sweating profusely and breathing heavily. His face had turned a ghostly white.

"The captain has the right blood, of course," Eli pointed out.

Stiger snapped a dark look at his friend.

"Only one of sufficient blood may retrieve the legion's honor," Father Thomas repeated, looking over at the captain. "Might you be related by blood to General Delvaris?"

Stiger nodded and turned his gaze back to the armor resting in the trunk. Every child by noble birth learned his own family history at an early age. It was drilled into him until he could recite it by memory. Stiger was no different. He could recite his family history going back to the founding of the empire. There had been nothing in the ancestor's room from General Delvaris, but that had not stopped the instructors from drilling the general's story into him. Up until a few moments ago, his great-great-grandfather, Ut'Hule Delvaris, had been a stain upon his family's honor. Now he was not so sure.

Glancing around at the monument erected on behalf of the Thirteenth, Stiger was beginning to suspect that his long-deceased relative had achieved something noble and of great import. What that was he had no idea.

"The gods move in mysterious ways," Father Thomas spoke. "As I am called to serve, I feel confident you were called here for a purpose."

Stiger met the paladin's gaze and nodded soberly. He could not deny the paladin's words. It was rare for an officer to be transferred from one legion to another, and yet that was what had occurred. Not for the first time, Stiger considered that providence had a guiding influence on his life.

The captain looked around the interior of the monument. He could not see any additional writing, signs, or engravings. He wanted to know what the Thirteenth and his ancestor had done to warrant such an honor.

"Do you have any idea what happened to the Thirteenth?" he asked Eli.

"There is nothing else that I can find," Eli admitted sadly. "Though I would hazard your relative and the legionaries of the Thirteenth achieved something of intense importance for the dwarves to erect this monument in their honor. From what I know of the dwarves... it takes much to move them."

"Then we take this with us," Stiger said, gesturing toward the eagle, sword, and chest. "It is time for the eagle to be returned to the emperor."

With that, Stiger stepped up to the sarcophagus, which was nearly as tall as he was, and reached out, taking hold of the staff, on which the imperial eagle was mounted. As he had felt with the chest, that same funny tingle ran up his arms. Again, it happened so quickly, Stiger was unsure it had occurred at all. Holding the staff firmly with both hands, he lifted it up into the air.

There was a sudden flash of intense white light around the eagle, followed by what sounded like a bell ringing throughout the monument. Stunned, Stiger stepped back, his eyes fixated upon the eagle held aloft. After a moment, he looked over at Eli, questioning.

"The ward has been broken," Eli said simply. "I believe anyone can now touch those items."

Stiger looked up the staff once again at the eagle. Each legion was personally presented one by the emperor himself. An eagle represented the collective honor of the legion and that of the empire. There were currently twenty-two legions in the empire, which meant there were only twenty-two eagles. Without knowing her fate, the Thirteenth had never been officially disbanded, just simply listed as "Vanished" and struck from the rolls, though her eagle was still listed among the twenty-two in the field. It was a convenient way for both the emperor and empire to not lose face. No matter what the status of the Thirteenth had been, while the eagle was still held, the Thirteenth lived.

Well, lived again, Stiger corrected his thinking. After their mission to Vrell, the eagle would be returned to the emperor. At that point, the emperor would decide the Thirteenth's ultimate fate. Without more to the story, Stiger suspected General Delvaris would remain disgraced, but at least the stain upon the family would be lessened. Perhaps it might even be enhanced by the mystery and recovery of the eagle, Stiger mused.

"You," Stiger said suddenly to Legionary Beck, who had nearly died just moments before. "I name you eagle-bearer."

The legionary's eyes went wide and he turned perhaps even paler than when the magical ward had nearly struck him down. To name a man eagle-bearer was one of the greatest honors a legionary could rise to. Eagle-bearers were treated as special men; they were saluted and received pay equivalent to that of an officer. The man held the honor of the legion in his hands and was expected to defend it with his life. That individual had sole responsibility for the eagle, and it would be in their presence at all times when not planted at legionary headquarters.

Stiger handed the standard to the legionary, who tentatively took it. "I bestow upon you great responsibility and trust."

"I accept the honor," the legionary said shakily, gripping the standard tightly with a fierce look in his eyes. "I will protect this eagle with my life."

Satisfied with the man's resolve, Stiger turned to Eli. "Is there anything else to see?"

"No," Eli admitted. "I believe we have seen all there is."

"Then it is time we depart," Stiger growled. "We need to return to the company. You two, get the trunk."

The two legionaries Stiger directed moved forward and, cautiously at first, touched the chest. When nothing happened, they closed the lid. Both rapidly hauled it up by the handles and easily carried it between them. Stiger reached for the sword and the folded cloak resting on the sarcophagus. He handed both to Legionary Starnes, who was not carrying anything.

"I will meet you outside shortly," Stiger informed them. "I would like a few moments with my ancestor and the gods."

The legionaries moved out immediately. Eli spared Stiger an odd look before following. Father Thomas said nothing but followed Eli.

Stiger watched them go and then turned back to the sarcophagus that held the remains of a man who, until recently, he had viewed poorly. He offered a prayer of thanks to the High Father and asked one day to learn the full story. He then touched the stone sarcophagus reverently. Honored ancestors meant everything to imperial families.

"I will return the eagle and with it your honor. On this I swear," Stiger announced. He hesitated a moment, then turned and began walking toward the double doors, his bootfalls echoing solidly off the walls. As he walked out, the magical light behind him began to fade.

Thank you...

Stiger froze. Had someone spoken? He turned to look back, unsure that he had even heard anything. He was clearly alone. Shaking his head, he decided he had imagined it and continued out.

FOURTEEN

Four days after the assault on the bandit camp and two days after Stiger's small party had rejoined the main body, the road began to climb and fall more steeply with each passing mile. They had entered a set of heavily forested foothills, which presaged the great mountains to come. With the cresting of each hill, snowcapped mountains could be seen in the distance.

There had been a great deal of excitement on the captain's return. Legionary Beck had placed himself proudly at the head of the column, marching with the golden eagle held aloft. The fight had given the men confidence. The hard marching had reinforced that feeling, and the eagle solidified it. The men felt pride in themselves and their achievements. The discovery of the Vanished, the eagle, and General Delvaris's tomb only confirmed that the entire affair was an auspicious event, in that the gods were giving their blessing to both the captain and the company. With the recovery of the eagle, they knew their company, the Eighty-Fifth, would become legend. Some had even begun openly wondering if their captain was Gods Blessed. The fact that a paladin marched with them only added to the feeling.

The suggestion that providence had blessed him made Stiger uncomfortable. His life had been anything but easy to be considered Gods Blessed. Stiger responded by driving the men even harder. So hard did they march, they began circulating a joke that they were not infantry but instead "foot cavalry." Stiger smiled every time he heard this, another sign they were taking pride in being part of the company.

The captain walked Nomad, sharing the miles and sweating alongside the men. He had placed himself near the middle of the column. He could see the Thirteenth's eagle at the head, glinting with golden flashes whenever a stitch of sunlight broke through the canopy. Up and down and up once again was the story of this day's march as the road traversed hill after hill. The closer they got to Vrell, the more pronounced the hills. Even worse, as a direct result of the grade, the road exhibited increasing signs of distress. Large portions were rutted or partially washed away, which meant care had to be taken where feet were placed.

Studying the road critically, Stiger understood the supply train would have their work cut out for them. Where he could, he had fallen trees and debris moved out of the way. This would help save time for the train, which was now several days behind. Once the train entered the hills, the wagons would be slowed due to the rugged condition of the road.

"You march hard, Captain," Father Thomas stated with a ready smile, having ridden up. Stiger nodded a greeting to the Holy Father as the paladin dismounted to walk alongside the captain.

"The men can do better," Stiger responded with a trace of a frown.

"Can't we all?" Father Thomas agreed, apparently sensing Stiger's meaning.

Stiger had avoided the paladin since their return, which was clearly why Father Thomas had sought him out. Stiger wondered if the paladin understood his discomfort.

Neither said anything for several minutes amid the ever-present crunch of many footfalls sprinkled with the occasional laugh as men joked and bantered to pass the time. Stiger glanced up at the sky, which had begun to cloud up. Perhaps they might get rained on, he considered. A light rain to help cool down might be welcome; however, the temperatures had begun dipping alarmingly each evening. A little relief now could mean an uncomfortable night later.

"When was the last time you spoke on your sins?" Father Thomas asked abruptly, referring to the sinner's ritual.

Stiger glanced briefly over at the paladin with a hooded expression. He did not immediately respond, but instead chose to weigh his response. He had not dealt with his sins in a good long while, and he wasn't sure he was ready to just yet.

"I am not entirely sure," Stiger finally said, deciding to answer directness with honesty. He would have preferred to avoid the conversation altogether. "The High Father is not my family's sole deity."

"A follower of the Old Order?" Father Thomas asked, with some surprise.

"My family are followers of the Order," Stiger confirmed, "though we honor the High Father. He is part of the Order, as you well know."

"I should have expected nothing different," Father Thomas said, with a slightly sardonic smile. "You come from an interesting family, my son."

"Don't we all?" Stiger responded rather blandly. There were times he wished he had been born into an ordinary household, one with very few expectations and responsibilities. How much simpler would life have been? How much pain would he have been spared?

"Some families are more interesting than others," Father Thomas breathed, smile leaving his face.

"Unfortunately," Stiger agreed with a sour expression.

"There is another way to look at it," Father Thomas offered. "Some are more blessed than others by being born to such families."

"That is one blessing I would gladly return." Stiger spoke barely above a whisper.

"Is it?" Father Thomas asked with a skeptical expression. "Would you really return such a blessing?"

Stiger grunted in reply and glanced away. Being a Stiger was both a blessing and a burden. His family was wealthy and powerful almost beyond belief, but for a Stiger, good fortune seemed to come at a painful price. Nomad nudged his shoulder gently as if in rebuke to his master's words and thoughts. Stiger cast his horse a brief look and reached up, patting his neck.

"Is it so terrible, being a Stiger?" Father Thomas asked sincerely. "You would not lie to one of the cloth, would you?"

"I found Father Griggs much more taciturn in nature," Stiger responded wryly.

Father Thomas let out a guffaw at that, which caused several nearby legionaries to glance over. Their captain was such a serious man that they sometimes thought him nearly incapable of jest. "I talk too much. Is that it?"

"I prefer to take religion on my own terms," Stiger answered, wishing to turn the subject away from his family. "I do not enjoy being pushed by others to worship as they wish me to."

"There are some who would brand you a heretic for a comment like that," Father Thomas said, probing for a response. "Such talk could be considered dangerous."

"Are you one of those people?" Stiger asked, looking meaningfully at the paladin.

"Oh, heavens no!" Father Thomas chuckled. "I am more pragmatic and tolerant in my approach to worship and belief structures. You see, in my calling, I have to be more … shall we say, understanding. Not all is evil that does not agree with the High Father's teachings."

"Is that so?"

"Life is not as black and white as the absolutists believe," Father Thomas replied.

"That is encouraging to hear. No doubt you are better educated than the fanatics," Stiger growled. This conversation was familiar ground. He'd had similar conversations with Father Griggs.

"Better educated than the absolutists," Father Thomas said with a wry nod. "Oh, heavens yes. As you are most likely aware, those of my order spend years in study and training."

"I expect, like Father Griggs, you will respect disparate beliefs and practices?" Stiger looked over at the paladin for assurance. "You will not attempt to force religion on my men and me?"

"Heavens no," Father Thomas replied, amused. "Belief is a choice, as is the decision to practice."

Stiger said nothing, but nodded. Nomad nudged his arm again, and the captain began scratching the horse's neck affectionately.

"I am, however, available to those who desire my counsel and spiritual direction," Father Thomas added. "I may also, from time to time, nudge those I believe faithful and in need of my services."

"Such as offering to conduct a sinner's ritual?" Stiger asked with a raised eyebrow.

"I am pleased we understand each other so well," Father Thomas replied enthusiastically, a sly smile playing across his face. "And to think, with such understanding we may even one day call each other friends."

Stiger had to chuckle at that one. Father Thomas was a likeable sort. The problem was that Stiger had also liked Father Griggs. Would it end up the same way?

"Perhaps we do understand each other," Stiger replied as they started up yet another hill.

Lost to his thoughts, Stiger smoked as he sat before his campfire. Most of the camp had bedded down for the night. A number of discordant snores could be heard from those slumbering nearby. Only the watch sentries moved about, marching off their rounds and keeping a sharp eye.

Stiger blew out a long stream of smoke and then looked over at General Delvaris's oak trunk a few feet away. It had been placed next to his bedroll. The general's sword, in its blue scabbard, lay atop the trunk. Ever since they had returned from the monument, Stiger had been reluctant to examine Delvaris's belongings. He rarely, if ever, avoided things, yet Stiger had been deeply troubled by the thought that providence had led him to Delvaris's monument. Something deep down and primal warned him to stay away from the trunk. At the same time, he felt a need to learn more about his ancestor. He was conflicted and it bothered him to no end.

Perhaps it was time. What was he afraid of?

Stiger stood and walked over to the chest, eyes on the ornately carved wooden scabbard lying across the top. He stood for a few moments looking down before reaching for it. Upon contact, a tingle ran up his arm. Stiger wondered briefly if he had imagined it. He had felt it before, and the more he thought about it, the more he was sure the feeling was real. Perhaps it was a remnant of the magic that had safeguarded it all this time?

He looked down on the trunk and contemplated opening it. After a few seconds, he decided to refrain from doing so. He would begin with the sword.

Pipe clamped in his teeth, he returned to his place before the fire and laid the weapon across his knees. He ran his fingers across the lacquered surface of the scabbard, feeling the grain of the wood. Strange, fascinating runes ran up and down its length, but it wasn't that which caught his attention. The figures of three magnificent dragons, meticulously carved into the wood, ran from the tip to the hilt. The detail of the workmanship was incredible. Each dragon was colored differently. One was gold, another black as night, and the third near the top, with its mouth agape as if striving to reach the hilt of the sword, was a deep forest green.

He had never seen its like. So incredible were the carvings that Stiger wondered on the master artisan who had crafted it. The closer he looked, the more detail he discovered. Flipping the scabbard over, the reverse side was similar, though these dragons were painted in different colors—copper, blue, and red. The red dragon near the top looked slightly different than the others. Stiger brought the scabbard closer and tilted it toward the fire to better catch the light. A warrior rode the red dragon's back, a sword held aloft. The warrior looked tiny in comparison to the dragon.

He briefly wondered what it would be like to ride such a creature, soaring high above the clouds. He had never seen a dragon and had not met anyone who had ever claimed to.

Dragons were rumored to live in the more remote regions of the world. Surely such a ride would be a terrifying and incredible experience.

Shaking his head at his flight of whimsy, he reached for the hilt. His hand comfortably wrapped around the finely corded grip. Stiger hesitated a moment, and then pulled the blade free. The sword hissed slightly as it came out, with a ringing sound that was music to his ears.

Stiger whistled softly at the sight of the blade and its finely crafted steel. Etched carefully into the steel, the same strange runes worked their way up and down the length of the blade. The sword was perfectly balanced and, testing the edge, he found it to be razor sharp, as if just whetted.

It was possibly the most impressive sword he had ever laid eyes upon. Stiger set aside his pipe, having long since burned out, and stood. He took a couple of practice swings, marveling at the blade's lightness and spot-on balance. It seemed to sing to him as it cut effortlessly through the air.

Though of excellent quality and made by a master, Stiger's own sword paled by comparison. What he held in his hands was nothing short of a masterpiece of sword smithing. It was, for lack of a better word, perfect.

Stiger made a decision. He would honor Delvaris by carrying the man's sword, at least until he returned home. At that time, Delvaris's armor, cloak, sword, and whatever possessions remained in the trunk would be properly displayed in his family's ancestor room.

"I will honor you by carrying your sword," Stiger said quietly to Delvaris's spirit.

At last, a soft voice hissed.

Stiger froze, hair standing on end, and then spun around.

There was no one there.

He slowly turned in a circle, scanning the camp beyond his fire. No one was nearby, save those sleeping and the sentries making their rounds. A breeze rustled through the treetops. After a moment, Stiger shrugged, convinced he was hearing things. It had likely been just the wind. He looked down on the short sword once again, marveling at its beauty and elegance.

Sitting back down before the fire, he reluctantly sheathed the sword and sat, staring into the depths of the fire. The contents of the trunk could wait for another day.

Eli had emerged from the forest with news on Vrell. He advised a halt.

The company had been marching for eight days since the assault on the bandit camp. In that time, Eli and his scouts had located two additional bandit camps. Both had been abandoned for some time. The camps looked undisturbed since the day the bandits had left. Stiger had never seen anything like it. It was as if the bandits had just up and left, leaving everything of value behind. Eli had been unable to find any useful clues.

They managed to salvage some equipment and supplies from the camps, but not much. It was an interesting mystery. Why had they left? Where had the bandits gone? It was unlikely they went deeper into the forest. Had they gone to Vrell? There was just no way to tell.

Column halted, the men fell out of ranks. Shields in their coverings were carefully rested against trees before the tired legionaries dropped to the ground along both sides of the road. It was near enough lunchtime that many of the legionaries began to rummage through their haversacks.

Between Cook's food and the scouts' foraging, the men had enough to eat.

Stiger sent word for Ikely and both sergeants to join them, to hear what Eli had to report on Vrell. They arrived shortly, along with Father Thomas. Each was dusty, sweaty, and weary. The hard pace was beginning to take its toll. His men were wearing down. Thankfully, the hard march out was almost over.

It was concerning that he had been led to believe that there would be great resistance along the road. There had been virtually none. The road could have been easily opened at any time. It was not like General Kromen did not have the strength to keep the road open. Even the small rebel force that had been operating in the area could easily have been brushed aside. So why had it not been done?

"Castle Vrell is ten miles distant," Eli reported when everyone had gathered around. "The castle is in a very formidable position, easily blocking the pass into the valley. I do not in the slightest jest when I tell you a handful could hold the pass against an army."

"That impressive, huh?" Stiger asked. He was curious to see this fortification. There had been a good number in the North, and Stiger had been impressed with their size and scope. He wondered how Castle Vrell compared.

"It is of dwarven construction," Eli added.

"I had always thought there were no such things as dwarves," Ikely said. Eli simply gave Ikely a flat look.

"What does that mean for us?" Stiger asked.

"We all need to be aware there is the very real probability of a dwarven kingdom somewhere nearby," Eli stated matter-of-factly. "Dwarves prefer to live in the mountains. Well, under them, actually. Though I must admit, it is entirely possible that such a kingdom is no more and all that remains is their labor. It has long been understood amongst my people that dwarves are few in number these days."

"Are they dangerous?" Ikely asked.

"They were once renowned for their ability and tenaciousness on the battlefield," Eli said. "I have heard it said that the dwarves fielded some of the most feared heavy infantry ever to march."

"If there is a dwarven kingdom around, do you think there is a chance we might encounter them?" Stiger asked.

Eli gave that a moment's consideration. "That is difficult to say. I think it is unlikely. Long ago, the dwarves retreated from the wider world. Should there prove to be a kingdom nearby, I rather suspect that, since humans have long occupied the valley and castle, they will probably ignore us as they have been ignoring everyone else.

"If we do meet them," Eli continued, "it is best to understand that dwarves are a difficult and proud people. They value their personal honor, which they call their life's legend, very highly. From what I understand, dwarven honor is somewhat complex. Only the clan's honor is more important than the individual's. They could prove troublesome if affronted."

"So, basically, don't offend them?" Stiger asked.

Eli nodded in confirmation.

"Have you ever met a dwarf?" Ranl asked, not as a challenge, but with sincere curiosity.

"No," Eli admitted. "I have never had the pleasure of being introduced."

"Then how do you know they exist?" Ikely asked.

"I was present when emissaries from one of their kingdoms were presented to the Elantric Warden," Eli responded simply. "I was a child at the time."

Stiger shook his head, wondering who or what the Elantric Warden was. "Alright," he said, holding up a hand to forestall any further discourse on the subject. Given an opportunity, Eli could go on for hours. "If Eli says dwarves exist, then they exist. After having seen the monument to the Thirteenth, I believe they exist. What of Castle Vrell?"

"The imperial standard flies from the castle's ramparts," Eli reported. "There are no patrols beyond the main gate, and no evidence of any occurring recently."

"Did you make contact with the garrison?" Stiger asked.

"I sent in Witchell and Bran," Eli answered, naming two of his scouts. "Both were admitted; however, they failed to come out."

"What about the rest?" Stiger asked. He had given specific instructions on how to handle contact with the garrison. With how he had been dispatched on this mission and with the paladin joining them, he was worried about what waited at Vrell.

"As ordered, I was careful not to let any of the garrison see myself or the other scouts," Eli explained. "The garrison were led to believe that the scouts were an advance party sent to make contact and report back."

"Then they were supposed to come out?" Ikely asked, looking between Stiger and Eli.

"Yes," Eli answered, a disturbed look passing across his youthful face. It took a lot to bother Eli. He had clearly grown close to his scouts. "They were to report that there was nothing amiss within the garrison. They did not return in the agreed upon two hours. We waited seven hours."

"That is not good," Stiger said with a heavy sigh. "Do you think the rebels might have possession of the castle?"

"It is a possibility..." Eli said, considering. "However, I feel it is unlikely. I was able to obtain a good look at those of the garrison who came out to meet our scouts. I believe them to be legionaries."

"So, either something is wrong in the garrison, or the commander detained our men for some strange reason," Stiger said.

"I sent two so that one could return and report," Eli said softly.

"I sense..." Father Thomas spoke up for the first time in a very soft tone. All eyes turned to the paladin. His eyes closed as he searched within himself. "This is part of why I am pulled to Vrell."

"There is something wrong with the garrison, isn't there?" Stiger asked sharply.

"Perhaps," Father Thomas answered, opening his eyes and looking seriously at those around him. "Or something within the castle. I sense evil nearby."

"Great...just great," Stiger growled before turning back to Eli. "Do you have any idea what it is like in the valley beyond?"

"No," Eli admitted. "I do not."

"Is there a way to get up and around the castle...perhaps into the valley itself?"

"The pass is steep, with near-sheer cliff faces on both sides. Any attempt to scale those faces would be seen," Eli explained. "I would need to take men around the pass and through the mountains. It would be impossible to get more than a few men over safely. Such an attempt would take several days."

Stiger frowned. Waiting several days was not really an option. If there was something wrong with the garrison, he needed to know now. The supply train was at least a week behind. If the train needed to turn around, it would be better for that to happen before it got too close to Vrell.

"Do you think they will let us in?" Stiger asked Eli, getting a sudden idea.

"I believe they are very interested in the supply train," Eli explained. "From where I was concealed, I could hear the conversation between the gate sergeant and our scouts. They seem desperate for resupply."

"We may be able to use that as leverage, then." Stiger grinned. "Perhaps the promise of supply will purchase us entry."

"Sir," Blake spoke up. "If there is something wrong with the garrison, why do we want to go in there?"

"Good question," Ikely agreed with a glance over at Father Thomas. "Father, no disrespect intended, but I am not terribly eager to find out what your trouble is that awaits us."

"None taken, son, yet ignoring problems rarely solves them," Father Thomas countered.

"We cannot return without at the least discovering if there is a problem," Stiger said firmly. "If there is something wrong with the garrison, we need to discover what it is and either fix it or return to report. With luck, our scouts were detained for some innocent reason. For all we know, the garrison commander is not even present and they are waiting for his return."

"I don't like it, sir," Ikely admitted. "They should not have kept our scouts... At least one should have returned."

"I don't like it either," Stiger agreed. "Duty requires us to investigate, and besides, I will not leave those men behind."

"Yes, sir," Ikely said.

"If there is trouble, let's see if we can get them to invite the fox into the hen house," Stiger said. "Sergeants, I want the men looking slovenly. I want them to present a dirty and unkempt look. Let the garrison see poor-quality legionaries with little regard for discipline. Just what they would expect to receive from the main encampment."

"I believe the men can manage that," Blake said with an evil grin. "Since we came all this way, it would be a real shame not to see the famed Vrell Valley."

Stiger chuckled before turning back to Eli. "Now, I want to hear everything about Castle Vrell and the garrison."

Fifteen

Stiger looked up at the ramparts of the castle, at least three hundred feet above. He whistled at the impressive nature of the fortification. The dwarves who had built Castle Vrell had been very clever. It looked as if they had taken a very large knife and removed a slice of mountainside right where two very large mountains came together, creating a pass where one had not existed previously. Then they had built an impressive castle at the mouth of the pass. The outer wall of the castle, spanning the width of the pass, had been erected in a curved shape that bulged outward in the center.

The faces of each mountain climbed steeply out and away from the wall, starting about twenty-five feet below the crest of the battlements. The dwarves had carefully shaped and then smoothed the two cliff faces, which had the effect of making the defensive nature of the outer castle wall that much more formidable. Not only was it an impressive bit of work, but also an astounding engineering accomplishment. Everything about Castle Vrell had an impenetrable look that screamed defensive power. Eli had not exaggerated when he had said that a handful could hold the pass against an army. Stiger had never seen anything like it.

This was the most powerful defensive position he had ever seen, and he could not imagine how long it had taken to construct. As Stiger studied the walls, he tried to think of ways one would successfully assault such a fortification. He had difficulty imagining scaling such tall walls or breaking through the main gate, set in the center and at the base of the wall. The main gate consisted of a metal portcullis placed just inside a tunnel under the wall. Short of bringing down the walls themselves—which seemed an unlikely prospect, as they looked incredibly thick—the tunnel seemed to be the only weak point.

The outer portcullis was being raised. Stiger could see another farther along the tunnel that had also been raised. Sunlight was shining from beyond it. A couple of men had lit torches inside the tunnel. The more Stiger thought about it, he wasn't even sure the tunnel could be considered a weakness. There were likely numerous murder holes inside the tunnel, making any assault that made it past the first portcullis a difficult and potentially impossible affair. The tunnel was long enough that it was possible that portions might even be safely collapsed or blocked. The thought of traveling through it made him a little uncomfortable.

Getting a sizable force around the castle and over the mountains encircling Vrell Valley would also be very difficult. The snowcapped mountains, perhaps as high as fourteen thousand feet or more, were some of the largest he had ever seen. Sending a sizeable contingent of men over them might take months to accomplish, let alone moving any sort of supply to sustain them.

Starving the defenders out would prove problematic, too. Vrell was so isolated that any besieging army would have supply problems of their own. In short, Stiger decided the easiest way to take such a castle would be from inside. The question was, how would an enemy get themselves inside? In the end, he concluded the effort to reduce such a position would be a massive undertaking and would likely take years of work and the commitment of thousands of men.

Eli stood next to his silent captain, also carefully studying the castle. Stiger's company, looking worse for wear, stretched out in a column, four deep, down the road and into the forest. Stiger had intentionally halted the column about three hundred feet from the wall. The men lazed about while they waited, looking to the unpracticed eye incompetent and of low quality. They were the near spitting image of what they had been when he had taken command. Stiger could tell they were enjoying the experience, hamming it up … perhaps a little too much.

A lieutenant, along with a sergeant, strode forth, emerging from the tunnel. The two approached Stiger, who was waiting impatiently by this point. He hated to be kept waiting.

The garrison officer saluted, fist to chest. He was a young man, barely out of his teens, and this was likely his first assignment. Stiger returned the salute. The lieutenant looked as if he had not had a good night's sleep in a long while. His face was etched with exhaustion and what Stiger took to be worry. Something was clearly not right with the garrison.

"I am Lieutenant Peal," he announced in a high-pitched voice, after having glanced at Stiger's men with ill-concealed contempt. He did not introduce the sergeant. Stiger noticed that neither the lieutenant nor the sergeant were armed, which was downright odd. They were both wearing their armor, though. The sergeant's armor was well cared for, as would be expected of a typical legionary veteran.

"Captain Stiger." He then turned slightly toward Eli. "May I introduce Lieutenant Eli'Far."

The lieutenant looked at Stiger sharply, eyes widening. Peal recovered quickly, face becoming an inscrutable mask. "A pleasure to meet you both. Welcome to Vrell, gentlemen."

"It was a long road." Stiger sighed in an exaggerated manner. "It is good to finally arrive."

"I can imagine," Peal said and hesitated, looking down the road and back into the forest. "I thought...I thought the supply train would be with you?"

"The train is lagging a few days behind," Stiger explained casually, feigning indifference. "We pushed ahead and cleared the road of bandits."

"With these?" the lieutenant asked in surprise, gesturing disdainfully at the slovenly bunch of legionaries. "I am surprised they could safely dig a latrine without constant direction."

"I have to work with what I am given," Stiger responded with a disgusted look at his own men. "Lieutenant, we will need lodging and food. It has been a long, hard march, with far too few creature comforts. Some wine and a bath will be most welcome."

The lieutenant glanced uncomfortably behind him before looking back at Stiger. He looked torn for a moment. "I was instructed to have the supply train enter at once, so that it could be unloaded before sundown. Your men were to remain—"

"Lieutenant," Stiger interrupted with mock exasperation. "That is not going happen until the train actually gets here."

"So, you want to bring your men inside the castle?" Peal asked unhappily.

"Of course," Stiger snorted, as if there were never any doubt of his intentions. "I am not going to leave them out here. We encountered bandits on the road, and there are likely rebels about."

"Very well." The lieutenant sighed heavily. It looked as if he wanted to tell Stiger something, but refrained from doing so. "You can take it up with the commandant. Captain Aveeno will see your men camped on the valley side of the pass."

"Not in the castle?" Stiger asked, glancing up at the fortification towering above them. The walls were so high that they were in the castle's shadow. "It certainly looks large enough to house my company. Lieutenant, the last thing I want to do is spend another night on hard ground."

"I am confident lodging can be arranged for you and your officers, sir," the lieutenant said, glancing over at the sergeant who had accompanied him. "However, space is limited inside the castle. Have no fear, we will find your men a good, safe spot to camp."

"That sounds acceptable," Stiger said, as if somewhat mollified. Something was definitely wrong, and he did not like it one bit.

"Excellent." The lieutenant flashed a relieved look. "If you care to take your men through—"

"Lieutenant," Stiger said, watching the young man more closely. "I sent forward a couple of scouts to make contact. I know they arrived. They were ordered to report back."

The lieutenant squirmed, clearly uncomfortable. He cleared his throat before speaking. "Sir, I have the unfortunate duty to inform you that they were caught stealing."

"What?" Stiger asked, his voice becoming deathly quiet, almost a whisper. "Stealing, you say?"

"Captain Aveeno has disciplined them for their theft," the lieutenant said, voice cracking slightly. The young man looked so frightened that Stiger thought he might bolt. Stiger glanced over at Eli. He did not believe a word about his men stealing.

"Though they are nearly worse than pigs wallowing in the mud," Stiger growled, forcing himself to contain his anger, "I discipline my own men."

"I…I…ah, I understand, sir," the lieutenant stuttered. "However, the commandant felt it best—"

"What did the good commandant prescribe as punishment?" Stiger interrupted.

"There is but one punishment here," the lieutenant answered, struggling to pull himself together.

"Well?" Stiger demanded when the man failed to continue.

"Death," the lieutenant whispered, nearly shaking in his boots.

"Death?" Stiger breathed in astonishment. He had expected a severe flogging, at the worst. His anger grew into a mounting rage and he took a menacing step closer to the lieutenant, who took a nervous step backward. "For theft? What did they steal?"

"I, ah…I do not know, sir," the lieutenant answered, sweat beading his brow. "I was on assignment in the valley at the time. You will have to take that up with the commandant, sir."

"I will," Stiger breathed, inches from the lieutenant's face. "You tell him I will do just that."

"Sergeant Boral." The lieutenant turned, taking another step back. "Kindly escort Captain Stiger and his men into the castle."

"Are you sure about that, Lieutenant?" the sergeant asked. "The commandant was quite clear with his orders."

"Do as you are ordered," the lieutenant snapped, a frightened look on his face. Stiger was shocked that the sergeant had actually questioned Peal's order so openly. Such things just did not occur in the legions.

"Yes, Lieutenant," Sergeant Boral answered stiffly.

"Captain," Lieutenant Peal said, taking another step backward to gain some space. He hastily saluted and did not wait for a return salute. "If you will excuse me, I must inform the commandant of your arrival and arrange for suitable quarters." With that, the lieutenant turned and almost ran back toward the tunnel. Eli and Stiger shared another brief look.

Sergeant Blake and Father Thomas came up just then. Stiger gave the paladin a sharp look. He was wearing his coarse brown priestly robes, which covered his armor and sword. The last time Stiger had seen Father Thomas wear his robes had been when he had arrived at camp. The paladin looked very much like a simple, though large, friar or wandering priest of the High Father. It was not uncommon to see such men on imperial roads or traveling with the legions.

Stiger frowned as he looked upon Sergeant Boral, who still had not budged an inch. The sergeant was a tough older man, with a thickened neck to prove an easy twenty years of service. He had a look of competence and coolness about him. Boral carried himself in such a way that told others he had seen a great deal and not much impressed him.

"Blake," Boral said, a smile cracking his face as he recognized Stiger's sergeant.

"Boral, you bastard," Blake exclaimed with a slow, matching smile. They briefly hugged, thumping each other on the back, as two old companions who had not seen the other in a great long while.

"I thought you went north with the Seventh," Blake asked when he stepped back.

"Got sent here instead." Boral's smile turned to a frown. "Wish I had been lucky and gone north, though."

"Captain, this man here is the best dice player I ever met," Blake said, "and a good man, too!"

"Blake lies too much," Boral replied. "My skill in dice is much overrated. It is only chance that favors me, sir."

"Chance? Seven levels, man!" Blake responded with a full-on grin. "I thought it was the loaded dice you rolled with."

"What's going on in there?" Stiger interrupted, nodding toward the castle.

"Don't do it, sir," Boral warned, sobering. "Stay out of Vrell or you will end up like your two scouts."

"What happened?" Stiger asked. He was still shaken at finding out his men had been put to death.

"The commandant," Boral said simply. "He's up and gone crazy."

"What do you mean?" Stiger asked. "Crazy how?"

"We have not had any word from the outside in months. Messengers left and never returned. What with the supply train being so late, he claimed the empire had abandoned us. Him and his cronies have started ruling Vrell as if it is their own little kingdom. About a month ago he began executing anyone who disagreed with him. That has everyone terrified they will be next."

"Is that what happened to my scouts?" Stiger asked. The scouts' arrival had provided direct proof the commandant was wrong.

" 'Fraid so, sir," the sergeant said sadly, looking down in the dirt and kicking at a loose stone. He looked back up at the captain.

"Then why are they letting us in?" Stiger asked, looking toward the retreating lieutenant's back.

"His orders were to have your men camp outside the walls. Only the train was to be admitted. The commandant wants it," the sergeant answered with a shrug. "They have food to get through the winter, but that means starving the good people in the valley. They outnumber the garrison and are a tough, hardy sort, if you take my meaning, sir.

We've begun having problems with them. To maintain control over the winter, I guess he needs that supply."

Stiger was silent a moment as he considered his next question. "So what happens once I take my company in?"

"If I had to guess, the commandant will have your men encamped in the valley, with no way out. You and your officers will be lodged in the keep and sent an invitation to dinner, where the commandant will probably have you killed or some other such nonsense." Boral shrugged. "Your men will be unable to help you. When the supply train gets here ... well, he will take it, control most of the food for the valley ... end of story."

"Why are you telling us this?" Stiger asked, not liking at all what he was hearing. Everything in the South seemed upside down. If Aveeno was playing king, it did not bode well for the empire holding Vrell, especially with the impressive nature of the fortification before him.

"I want out," the sergeant answered plainly. "I swore an oath to the empire, not to a madman. All I ask is to complete my service and retire with my pension."

Stiger was silent a moment as he considered his options. "How many of the garrison are of a like mind?"

"Most. Good men they are, sir," Boral assured him, glancing back at the castle. "The majority are trapped in camps on the valley side. The commandant and his cronies terrorize them into following along."

"How many support the commandant?" Stiger asked, considering his earlier thoughts on how the best way to take Castle Vrell was from the inside. Well ... he had just been invited inside, hadn't he?

"Around forty of them support Captain Aveeno," the sergeant answered after a moment's consideration. "You will find most of 'em bastards in the castle."

Stiger turned, sharing another glance with Eli, who offered Stiger a slight nod of encouragement. Stiger rubbed his stubbly jaw as he considered his options, then turned back to the sergeant.

"Do you know where Captain Aveeno will be?" Stiger asked.

"What are you thinking of doing?" the sergeant asked, glancing between Stiger and the others. "After what I just told you, surely you are not crazy enough to go in there!"

"He is," Blake answered with a proud smile, then hesitated, turning toward his captain, embarrassed. "Sorry, sir...I did not mean to call you crazy."

"I have been called worse," Stiger said. "Well, Sergeant? Do you know where Aveeno will be?"

"With these men?" Sergeant Boral asked incredulously, looking at the captain's men lazing about. They looked terrible—covered in dirt, filth, and mud—like they had not seen a bath in weeks and, worse, did not care to see one. "They are rabble."

"Looks can be deceiving," Stiger replied.

Sergeant Boral looked shrewdly at the captain and then at Sergeant Blake, who nodded in agreement. After a moment, he shrugged. "Seven levels...I can't believe I am going to do this. I can lead you to the commandant," Boral stated, resolved. "They will not be expecting trouble. If you give Captain Aveeno long enough to rally them, the garrison will fight you out of fear alone."

"How many men are in the castle?" Stiger asked.

"Around three hundred," Sergeant Boral answered immediately. "The commandant does not trust much of the garrison, and as I said, he has the rest deployed around the valley. There is no other way out of the valley, which means they are effectively at his mercy."

"What of Lieutenant Peal?" Stiger asked.

"A frightened man," Sergeant Boral said. "He is lucky to have survived the purge of officers. He's so young and green, I don't think they consider him a threat. All in all, though, he is not a bad sort."

"Where will Captain Aveeno be once we get inside the castle?" Eli asked, getting back to the point.

"At this time of day, he will be holding court in the great hall," Boral answered with a snort. "Hearing grievances from the villagers in the valley. Thinks he's important now."

"Can you lead us to him?" Stiger asked.

"Yes, sir, I can and will," Boral said. "The tunnel leads to the main courtyard. Once in the main courtyard, we will have to get into the keep and climb three floors to get there. It is on the backside of the castle and overlooks the valley side of the pass. Perhaps a five-minute walk. There are several sturdy doors that could be barred. We may need to batter our way through."

"Is there any way to escape the castle?" Eli asked.

"There are two entrances to the castle, one gate to the valley side and this one here." Boral jerked a thumb toward the gate behind him. "The main courtyard is the center of the castle. It leads to the stables, barracks, walls, and the keep. If you secure both entrances, no one will get out, other than to throw themselves from the walls, which would prove a tad bit unhealthy."

"Once inside, is there anyone we can immediately trust?" Stiger asked with a glance up at the walls. Several legionaries were leaning over the battlements, looking down upon them. They were probably wondering why Stiger's men were taking so long to get moving.

"No, sir," Boral answered. "Anyone you come across could be a collaborator, and I won't be able to point them all out to you in the heat of the moment. I would not trust anyone, at least until the commandant is dead. Whatever you do, sir, please do not take him alive."

"Why not?" Stiger asked, shocked that a sergeant was asking him to make sure he killed a fellow officer and nobleman. First Boral had questioned Lieutenant Peal, and now he was advocating killing the commandant. "Should he not stand trial for what he has done?"

"He has magic, sir," the sergeant answered matter-of-factly. "I swear it. Some of the officers tried to arrest him for acting kinglike and he killed them with a simple touch. Some say he took their very souls."

Stiger shot a glance over at Father Thomas, who said nothing, but looked deadly serious, a change from his normal jovial demeanor. Eli looked grim as well. To an elf, one's soul was especially precious, and the mere mention of stealing one was unsettling.

"Sergeant Boral will lead us and the first three files into the keep in search of Captain Aveeno," Stiger ordered, feeling the tightness in his stomach that always presaged a fight. "Father Thomas, I think you had better come with us."

"I fear that might not be such a bad idea," the paladin responded grimly.

"Lieutenant Eli'Far will also accompany us," Stiger continued. He had left several men with the eagle and mules back in the forest. "Sergeant Blake, you are with us as well. Lieutenant Ikely, you will secure the main courtyard and both entrances to the castle with the rest of the men. Do not venture beyond the courtyard unless you need to do so. Try to keep your men together. If anyone resists, use force. Otherwise, allow them to surrender. Once we have dealt with Captain Aveeno, we will worry about securing the rest of the castle. Any questions?"

There were none.

"This is likely to get ugly," Stiger continued after a moment. "We have to be fast and utterly ruthless. Make sure the men understand. Now, let's get moving. We have a castle to storm."

They broke up, with the sergeants and corporals shouting orders mixed with curses for the benefit of those watching above. The men sullenly and slowly fell in, as if they resented the interruption of their rest. Above, on the walls, Stiger could see several sentries watching closely.

Stiger handed Nomad's reins off to a legionary and moved toward the head of the column, with Sergeant Boral in tow. Word had spread quickly, and the men eyed their captain grimly as he joined them. Bennet was one of the first men in the column, which was a spot of honor for his file. Stiger noted it and nodded to the man who had once tried to assassinate him.

"I have your back, sir," Bennet said quietly, eyeing Sergeant Boral with menace.

"I am a friend," the sergeant said, holding up his hands to show that he held no ill will for the captain.

"When we come up to them, I would like you and the others to quietly subdue those two men who are standing by the portcullis," Stiger said to Bennet, making sure not to look in the direction of the two sentries. The two had opened the outer gates behind the portcullis and were presumably remaining to close it after the company passed through.

"Consider it done, sir," Bennet said with a grin. The others, just as dirty and unkempt as Bennet, nodded with enthusiasm. Within minutes, the column began moving toward the castle. Stiger made sure that he walked slightly to the side, four men back, to give the men up front room to act. Eli was at his shoulder. Not unsurprisingly, Father Thomas was just behind Eli, looking like a peaceful friar and far from the holy warrior that he was. His robes did an excellent job of concealing the armor he wore underneath.

The two garrison legionaries manning the inner gate behind the portcullis looked bored as the column approached. They also looked thin and underfed, Stiger noted, wondering if the entire garrison was suffering so.

The column marched into the dark, torch-lit tunnel. The tunnel was chilly and damp, and the tromping of many feet on stone was near deafening. Stiger looked up at the massive portcullis and dark murder holes above and to the sides. Many of his men would not be out of the tunnel before the action began. He hoped that the murder holes were not manned.

Bennet and several others neatly stepped out of the column and back to the two sentries. Stiger hardly heard the muffled thumps as his men violently but efficiently silenced the first two sentries. Boral appeared shocked at how quickly the two had been taken down.

It seemed to take forever, but then Stiger and the front of the column emerged into the bright sunlight of the castle courtyard. To say the courtyard was large would have been an understatement. An entire legionary regiment could have easily assembled within the courtyard's confines without feeling the least bit crowded. The men's metal-studded sandals, magnified by the interior walls of the castle, sounded loud on the granite paving stones.

The castle itself rose to grand heights around them, with stone staircases leading directly up to battlements. On both sides, heavy wooden doors led inward to the bowels of the keep and what appeared to be barracks, stables, and general living quarters. Some of the doors were open and some were closed. The ones to the keep appeared to be open.

Directly ahead, the entrance tunnel to the valley was sealed; the portcullis was down. That simplified things, the captain thought, relieved. No one would be escaping in that direction.

Two garrison legionaries were leisurely moving toward the valley gate, talking as they strolled forward. Stiger supposed that once the entrance to the pass was closed, the valley gate would be opened so that his company could pass right through. That would not be happening. He and his men were here to stay.

Stiger studied the area critically. Several men, all garrison legionaries, milled about, waiting for Stiger's men to emerge from the tunnel. A few were sergeants and corporals, who, in contrast to their men, looked very well-fed. Peal was nowhere to be seen. Stiger also noted a line of ten archers had been posted on a large second-story staircase, apparently ready, if needed, to be called into action. They looked bored and unimpressed by the newly arrived company.

"Where do you think you are going?" a garrison sergeant, who had been waiting, arrogantly demanded of Blake and a handful of others who broke ranks. Blake walked right up to sergeant, a disarming smile of greeting on his face, and without hesitation or any hint of a warning slammed his fist right into the sergeant's nose. Blood sprayed as the man's nose broke. Grabbing the man's shoulders before he could fall backward, Blake pulled him forward and followed up with a knee to the chest and then a kick for good measure as the sergeant went down. With that, Stiger's men surged forward. The archers hesitated, shocked at the sudden explosion of violence below them in the courtyard and unsure of what to do. These were legionaries attacking legionaries.

Several, tired of the hell captain Aveeno and his cronies had put them through these past few weeks, quickly threw down their bows as Stiger's men drew swords and advanced on them, climbing the stairs. The archers fled higher up the staircases toward the battlements above, Stiger's men after them.

In a matter of forty heartbeats, the courtyard itself was secure, with several of the garrison bleeding and unconscious on the ground. The rest were being rapidly herded together, prodded by swords and shoves. They were quickly and efficiently stripped of their weapons.

A corporal who had surrendered threw a punch at one of Stiger's legionaries. Without hesitation, another of his legionaries rammed a sword into the man's back. The corporal screamed, falling off the sword, blood spraying as he collapsed to the ground. That was enough for the rest, who complied without hesitation with these slovenly yet dangerous-looking men.

Up along the battlements, there were several shouts. A steel-tipped arrow fired from above snapped into a paving stone with an audible crack. The missile had landed just feet from the captain. Lieutenant Ikely shouted orders and several additional files went charging up the steps to secure the battlements.

"This way!" Boral shouted, pointing toward a large open door. "Hurry!"

Stiger ordered his men forward. They charged the door, swords drawn, with the captain following closely. Another arrow landed nearby, this time with a meaty thwack, striking one of Stiger's men in the neck as he was charging up the steps to the battlements. Out of the corner of his eye, Stiger saw the legionary fall to the courtyard, landing in a heap. The man never even screamed as he fell.

Rage bubbled up inside the captain. He wanted to stop and direct the action for the battlements, but knew he could not. He would have to trust Ikely to handle it. There were more pressing matters to attend to. Captain Aveeno, the man responsible, was his objective. One way or another, Stiger vowed, the garrison commandant would pay for what he had done.

One of Aveeno's men appeared suddenly, attempting to swing the door to the keep shut. Stiger's men slammed into it, forcing the door and the man back. He was quickly cut down and lay bleeding in an expanding pool of blood.

Stepping over the body, Stiger and his men were in the keep. Oil lanterns and lamps lit the interior with an eerie, soft, flickering yellow glow. A hallway stretched out before them, along with two staircases leading upward in opposite directions. A shout rang out down the hallway as someone turned and ran in fright.

"Hurry!" Boral called, starting up a staircase. The men followed the sergeant. They charged up the stairs and through the keep, with Boral leading the way. At several points they encountered a number of the garrison. Any who resisted were rapidly cut down. If not, they were thrown down the stairs or simply disarmed and roughly pushed aside, to be collected later.

Moving rapidly, they passed through several doors, which, had they been shut, would have proved a significant obstacle. The doors were made of a stout, heavy oak, framed and reinforced with metal supports. Castle servants fled screaming before them as they advanced through the keep. A few cowered in corners as Stiger and his men stormed by.

The group burst out onto a landing, with Boral pointing the way forward through a large doorway. Stiger's men exploded through it, with the captain only a few feet behind.

They found themselves in the keep's great hall, which was filled with people. Most appeared to be not of the garrison, but civilians from the valley. They looked in shock at Stiger and his men. Several of the women screamed, with most everyone backing away.

Stiger and his men found themselves confronted by their first real, organized resistance. Seven of Captain Aveeno's legionaries rushed forward, swords swinging as they pushed their way through the civilians. None were wearing armor or carrying shields. They wore only their service tunics.

Stiger's men met the charge, shields forward, swords jabbing and slashing efficiently. Stiger stepped forward and caught a sword thrust that had been aimed at one of his legionaries. He deftly turned the stroke aside before jabbing it into the man's belly. The man screamed and fell backward. Eli's sword flashed out, lightning fast, catching a stroke meant for the captain. Stiger ducked back and to the side, striking at another sword. Sergeant Blake and several other legionaries appeared, having been delayed by disarming a man they had encountered on the landing. They pushed the captain back and stepped forward, hacking at the enemy.

It was all over in seconds, with all seven of Aveeno's men dead or dying at their feet. Weapons were kicked away from the wounded. Blake finished one off with a quick stab to the throat. The man had had a vicious belly wound and Blake had meant it to be a mercy killing, but the act had the effect of badly frightening the civilians even further.

Stiger took a good look around the room. Perhaps thirty or forty civilians and servants were cowering along the sides of the great hall, which was nearly empty of furniture. A fire burned in a large central fire pit in the middle of the room. Smoke curled lazily upward toward a chimney set in the ceiling above. Along the back wall, a row of windows looked out over the valley. Near these windows sat a great big throne, with a tiger's pelt draped over the back.

A man in an officer's tunic sat upon the throne. In front of him stood two legionary lieutenants, both with their swords drawn. Pure malice was written across their faces.

"Silence!" the man on the throne thundered at the screaming and moaning of the wounded legionaries and frightened civilians. A moment of silence settled upon the great hall.

"Captain Aveeno, I presume?" Stiger pushed himself through his line of legionaries. Rage burned in his heart. There were several things that Stiger wanted to personally do to this man. At the very least, Aveeno would pay for the deaths of Eli's scouts, not to mention the betrayal of his oath. Eli and Father Thomas moved with him as he advanced across the room and past the fire pit. Oddly, Stiger's men seemed frozen in place.

"Finally. I thought you would never come!" Captain Aveeno issued a wicked laugh.

"I am Captain Stiger," Stiger growled. "You will answer for the murder of my people."

"You care about your revolting men?" Aveeno laughed, spittle flying. "An officer who cares about those beneath his feet … how touching and enlightening!"

Stiger said nothing, but continued forward with Eli and Father Thomas flanking him.

"Since you care, you should know your scouts died screaming, and that I did the deed myself," Aveeno snarled, standing up from his throne. He pulled forth a wicked-looking sword that had been resting against the throne. It had been hidden from view. The sword was black as night, and seemed to absorb light as Aveeno waved it before their eyes. Hate and malice radiated forth, almost wavelike.

"They sold you out," Aveeno laughed. "You and your pet elf. A Stiger! Ha! I could not believe my luck! A spoiled, noble brat living off the legend of your dying family name."

"They told you nothing," Stiger snarled.

"They told me everything!" Aveeno laughed cruelly. "Your blood will honor my master, but first you will die begging for mercy at my feet as your scouts did!"

Father Thomas, who had been moving with Stiger, took one look at the commandant's sword and pulled Stiger up short. Stiger shot the paladin a look of pure rage, furious at having been interrupted from unloading his anger on Aveeno. Stiger jerked his shoulder in an attempt to pull away, but Father Thomas's grasp was ironclad. The captain's rage turned from Aveeno to the paladin. Stiger raised his sword to strike.

Time stopped, with everyone other than Stiger and Father Thomas seemingly frozen. An ice-cold feeling exploded through the captain. The cold surged forth from where the paladin's vice-like hand gripped his shoulder. Stiger cried out in agony, his vision going white as the paladin's power hammered through him. The pain lasted for what seemed like an eternity, but in reality was only a moment. Almost as quickly as the agony had begun, it was replaced by a cooling and calming sensation that flowed throughout his entire body. A sense of calm and serenity with the world settled in his soul. The captain's rage melted away. Stiger blinked in surprise at the paladin, who offered an understanding look in return.

"Your soul was under assault," the paladin explained quietly. "No longer. The High Father has freed you."

Stiger was at a loss for words. The paladin's power continued to surge through him, relaxing and calming. So incredible was the feeling, he was almost unable to comprehend

Father Thomas's words. Nothing seemed to matter, other than the feeling of peace and serenity.

"This fight is mine and mine alone, my son," the paladin said softly, barely loud enough for the captain to hear. He released Stiger.

Time started once again as the paladin stepped forward to confront Aveeno. It had all happened so fast, and yet to Stiger it seemed like an age had passed. The surge in power faded, but the feeling of peace and wellbeing remained, though diminished somewhat. Stiger glanced over at Eli, who also had a look of astonishment on his face. Had he been touched by the paladin's power as well?

"Are you going to let a traveling priest fight your battles for you?" Aveeno seethed, having witnessed the exchange but clearly not understanding it. "I don't know why I expected better from a Stiger!"

What would have normally stung his pride failed to pierce him. At this very moment, nothing could have upset or provoked Stiger to anger. He felt at peace with the world.

"Your fight is with me, filth," Father Thomas said in a voice that echoed across the great hall. Ignoring the large sabre belted to his side, the paladin held forth his hand, and abruptly a great golden war hammer shimmered into existence. It was so large Stiger was amazed the paladin could even hold it. "I believe it is time for you to reveal your true form," the paladin said.

The war hammer emitted a flash of white light that was so blindingly intense Stiger and everyone else in the great hall was forced to shield their eyes. When the flash had passed, Stiger saw the crumpled form of Aveeno's body lying before the throne. Shockingly, the body was shrunken like an old grape, with steam rising upward from the remains.

The two lieutenants were also down, their bodies smoking as well, but whole in form.

Where a moment before there had been nothing, a shadowy figure coalesced from Aveeno's remains, as if pulling itself together into a coherent whole. It slowly stood, terribly hunched and impossibly twisted, facing Father Thomas. It was so ugly and misshapen that Stiger's mind could not seem to focus on its features. Abstractly, Stiger understood he was looking upon the face of pure evil, and yet he still felt calm, relaxed, and untroubled.

Father Thomas and the thing were just feet apart.

"Priest...you think to challenge my powers?" The shadowy figure hissed a terrible laugh, almost serpent-like. "A holy relic alone is no match for my power!"

"I intend to banish you, filth...vile servant of Castor," the paladin answered, calmly but firmly.

The hunched, shadowy figure raised the wicked black blade that Aveeno had been holding moments before. "You are no simple priest!" the figure sneered, stepping from the steaming remains of Aveeno. It hissed in malice, which seemed to radiate forth like heat on a hot summer's day. "I shall be rewarded for taking your head!"

"You will take nothing but the High Father's greetings to your master," Father Thomas countered. "I will send you back from whence you came!"

With an incredible shrieking scream of rage, dripping with hate and pure loathing, the shadowy, twisted figure lunged forward with an inhuman speed that was shocking to witness, and struck at Father Thomas. The paladin reacted with similar speed. Both the black sword and the golden war hammer crashed together with the sound of thunder.

Two powers, well beyond mortal comprehension, came together in a titanic moment. Black and white lightning exploded throughout the great hall. The world stopped, ended, and then began again all in the same moment as a sound too terrible to comprehend ripped through the room. It sounded as if all of the tormented souls from the underworld cried out as one.

A concussive blast knocked everyone off their feet.

WAKE! a voice hissed, crying out in desperation. *GET UP!*

Stiger's eyes snapped open. He was lying on a hard stone floor and every part of his body ached terribly. He had no idea how long he had been out. The feeling of serenity had been taken cruelly away. He slowly picked himself up and looked around in confusion. He was still in the great hall and his sword was still in his hand. Besides himself, only Father Thomas and the misshapen figure were on their feet. They were fighting furiously, midnight blade against golden hammer. Stiger stood there dumbly for a moment, his brain refusing to believe what he was seeing.

Whenever the two weapons made contact with the other, the building shook with the impact. The sound was very much like a smith pounding on his anvil. Dust and loose mortar fell in a shower from the ceiling. Sparks and multi-colored light exploded outward in a cascade from the point of each contact.

Father Thomas was bleeding from multiple wounds. He was being pressed hard by the misshapen figure, who was also wounded. Blood darker than a moonless night dripped and splashed onto the floor, hissing and smoking where it made contact with the stone.

Wield me! the voice spoke once again, and Stiger somehow knew it was coming from his sword. The voice was becoming louder, more insistent. He looked down upon the blade in his hand and was startled to see it glowing a soft pale blue.

Forged for a purpose, forged for a reason, forged for a will! Your will is my will and mine is yours! Together we are one! WIELD ME!

Looking on the battle raging before him, Stiger honestly did not know what he could do. The weapons the paladin and the figure wielded were beyond his ability to comprehend. They were supernatural. How could he battle this evil without such a weapon?

The room abruptly faded from view and Stiger found himself on a field of battle. Two armies fought bitterly against one another in a blur of motion and color. Stiger could not see the action clearly, but he somehow knew intuitively that they were fighting. It was as if the two armies were shrouded in fog.

Stiger abruptly found himself at the center, where the two armies met. He saw a man who looked like himself, wearing a legionary general's armor, blue cloak fluttering in the wind. The general was wielding the sword Stiger held in his hand, of that he was sure, though he knew not how. The general faced an abomination, twisted and misshapen like the figure Father Thomas now fought. The general was wounded, a hand held to his side, in an attempt to staunch the flow of his life blood.

Stiger sensed it was a mortal wound.

Watch, the voice hissed from nowhere and everywhere at once and Stiger realized with alarm it was in his head.

The twisted figure approached the general, carrying an impossibly large dark sword, black as night. The figure radiated hate. Stiger could sense its feeling of triumph as it took a last step forward to finish what it had started and strike down the general. Lightning fast, it struck. The general brought his sword up to block the killing blow. Stiger thought nothing could withstand the power of such a strike. Surely the general's blade would break!

The black sword hammered down onto the general's sword and then shockingly shattered into smoke with an audible hiss, much like steam escaping a tea kettle. The general seemed stunned that he still lived and stood there staring in surprise as the smoke rapidly curled about his sword before dissipating. The figure looked just as shocked, its moment of triumph rudely torn from its grasp.

The moment passed, and with a look of great determination, the general stabbed his sword forward into the evil figure's chest. The creature screamed horribly, the sound of tormented souls crying out from the great beyond. There was a thunderclap, and the evil figure was no more.

The general stood for a moment, then swayed and fell to his knees. He dropped his sword as his final moments of life ticked away.

The vision of the battlefield faded before his eyes and Stiger found himself returned.

The voice had shown him how to defeat the creature.

Now! the voice hissed desperately. *STRIKE NOW!*

Stiger took a step forward, his muscles crying out in agony. His entire body ached terribly. Moving forward toward the mystical melee between the paladin and the creature of evil was an incredible struggle. Stiger felt as if the air was somehow thicker. He took another step and suddenly it became easier to move.

Father Thomas threw out a hand at the figure and the room exploded with blinding light. The figure cringed for a fraction of a second and then countered. The room descended into absolute darkness. Stiger blinked. His sword flared brilliantly and the darkness faded, though Father Thomas still appeared to be affected and staggered backward, blindly waving his great hammer back and forth where he thought the creature was.

The figure, oblivious of Stiger, moved to the paladin's side in the captain's direction and raised the wicked-looking blade in preparation to strike. Stiger lunged forward and blocked the blow.

Upon contact, the figure's sword evaporated into smoke. It turned in shock toward Stiger and snarled viciously.

Stiger swung down and stabbed the creature. It cried out in rage and fell back, Stiger's blade coming free and hissing foully as the black blood boiled off the steel. He had expected the strike to kill or send it back from whence it came as it had done in the vision. He stabbed again and the creature dodged.

Father Thomas blinked and suddenly it became apparent to Stiger the paladin once more had use of his eyes. A savage blow knocked Stiger aside as the figure lashed out with a powerful fist, screaming with rage as it focused its anger on Stiger. He staggered backward, his vision swimming.

The paladin took advantage of the distraction and swung his great golden hammer forward.

It connected. With the sound of a bell tolling, the room shook as a brilliant light exploded from the point of contact, completely blinding Stiger.

The creature exploded into smoke.

A fraction of a second later, a tremendous concussion knocked him down. Stiger's head connected with the floor and he knew no more.

He opened his eyes. He was once again lying on the cold, hard stone floor. If it was possible, every part of his body ached even worse than before. Disoriented, Stiger dragged himself to his feet. Others were beginning to stir. Memories began to return as he saw Father Thomas kneeling before the throne that Aveeno had recently occupied.

The paladin seemed to be in prayer. He no longer wore his priestly robes. Those had been cast aside and lay in a heap only a few feet away. The paladin's armor gleamed with a soft whitish light that throbbed slightly. Stiger could only describe the light as "holy" in its source. The paladin's wounds were gone, vanished as if they had never been.

Eli stood off to the side, watching the paladin silently. He cast a glance over at Stiger as the captain approached. Together they watched, mute, as the light emanating from the paladin's armor dimmed and then faded away altogether. Neither dared speak.

Father Thomas stood slowly, as an old man would. He turned to Stiger. His face was drawn and lined with exhaustion. His right eyelid twitched uncontrollably and his hands shook.

"What happened?" Stiger croaked after a moment, throat dry.

Memories returned of the battle between the figure and Father Thomas. Stiger looked down on his sword. The room spun slightly. He shook his head, as if clearing cobwebs from a long night's sleep. Did that really happen?

"A servant of Castor infested Aveeno's body," the paladin explained tiredly, voice etched with deep exhaustion. "With the grace of the High Father, both are no more."

"A miracle," Eli breathed reverently. "We have been blessed."

Stiger looked over to where Captain Aveeno's body and that of the hunched abomination had been. There was nothing remaining of either. It was as if both had never existed. All that remained was the tiger pelt draped over the back of the throne. Even the bodies of Aveeno's two lieutenants were gone—vanished.

"With the High Father's help, their remains have been removed," Father Thomas explained. "Had I left any-thing...it was quite possible what remained might have infected others."

The captain shivered. Castor was evil incarnate. The dark god was known for spreading suffering, torment, and pain. Castor's followers were a twisted lot, committing vile atrocities in the name of their dark lord in return for power. They had been lucky Father Thomas had been with them.

"Glad you kept me around?" Father Thomas asked, guessing the captain's line of thought.

Before Stiger could reply, the paladin lurched and then fell forward, collapsing. Stiger caught him and eased the man gently to the ground.

"I am afraid that I shall be of little help for the foresee-able future," Father Thomas breathed in a weakened voice. "I have given all of my energy and must now rest to recover. No matter how long I sleep, try to keep from disturbing me."

"We will keep you safe," Stiger affirmed.

"Thank you, my son," Father Thomas said, with the faintest hint of a smile. His eyes began to roll back and then suddenly snapped back into focus. "There may be more of Castor's contamination about...be cautious of strange items, like the sword Aveeno wielded. Do not touch any-thing that looks out of the ordinary."

"We won't, Father," Stiger promised. "Now, if you will, please rest."

"Thank you for your help..." Father Thomas closed his eyes with a small sigh and immediately entered into a deep sleep.

Stiger looked up at Eli, who had knelt by his side.

Bennet and several additional legionaries burst into the hall, swords drawn. Those who had entered with Stiger were still shaken terribly, as were the villagers. Some were still struggling to stand.

"Are you all right, sir?" Bennet asked, looking over the dead and wounded of Captain Aveeno's supporters who had first challenged them when they had burst into the great hall.

"Yes, I believe we are," Stiger said, taking a deep breath.

"What happened?" Bennet asked, looking around.

"Father Thomas defeated a servant of Castor," Eli answered.

"Castor?" Bennet gasped in horror and looked down at the sleeping paladin. Eyes wide in shock, several of the legionaries with him made the sign of the High Father. The horror was quickly replaced with a look of incredible respect.

"Father Thomas needs to be watched over," Stiger said, standing up. His muscles protested. "He must rest and not be disturbed."

"Me and the boys will watch over the good father, sir," Bennet assured his captain. "No harm will come to him."

Stiger nodded and stepped back, allowing Bennet to care for the paladin. The captain blinked and shook his head, trying to clear his mind. He felt as if he had slept for a week and was still somewhat disoriented. A shout outside the doorway, followed by the sound of sword on sword, shattered the moment.

"Eli, Blake, Boral...you men!" Stiger snapped. He walked over to where he had dropped his sword and picked it up. Stiger looked down upon Delvaris's blade. It no longer glowed. Had he dreamed it all?

Stiger shook his head. He had a powerful headache.

"Let's go find out how the rest of the fight is going."

Blake, wobbling a little, stepped over and followed the captain out of the room. Sergeant Boral, hand on his forehead, shook his head, trying to recover his wits. After a moment, he too followed, wide-eyed at what he had just witnessed.

Sixteen

Stiger found Ikely in the courtyard. The lieutenant looked more than satisfied as he greeted his captain. He seemed confident, in control, and in great spirits. The courtyard was packed full of men. Stiger guessed there were around two hundred prisoners under guard, all sitting in the middle of the courtyard. They had been stripped of their armor and weapons. Some of the prisoners were sporting nasty bruises or nursing minor wounds. The company's surgeon's mate was making his way through the prisoners, working on the more serious wounds.

Several of Eli's scouts, armed with their small bows, stood on the battlements above, looking down on the prisoners with a casual competence. A large pile of weapons and shields sat off to one side. Bodies had been lined up next to the pile. Several of the bodies sported arrows, testifying to the accuracy of the scouts' work.

"Sir," the lieutenant reported. "Most surrendered without a fight. We have secured the courtyard, both gates, the stables, and the battlements. I thought it best we begin cleaning out the barracks. Sergeant Ranl began sweeping them a few minutes ago." As he reported this, several additional prisoners, under the watchful eyes of a guard, emerged from the barracks into the courtyard.

"Very good, Lieutenant," Stiger said, pleased with his subordinate's initiative. "How many casualties did we take?"

"I have two dead and four wounded, sir," he reported, handing over a paper with the names of the dead written on it.

"How many of the garrison?"

"Out here...around thirty-two of the garrison who chose resistance are deceased. I have not yet had the wounded counted."

"I see."

"You should know that some of the prisoners turned on their own. Several were killed before we could intervene. I had to separate that group from the rest." He nodded toward a separate group of ten men, under heavy guard. Unlike the mass of other prisoners, each one had their hands bound securely behind their backs with rope. Several in the group appeared to have been beaten rather badly.

"Captain Aveeno's bullies, I take it?" Stiger said.

"It appears that way. They seem to have compromised themselves."

Stiger had a feeling he would soon be ordering the execution of those ten. An investigation would have to be initiated to determine the facts. The executions would likely follow.

"Did you manage to locate Captain Aveeno?" the lieutenant asked with some interest.

"Yes," Stiger answered. "Father Thomas dealt with him. He is no more."

Ikely raised an eyebrow at that, but said nothing further.

"Aveeno was a servant of Castor," Stiger explained.

"Good gods!" Ikely exclaimed. "Really?"

"Spread the word that if anyone comes across any strange items, they are to leave them alone until Father Thomas can verify they are safe." Stiger made a mental note that as soon as the paladin was capable, he would make sure that each of Aveeno's bullies was carefully screened for any lurking evil.

"I will, sir."

"Sergeant Boral." Stiger turned to the man, who had been following him, along with Eli. Blake had separated himself from them a few minutes before and taken some additional men at the captain's orders to thoroughly search the keep. "Would you be kind enough to assist Lieutenant Ikely here with the search and securing of the rest of the castle?"

"It will be my pleasure, sir," the sergeant said.

"When the castle is secure," Stiger continued, "I would like your thoughts on the forces in the valley and, specifically, who I can trust."

"It would be an honor, sir," the sergeant responded, snapping to attention and saluting rather smartly. "Thank you, sir, for freeing us."

Stiger nodded and stepped away from the lieutenant and sergeant, working his way around the prisoners, who eyed him carefully. Eli trailed a few steps behind. Stiger doubted they knew his name yet, which was a good thing. They might begin to fear for their lives, which would make them potentially desperate. Desperate men could behave stupidly. He shook his head at the mess that Aveeno had left him. He hoped and rather suspected that these men could be rehabilitated. With the current poor state of the Southern legions, he had a suspicion that soon every able-bodied legionary would be needed.

If what General Kromen had told him was true, there were close to a thousand legionaries garrisoning the castle and valley. With Aveeno dead, and as the senior officer in the area, Stiger was now responsible for them all. What had started as a simple resupply run had turned into much more. He was now effectively the garrison commandant, at least until relieved.

"Eli." Stiger stopped and turned to his friend. "Would you kindly send one of your scouts to update the supply train? Also, see that the eagle is brought in."

"I will," Eli said, and then suddenly flashed a grin. "Congratulations on storming your first castle."

"It is a bit more intimidating than those forts we assaulted in Abath, isn't it?" He returned his friend's grin. "Does it matter that they opened the front door for us?"

"Should you refrain from mentioning that little detail, then certainly I shall as well," Eli promised with a wink and went off to find a scout. Stiger watched him go.

"Well," Stiger said quietly to himself, "I have taken my first castle. Now... what do I do with it?"

Stiger had set up his headquarters in a very large room on the fifth floor of the keep. It had somehow felt wrong to take the great hall as his headquarters. Someone had found a large, solid wooden table and several chairs to serve as a place for the captain to work.

He suspected that the room had once been a bedroom with an adjoining sitting room. Sergeant Ranl had secured a desk and chair and taken up a station to work from the sitting room like it was an office. Ranl was acting as Stiger's direct assistant.

Two armed guards stood before the door at the entrance. Ikely had seen to posting guards throughout the keep and castle. He had also set up random patrols in the hopes of catching anyone lurking about. Several of Aveeno's thugs had been discovered hiding in the keep. There was no guarantee there were not more about.

Though a day after the fight, Stiger was reasonably confident the castle was secure. Under heavy guard, the bad actors had been locked up in the castle dungeons. It had helped that the rank and file had not hesitated to point out the ringleaders, thugs, and bullies who had collaborated with the corrupted Captain Aveeno.

Lieutenant Peal stood at attention before Stiger, sweating despite the cool air blowing in through the open shutters. The man was literally quaking in fear as he waited to learn his fate. Stiger coldly considered the lieutenant, nearly a broken man, for a few more heartbeats. Peal had clearly not been in Aveeno's camp, but seemed to have been a small enough fish to have escaped. Perhaps the man could be rehabilitated, Stiger wondered, though judging by the quaking, he might only be good for administrative work. Well, he thought, there was only one way to tell the man's worth.

"I am going to give you a second chance," Stiger growled. "Several of the men have to one degree or another vouched for you, including Sergeant Boral."

"Thank you, sir." Peal breathed a huge sigh of relief, shoulders slumping.

"The rank and file who did not collaborate will also be given an opportunity to continue to serve the empire. You will set up a proper camp on the valley side of the walls and begin training the men up. I will assign you Sergeant Boral. Sergeant Blake will also assist you with training. I suggest you listen carefully to their advice. Both men have far more experience at this sort of thing than you do."

"Yes, sir."

"I will loan out a few of my corporals to help you whip the men into shape. I expect that, in my spare time, I will work with you as well."

"I will not let you down, sir," the lieutenant said eagerly.

Stiger noticed how young Peal was—probably seventeen, maybe even sixteen. His parents had likely purchased his commission. Yet his age did not matter. He was imperial nobility and, as such, much was expected. The honor of his house, though a minor one, demanded nothing less.

"I should hope not," Stiger said coldly. "You are lucky to have a second chance. Do not disappoint me."

"I won't, sir."

"Sergeant Ranl has your orders."

The lieutenant saluted and quickly stepped out of the room to speak with the sergeant. Stiger had assigned the lieutenant close to two hundred men who had been captured in the castle itself. He had already spoken with those men earlier this morning and offered them a chance to once again serve. No one had refused. Upon learning they would be spared death or, worse, a life of slavery, they had cheered themselves hoarse, many thanking him profusely.

Unfortunately for Stiger, Peal was the only officer available. Promoting a man from the ranks was not possible, so in the end the lieutenant had been his only choice. Captain Aveeno had either executed or corrupted the other officers in the keep. All of those men had either died with him in the great hall or elsewhere in the castle.

Stiger would have to work closely with Peal to make sure he could handle his assignment. Should he prove to be incapable of handling the men, Stiger would be in a bind. He was hoping there were a few officers of worth in the valley on whom he could rely to help.

"What of the rest of the garrison?" Eli asked, looking out the window at the magnificent view of the large, lush valley below. Though winter was nearly upon them, the mountains shielded the valley somewhat. Eli was referring to the troops occupying the three forts in the valley. There were around seven hundred men in those forts. Stiger had sent Blake to those posts, along with written orders.

"According to Boral," Stiger sighed, "none of the formations assigned to the garrison are commanded by anyone higher than a lieutenant. Aveeno killed anyone senior. Boral tells me most are good men, though there are a few of Aveeno's watchdogs who will have to be dealt with."

"Do you think they will accept your command?"

"They don't have a choice," Stiger responded. Aveeno's reign of terror was over, and as such, he expected no resistance from the officers. With the remaining officers on board, the men should fall gratefully in line.

Eli said nothing in reply, but turned back to the window and the magnificent view. Stiger had spent some time studying the same view. The valley was much larger than he had expected, at least twenty miles in length and ten miles in width. A brilliant blue river snaked its way through the middle.

"Sir," Sergeant Ranl said from the doorway. "Councilman Bester is here at your request."

Stiger stood as the councilman was led in and introductions were made. The councilman was a short, balding man in his middling years and slightly pudgy. The man looked of much different stock than most Southerners. In fact, he could have passed for an imperial citizen.

Bester represented those who lived in the valley. Stiger understood he owned a large mill. The man had been in the great hall when Stiger had taken the castle, and he looked more than a little uncertain about meeting with the captain.

The relationship between the residents of the valley and the garrison was in a terrible state. The garrison had been taking whatever it wanted from the people of the valley. There had even been some attacks on members of the garrison, and the beginning typical reprisals.

The captain had no idea how long he would be in command of Vrell. It was entirely possible that General Kromen or General Mammot, whoever was now in command, would view this as an opportunity to get rid of a potential headache by leaving Stiger in command. Thinking about that worried him. Though it was more likely they would promote one of their favorites instead.

Either way, Stiger expected to be in command of Vrell for at least two to three months. That meant this meeting was important. He wanted to get things off on the right foot and begin to repair the damage that Aveeno had inflicted. The last thing he wanted was to have to clamp down on a hostile population while he got the remnants of the garrison under control.

"You are wondering if I will be worse than Captain Aveeno?" Stiger asked, holding up a hand to forestall a response that would obviously be to deny any such thing. "Let me assure you, I am not anything like the late Aveeno. I understand that the residents of this valley have been treated poorly. That changes immediately. As long as I am in command, your people and property will be respected, as they were prior to the rebellion."

"We will very much appreciate that, Captain," Councilman Bester said neutrally. Stiger could tell the man wanted to believe him, but they had built no mutual basis for trust yet. Good faith would be developed over time. "The valley supported the empire, not the rebellion."

"I was aware of that." Stiger motioned for Bester to take a chair at the table. Stiger took a seat on the other side of the table and continued. "I would like to earn that support back. Should any of my men step out of line or mistreat your people, I expect to hear of it, and those involved will be swiftly disciplined."

Bester said nothing.

"As long as the residents of the valley respect us," Stiger continued, "my legionaries will respect your people. I expect no attacks on my people and, simply put, we will not molest you."

"We want nothing of the rebellion," the councilman said emphatically. "The rebellion has only brought us trouble and heartache."

"That is encouraging to hear," Stiger said.

"What of those of the garrison who have already done harm?" Bester asked.

"Captain Aveeno's thugs will be dealt with," Stiger answered.

"Is what I hear true, Captain?" Bester asked.

"About Captain Aveeno being an agent of Castor?" Stiger breathed heavily. "You were there. You saw it with your own eyes. Father Thomas removed that filth from this world."

"Then it is true," the councilman said. "This Father Thomas is a paladin of the High Father?"

"Yes, he is."

"I would very much like to meet him."

"He is still recovering from his battle with evil," Stiger explained. "However, I am confident he would be willing to meet with you when he is well enough to do so."

"Thank you, Captain, I would appreciate that."

"I am not sure how long I will be here—most likely at least two to three months, until a replacement can be appointed," Stiger said, changing the subject. "In that time, I would like to build a working relationship with you and the people of the valley. Perhaps even a written agreement that, if accepted by the commanding general of the South, would have lasting repercussions for the peace of the valley and how the garrison interacts with your people after I leave."

"I would be willing to work with you," Bester said, still looking as though he was afraid to trust.

"The captain is an honorable man," Eli added, turning from the window and showing his face for the first time. The councilman's eyes widened.

"An elf!" Bester exclaimed, standing in astonishment. "You must be an elf! I never thought I would meet an elf."

Eli approached the table and offered a slight bow. "I am Lieutenant Eli'Far."

"You keep interesting company, Captain," Bester said, not taking his eyes off Eli.

"'Interesting' does not do justice to this one's life," Eli said with a close-mouthed smile. It seemed that he just could not resist a friendly jab.

"Can we work together, Councilman Bester?" Stiger asked. "Can you keep the peace of the valley long enough for me to gain control of the entire garrison?"

"I will do what I can," Bester said, dragging his eyes away from Eli and back to Stiger. He sat once again. "I will need to speak with a number of people. Captain Aveeno confiscated all of the horses. It would be most helpful if I could borrow one, along with a pass to travel freely."

"I am sure we can find you a horse from the stables," Stiger said. "I have already sent orders nullifying the requirement of passes. You should have no problem traveling freely."

"Thank you for that, Captain."

"What else can I do to help the people of the valley?"

"Help?" Bester asked and laughed nervously. "Do you really mean that?"

"Yes," Stiger said sincerely. "I mean what I say."

"Captain Aveeno confiscated much of our food stores and animals," Bester admitted grimly. "We are looking at a hard winter."

Stiger had learned that Captain Aveeno had amassed a hoard of food to keep the garrison fed throughout the winter. It was another way to keep them loyal. Aveeno had made a real mess of things, Stiger thought with frustration and anger. Or perhaps it had been the creature controlling him. Stiger found the concept of losing control to such an agent of evil frightening. When Father Thomas woke, Stiger planned to speak with him at length about it. Regardless, once the supply train arrived, the cache of stores the garrison had confiscated would be mostly irrelevant.

"I will return all that I can," Stiger said. "We have a supply train that will arrive within the next few days. I do not see food for your people or the garrison being an issue this winter."

"Thank you, Captain," Bester said, brightening. There was still distrust in his eyes, but Stiger could also now see a glimmer of hope. "That will go a long way toward building faith."

"I hope to do much more," Stiger responded. "I would like to meet with your full council to work out a permanent agreement."

"I do not think arranging a meeting will be a problem," Councilman Bester said. "Do you wish to hold it here or in the valley?"

"The castle would be best, I think," Stiger replied, then decided a concession might be in order. "However, if the council is more comfortable, I will travel to a place of your choosing in the valley."

"Excuse me, sir," Ranl interrupted, poking his head into the room. "Legionary Beck is here with the eagle."

"Send him in."

So strong was the Thirteenth's history with the legions that Stiger had made sure that the men of the castle garrison whom he had given a second chance had an opportunity to see it. Legionary Beck was now returning with it. Stiger hoped the eagle, as a symbol, would help cement his control and reinforce loyalty to the empire.

Beck entered rapidly. A stand for the eagle's pole had been fashioned in the corner. Bester's eyes widened as he saw the eagle. He gave the captain a calculating look, which Stiger noticed. Bester glanced back at the eagle, which Beck set in its stand. The legionary saluted his captain before he left.

"Forgive my misunderstanding, Captain Stiger, but I had thought you were the senior officer," Bester said smoothly. "Should I be speaking with the general in charge of the legion?"

"Councilman Bester, I am the senior officer in charge," Stiger said with a frown. "I was under the impression we had already established that fact."

"I understood that imperial eagles traveled with the general commanding the legion," Bester explained, gesturing at the eagle. "Am I mistaken?"

"No, you are quite correct." Stiger exchanged a quick glance with Eli. "This eagle was lost with the Thirteenth. We were able to recover it on our march here and will be returning it to the emperor."

"A lost eagle … very interesting," Bester said, a strange expression crossing his face. "I did not realize the legions ever misplaced their eagles."

"They typically do not," Stiger said, his tone harder than he wished. The man was playing with him for some reason. He softened his tone. "The Thirteenth Legion was lost in the South many years ago, along with her eagle."

"I see." Bester made a show of glancing over at the window. "It is late afternoon. There are a number of people I must speak with to arrange a council meeting. The first is in Rivertown, and if I leave now I should get there by nightfall."

"Of course," Stiger said, standing. The councilman stood as well. "When can I expect your return and word on the meeting with the council?"

"Three or four days should be sufficient," the councilman said, with a glance at the eagle. "When I see you next, I would love to hear more about this 'lost' eagle and how you recovered it."

"Sergeant Ranl," Stiger called.

"Sir?" The sergeant appeared in the doorway.

"Please see that Councilman Bester gets a good horse along with a saddle, rations, and sufficient feed from the castle stables."

"I will, sir," Sergeant Ranl said.

"It was a pleasure meeting you." Stiger offered Bester his hand, which the councilman shook.

"The same for both of you." Bester's eyes lingered a moment on Eli before his gaze shifted to the eagle again. Stiger thought he caught a slight shake of the man's head as he walked out.

Stiger sat down and was silent, thinking. Eli took Bester's former seat.

"I believe he has seen this eagle before," Eli said, tapping the table with an idle finger.

"Perhaps," Stiger said, pouring himself a mug of wine from a pitcher on the table. He took a sip and savored its taste, finding it quite good. One of the castle servants had explained that it was made here in the valley. The wine rivaled some of the best of imperial vintages that were available in Mal'Zeel. Once the rebellion in the South was resolved, Stiger intended to send an agent to purchase an interest in its production and begin importing it to the heart of the empire. With any luck, it would prove a sound investment.

"Perhaps," Stiger said again, considering Bester. "Perhaps not."

Eli poured himself a mug of wine. "The people of this valley must have suffered terribly." He took a sip, then returned to the window and looked out over the valley.

"I clearly have a lot of work to do to gain their trust," Stiger said.

"Fixing roads, roofs, and helping to take in what remains of the harvest might be a good start," Eli suggested.

"Between training, it would certainly keep the men busy, and we both know busy means out of trouble."

"The South has proven to be very different than the North," Eli said wistfully, turning back to the window.

"More like all upside down," Stiger responded.

SEVENTEEN

The officers commanding the three forts in the valley had arrived, according to the summons Stiger had sent them. All three were very relieved Captain Aveeno was no more and that the madness had ended. They were all young, this being their first assignment. Stiger spent time with each of the lieutenants, learning about what they had been through and the state of their men. All three seemed to be good men, though jaded by recent events. They were still very wet behind the ears.

Unsurprisingly, Stiger confirmed, there was tremendous hostility between the people living in the valley and the garrison. He intended to rectify that, but it would take time. He knew he had a lot to do. By order of seniority, he was responsible for the entire garrison and the civilian population in the valley. Oddly, there were no allied auxiliaries comprising part of the garrison. Most garrisons were primarily made up of auxiliaries, with only a handful of legionaries to act as a backbone. It was all very strange.

Stiger had called a meeting, which included all of the lieutenants, along with their lead sergeants. This also included Eli, Ikely, Peal, Ranl, and Blake. Stiger had also invited Boral.

They stood around the large table in the room that served as his headquarters. A map of the valley was spread across the table. It was an old map that Ranl had found in the castle's dusty library, which had apparently sat unused for years. Stiger had placed stones on the map, indicating the locations of the three forts. From his interviews, he had learned they were nothing but simple, rough wooden structures without walls.

"I expect you to construct proper legionary fortifications," Stiger ordered. "In between training your men, you will work on this daily. The civilians in the valley are hostile. Until we can change that attitude, I want our men protected and confined behind the walls."

"Sir," Lieutenant Banister spoke up. He commanded one of the infantry companies. "Captain Aveeno selected the locations for our forts. They are not in the best areas. Mine, for instance, has no access to fresh water. I must send a daily wagon at least two miles to fetch water."

"Find a more suitable site," Stiger ordered. "Be mindful of the civilians, though. We need to build bridges and not burn them."

Stiger thought for a moment. The company garrisoning the castle had been in poor shape. He suspected those in the valley were in the same condition. Seven levels, he thought, the legions of the South were simply rotten. He struggled for a moment with what he wanted to say. These lieutenants were fairly fresh men, with little real experience. Their more experienced seniors had all been cut down. Stiger decided to come out and say what needed saying.

"Having come from the North, I have been personally appalled by the conditions here in the South. I want you to understand I will not tolerate slovenly and lax standards. Your men are legionaries. I expect them to look and act the part. I also expect you to get your men into proper shape. Is that understood?"

There was a chorus of yeses. Stiger was in command. It was that simple.

"I have provided each of you a 'suggested' schedule of training." Stiger paused. He knew the men would resent the training, as his own company had. Each of the garrison companies would have to be rebuilt from the ground up. That would take time. He hoped the people in the valley would give him time and that the bad feelings had not reached the tipping point yet.

"Keeping the boys busy will also keep them out of trouble," Boral added.

Stiger actually smiled. He was beginning to take a shine to this man. In private, Blake had gone out of his way to vouch for Boral.

"Exactly," Stiger agreed. "From what I understand, you are short sergeants and corporals. Promote additional corporals from men you trust and can rely on. Any candidates for sergeant I would like to meet before giving my approval."

Stiger was asking a lot from these young officers. A typical company was led by three officers, one captain, and two lieutenants. Until replacements arrived, they would be running the show by themselves. This was garrison duty, and hopefully things would remain quiet.

"Sir," Cannol said after a moment. He commanded the cavalry company. Why General Kromen had detailed a cavalry company to garrison duty was beyond Stiger. It seemed a waste, unless they had been initially meant to patrol the road—but even that was a waste, since the road was bracketed almost entirely by forest. Foot soldiers would have been better suited to keeping the road clear. "About helping the locals..."

"Yes?"

"How do you want us to fit that in with the training schedule you have outlined?"

"I expect you to rotate detachments in and out of the training schedule."

"Are you sure you want us to help these people?" Lieutenant Brent asked. "They hate us."

"I know," Stiger responded. "We need to change that. We need a quiet posting here, especially after the animosity that has been stirred up. They outnumber us. It could get ugly, and I believe we are not prepared for a revolt here in the valley."

"I am in agreement with you, sir," Cannol said, and the other two garrison lieutenants nodded.

"I have spoken with Councilman Bester and laid the foundation for a better relationship. Look at it this way: Winter is coming. Without a return of their food stores, these people are facing starvation. Returning the food should go a long way to smoothing things over. Helping to repair roofs, barns, fences, gathering firewood … the little things will help further change their view of the empire. We need to win these people over with a little kindness and respect. I would rather have these people working with us than against us. Do all of you understand?"

There were nods around the table. Despite the nods, Stiger knew that they harbored reservations. He would be forced to check on their progress to confirm they were doing as he intended. It would not be easy. Seven levels, nothing ever done right was easy.

"Good," Stiger said. He leaned over the map and traced a line that represented a road. "I have a question. This road leading north into the mountains—where does it lead?"

There were surprised expressions all around as everyone looked closely at the map. Nothing on the map indicated there was anything at the end of the road. It was damn strange—a road to nowhere.

"My fort is the closest and I know of no road, sir," Cannol answered with a frown. "Hillside and trees are all that's up that way."

"The map looks very old," Brent said. "Perhaps there was a road but no longer? It's all forest up there anyway, so it is possible there was once a logging road. That could be it, sir."

Eli exchanged a look with Stiger. The captain knew what his friend was thinking: dwarves. The map was extremely old and showed its age. It was possible that it was even of dwarven manufacture.

"Something is, or was, there," Stiger stated. "You don't go to the effort to build a road to nowhere and then mark it on a map like this one. I seriously doubt whoever drew this map would bother to mark down a simple logging road. Eli, send a couple of your scouts to see what they can discover."

"What do you expect to find, sir?" Cannol asked.

"Dwarves," Eli answered quietly and got surprised looks in return.

"You are jesting," Brent said with a laugh. "Dwarves? Seriously."

"Fairy tales," Cannol chuckled, then cut it off at the serious look Stiger gave him.

"They built this castle," Eli stated, gesturing around them. "Dwarves are very much a real race—"

"The lieutenant," Stiger interrupted, raising a hand to forestall any further protest, "has had personal experience with dwarves." He paused, glancing around the table. "It is quite possible there is a dwarven settlement nearby. On the other hand, when we go looking, we might just find abandoned ruins and structures like this castle. They may have moved on. Until we look, we won't know for certain."

There was a knock at the open door. Father Thomas stood in the entrance, wearing a simple tunic. He was unarmed. All eyes turned to him. It was the first time Stiger had seen the paladin unarmed and without his armor. It was also the first time the man had been up and about since the battle. He looked worn, and somehow older.

"May I introduce Father Thomas," Stiger announced.

Stiger knew all the men in the room had heard how Father Thomas and Stiger had fought the evil within Captain Aveeno. More than a few blinked in astonishment or dropped their jaws. Stiger could guess they had expected a mountain of a man in shining armor—an impressive warrior of the High Father. Instead they received a middle-aged, physically fit man who could pass for a legionary officer out of uniform.

"Captain," Father Thomas said, approaching the table. Since no one was sitting, he took the nearest available chair. He lowered himself carefully into it. "I apologize for my lengthy absence. Fighting the agent of Castor took a lot out of me."

"I've been wondering about that," Stiger said. "Was Captain Aveeno possessed by this evil from Castor, or was he the agent?"

"I would not exactly say *possessed*," Father Thomas replied sadly. "Castor works more subtly. I suppose Captain Aveeno was likely more of a willing participant at first, perhaps in an attempt to satisfy his own ambition. You see, once Castor gains access to part of one's soul, the darkness spreads like a cancer, until the host is completely under the Twisted One's dominion, permitting, or really opening, a conduit for a minion. Think of it as an evil spirit who enters our world and takes control of the host. Had the corruption continued, this entire valley would have fallen under Castor's power."

Several of the men at the table turned pale. Boral, having witnessed the struggle first-hand, made the warding sign of the High Father.

"How exactly did he become a follower of Castor?" Ikely asked.

"That, I am afraid, we will likely never know," Father Thomas admitted with a shrug. "Perhaps he came across a priest at some point and sought a favor, or perhaps it was something altogether different."

"A priest of Castor?" Brent exclaimed, shocked.

"A horrid thought," Cannol breathed, equally appalled.

"Yes, it is," Father Thomas agreed distantly. "Though this was somewhat different. It felt almost as though Castor was attempting to establish a more solid presence in this world. Such an attempt has not been seen for a very long time."

"Father," Brent said, stepping forward, "may I be the first to thank you for delivering us from evil?"

"The High Father deserves your thanks," Father Thomas stated firmly. "I am only his humble instrument, and a blunt one at that."

"Then I will offer thanks to both." The lieutenant offered and shook Father Thomas's hand. One by one, the others did as well.

EIGHTEEN

Stiger's company was drawn up for review in the main courtyard of the castle. With the exception of a few men posted on the ramparts and those assigned to escort the supply train, all of his men were present. They were clean and their equipment was maintained. From the look in their eyes, they considered themselves hard-charging veterans who had proven themselves in two fights, one of which resulted in the capture of a castle. They had shown they could march harder than any other company in the South, and they knew it.

A real battle would be the true test of their mettle, yet Stiger was pleased. He was proud of how far they had come. He intended to keep working the men, focusing on improvement. The more he thought about it, the more it seemed likely General Kromen or General Mammot would give the garrison to one of their cronies as a reward. Stiger wanted nothing more than a challenge, and that meant getting out in the field with his men. The more effective his company, the greater chance they would remain in the field and away from the main legionary encampment.

"What is that?" Stiger turned toward Ikely, who was standing to his right. The company was drawn up at attention. The captain was pointing at the Eighty-Fifth's standard-bearer, who stood next to Beck with the Thirteenth's eagle.

The sun broke through a cloud at that moment, and the golden eagle lit up brilliantly under the sunlight.

"That, sir, I do believe, is our standard," Ikely answered, without a hint of a smile.

"I know our standard," Stiger growled, not appreciating the lieutenant's cheek. A crossbar had been added, and something was draped around and over the bar. "What is that thing draped across it?"

"I believe the boys...ah... *liberated* the tiger pelt from Captain Aveeno's throne," the lieutenant explained with a straight face.

"I see," Stiger said with a slight frown.

"They have also settled upon a name for the company," the lieutenant added.

"A name?"

Stiger was genuinely surprised. Legionary companies occasionally named themselves, usually only when the men felt they had done something impressive. Named companies were considered blessed by the gods. Tradition prohibited officers from influencing the process. As such, naming a company was a very important affair, and it was considered bad form for a company to take a name without having achieved something noteworthy. It was widely believed that doing so would incur divine disfavor. Companies who violated tradition were shunned and suffered serious runs of bad luck, from accidents to terrible assignments. Men from other companies wanted nothing to do with them, as bad luck could be contagious.

"So," Stiger continued, his frown deepening, "having force-marched to Vrell, cleared a forest of bandits, recovered an imperial eagle, assaulted and captured a castle—not to mention assisted a paladin of the High Father to defeat a minion of the evil god Castor—qualifies my company for a name? Do you think they have done enough to avoid divine disfavor? Would the gods approve?"

"Yes, sir," Lieutenant Ikely said, still staring forward. "I believe the gods smile upon us, and it seems the men feel our company has earned a name."

"Will the gods approve?" Stiger asked, turning to face the men.

The men shouted a resounding, "Yes!"

"And what name?" Stiger asked. He had never commanded a named company before. This was only his second command. Such names were usually fierce, like the Bastards of the Fifth or the Abath Avengers. What had the men settled on? he wondered.

"Stiger's Tigers," the men shouted in unison.

Stiger was silent for several moments, the shouts still ringing around the courtyard's walls.

"Should have been Stiger's Bastards," he said, a rare grin suddenly cracking his weather-hardened face, scar tugging at his cheek. "I do believe that Stiger's Tigers will do."

The men cheered at that, and it made Stiger's heart warm.

Rarely, if ever, did a company name themselves after their commanding officer. Such an event meant that they respected their commander greatly and believed in him. Stiger let them cheer for a moment or two more before returning to business.

"Let's begin the inspection," Stiger said to Lieutenant Ikely, stepping forward and up to the first man. Bennet could not suppress his grin or his foul breath as Stiger looked him over. Everything was perfect. Stiger gave Bennet a nod, and moved on to the next man.

The men were his and he was theirs.

Stiger was sitting at the table in his office, writing out a detailed report to Generals Kromen and Mammot. The sun had long since set. A fire blazed in the hearth, heating the room. The windows had been shuttered, as the temperature had dropped to near freezing. Winter was nearing with each passing day, and up here in the mountains, at higher elevation, it would arrive early. Two lamps burned brightly, providing the room plenty of illumination. A dented pewter mug of brandy sat before him. A thorough search of the castle had revealed the ancient casks, along with a barrel hoard of valley ale. The sergeants had wisely put it all under guard.

Next to the mug lay the sword, snug in its ornate wooden scabbard. Stiger glanced over at the weapon. The sword had not spoken since the battle with the agent of Castor. It was clearly a powerful relic, magical or perhaps even spiritual in nature, given that he had challenged a god's minion with it. He was somewhat concerned about asking Father Thomas to examine the weapon.

The paladin had been to meet with him and had not mentioned the sword, though Stiger had caught him eyeing it carefully. Surely if it were an item of evil, Father Thomas would have said something. Still, Stiger knew he would have to eventually ask, but something he could not put words to kept him from doing so. Stiger put the sword and the voice from his mind and returned to work.

Stiger had delayed writing his official report for several days. He had wanted the supply train to arrive so that he could report his mission to resupply Castle Vrell a success. He had also wanted to get a handle on the forces garrisoning the valley so that his report would be more complete.

The train had finally arrived that afternoon, and Stiger had begun writing the long-delayed report. At this late hour, the courtyard was still a scene of chaos as wagons were driven in and unloaded. Stiger had sent for Lieutenant Peal's company to assist with the unloading. He had also left his lieutenants and sergeants to supervise so that he could write out his report. In the morning, he would dispatch a messenger and then begin the long wait for a reply.

He was busily scratching away at the parchment with a charcoal pencil when he heard hurried boots in the corridor outside. Guards were still posted outside his headquarters. He could hear them asking muffled questions before the door to the study opened. In walked Lan, Eli, and a very dusty, road-weary cavalry trooper.

"Sir," the cavalry trooper said, saluting, exhaustion heavy in his voice. "They're gone! The legions are gone!"

Stiger dropped the charcoal pencil and looked at Lan, not understanding.

"As requested, I detached Terrance here back to the main encampment with your dispatch about clearing out the bandit camp," Lan said.

"I went to the encampment as ordered, sir," the trooper explained wearily. He was so exhausted that he leaned on the table for support. "The legions are gone, sir, and the encampment empty."

"The fighting season is almost upon us," Stiger said hopefully.

"They went north, sir, not south," the trooper continued. "The road is all torn up in that direction."

"North?" Stiger asked, incredulous. Why would the army march north? Marching north was pulling back and ceding more territory to the rebels.

Stiger had been part of armies that made unexpected movements in response to an enemy, but this was different. With those unexpected movements, messengers were always dispatched to isolated outposts or units out in the field. The captain clamped down on the stem of his pipe with his teeth as anger began to overcome his surprise. They had been abandoned!

"You came across no messengers?" he asked.

"No, sir," the trooper said emphatically.

"Why didn't you follow the army?" Stiger asked as a thought occurred to him. That would have been the natural thing for the man to have done. There must have been a reason he had not. Stiger was afraid to hear it.

"The whole cursed rebel army showed up," the trooper explained wearily. "The rebels are marching north! I stayed hidden in the forest, watching them for some time. But that is not the worst of it, sir…"

Stiger closed his eyes momentarily, knowing what was coming.

"Part of the rebel army is marching here, sir, to Vrell."

"You are sure of it?" Stiger asked.

"I am," the man breathed, "at least twenty thousand foot. I stayed hidden in the forest and counted companies, sir."

Stiger stood, took a puff off his pipe, and walked over to the hearth. His mind was racing. He could understand retreating north. The Southern legions were in no condition for a standup battle with the rebel army. That had been abundantly clear when he had seen the condition of the main encampment. What bothered him was being abandoned.

Kromen and Mammot had to have known the rebel army was preparing to move north. There was no way they could not have known! The Southern legions were in no condition for a fight, which meant they knew in advance they were going to retreat when the roads solidified and the fighting season began. They had sent him, a potential headache, to Vrell to get him out of the way. Yet in reality, they had effectively sent him here to die. The rage he felt at being so callously and intentionally abandoned burned hotter the more he thought about it.

Stiger and the garrison were trapped. The enemy was coming and, if true, in overwhelming numbers.

Stiger continued to stare into the fire as he turned over the situation in his mind. He held the most fortified position in the entire South, with over one thousand men at hand and winter coming. Winter in the South was typically the fighting season, but Vrell was in the mountains. At the higher elevations, the winter would be severe, and Vrell was far from any source of enemy supply. He chuckled suddenly, realizing that he would be staying in Vrell much longer than he had planned or hoped.

"Sir?" Lan asked, apparently worried at hearing his captain chuckle. "What do we do?"

"We fight," Stiger growled, turning back from the fire.

"Fight, sir?" Lan asked.

"We hold the castle, the most fortified position in the South. What we do, Lieutenant, is fight!"

"The legions will return," Eli added. "They always come back."

"Of course," Stiger snapped. "We have a duty to defend Vrell and hold it."

"That could be years," Lan stated.

"Then we hold it for years," Stiger said. He turned to Blake, who had followed Lan and the trooper in. "Sergeant Blake, send for two of Eli's scouts. We need to get word of our condition here to the legions before it is too late to sneak word out."

"Yes, sir," Blake said, and left.

"How far is the enemy?" Stiger asked the trooper.

"Two weeks' hard march, maybe," he reported. "Likely three to four. They seemed in no hurry."

"Eli," Stiger said suddenly. "We need to make their life marching here hell, and slow them down long enough for winter to arrive."

"I can think of several places we can ambush the rebel column," Eli said, nodding, "and a few of my scouts harassing them with bows could slow them down even further."

"Excellent," Stiger said. "We will also need axe parties felling trees across the road." Stiger started pacing the room. "I think our best chance to really cut them up will be in the foothills. You could hide an army in those hills. We can—"

"You can't be serious, sir," Lan broke in. "You are going to attack an enemy army?"

"I am going to do much more than that, Lieutenant." Stiger turned to the cavalry officer. "I am going to make them regret they ever heard of Vrell."

Epilogue

"Open it up," Braddock snapped. One of his guards obediently stepped forward and unlocked the steel door. He leaned heavily on it and pushed. Metal hinges groaned and shrieked as the heavy door swung outward and open. Sunlight forced Braddock to shield his eyes as a strong, cold wind blasted into the room, kicking up centuries of undisturbed dust.

Squinting, Braddock stomped out onto the small terrace carved into the side of the mountain that had long ago served as a watch post. From below in the valley the watch post was invisible, as it had been intended to be. A small wall enclosed the terrace.

He laid his hands on the wall and looked down. Vrell Valley spread out before him in all its green, bountiful grandeur. He had spent much of his youth in the valley, for once the land had been his people's.

"This brings back memories, my Thane," Garrack said, emerging onto the terrace and leaning against the wall.

"That it does." Braddock glanced over at his oldest friend and closest confidant before turning his gaze back down on the valley below. "That it does."

They were silent for a time, both lost in their own thoughts. A strong gust of wind swirled around them.

"Evil has entered our valley," Braddock said sadly, breaking the silence as he gazed down upon the great citadel guarding the pass to the wider world. The humans called it Castle Vrell. His people called it something different. It did not matter. What did matter was what was coming.

"The clans are assembling as called," Garrack growled angrily. "For the first time in three centuries, we field a unified army. You will cleanse this valley of its stench and restore the Compact."

"That I will," Braddock affirmed, slamming a mailed fist down upon the ancient wall. "Before our gods, I swear it!"

End of Book One

Enjoy this preview of Book Two:

The Stiger Chronicles

*Originally published as Chronicles of an
Imperial Legionary Officer*

Book 2

THE TIGER

ONE

Marcus thought it a pleasant spot. The air was crisp, cool, and the scent of the forest was strong. Wind rustled through the tree canopy above, setting off a shower of brightly colored late autumn leaves.

The scout, Marcus, remained still, kneeling on the forest floor, watching silently as the leaves slowly settled. The display that nature put on was simply magnificent. He felt blessed to be here, in the Sentinel Forest, to witness it, and his heart swelled at the beauty surrounding him. Silently he offered a brief prayer of thanks to the High Father.

A bird called in the distance. He listened to its beautiful song. For a moment he felt that the bird was singing exclusively for his entertainment. The bird started and stopped, only to begin once again. In search of insects for a morning meal, a woodpecker abruptly began hammering away somewhere off in the distance. Such were the sounds and ways of the forest.

Lieutenant Eli'Far, an elven ranger, had opened his eyes to the ways of the forest and taught him to watch, listen, smell... to feel the forest as if it were a living being. The process involved calming the mind and letting go. It was almost like a form of meditation. Marcus found it difficult to put the experience into words, but he was beginning to understand and sense what the lieutenant was teaching him.

He had spent two years in the company before Captain Stiger had assumed command of the Eighty-Fifth. At the time Marcus had thought himself to be quite good as a scout. With hindsight, he now recognized he had been a bumbling amateur. The captain and Eli had brought change to the company, and for that he was grateful.

Eli had taught him that life in the forest, at its base level, followed a pattern. Someone properly attuned to the forest could spot the moment when something disturbed the pattern. It was this disturbance that he had been trained to watch for and one among many other important things that Eli had imparted. Incredibly honored to receive instruction from one of the High Born, Marcus had done his best to be a good student. He had always been a quick learner. He paid as close attention to the elf as humanly possible. Marcus did everything he could to put to practice what Eli had taught him. What at first had seemed inhumanly possible soon became second nature for Marcus as he became more proficient in the ways of the ranger. He was a better scout for it and without question the best in the company. He felt sure it was one of the reasons he had been promoted to scout corporal.

He loved being a company scout and the freedom that came with the job. While scouting and on detached duty, he was not required to wear his armor. Instead, he and the others were permitted to wear their service tunics with light leathers that provided limited protection but were infinitely more comfortable. Unlike the majority of the company, they had also been issued boots, a serious improvement over standard issue sandals, particularly in the winter.

A strong gust of wind blew through the canopy, setting off another shower of leaves. Marcus breathed in deeply through his nose and slowly exhaled. It had rained the night before. He could smell the moist earth, moss, and the occasional pine amongst the great old trees. A moose could be heard braying distantly. Marcus had never seen one before coming to the South. They were impressive animals, weighing as much as two thousand pounds. Like the man-eating cats that also lived in this forest, he had learned they were to be respected.

Marcus considered for a moment that he had come a long way from the slums of Mal'Zeel. He had been a criminal and had been sentenced to a term with the legions. That now seemed a lifetime ago. The magistrate had given him a choice, two years forced labor in a lead mine or a twenty-five year term with the legions. In essence, the magistrate was doing his best to give Marcus a fresh start, a chance to make something of himself, though at the time he had not seen it that way.

Marcus had never seriously contemplated joining the legions. Who wanted to voluntarily sign up for a twenty-five-year term of service? Life with the legions was hard, with the potential to be carved up by some distant battle-crazed barbarian. The slums of Mal'Zeel were awash with legionary cripples who were missing limbs or suffering from some debilitating injury. Such men, deemed unable to march, were discharged with a small monthly disability benefit and whatever pension funds they had accrued during their service. Having not completed their signed twenty-five-year term, they were not entitled to any lands. Unable to work, even if they could find a job, they survived on the grain dole and simply drank or diced their meager monies away. Such wretches were shadows of their former selves. He had pitied them. Still, Marcus had not hesitated to accept the offer of a term with the legions. Forced labor in a mine was the same as a death sentence.

I am a very different person now.

He had already resolved, should the opportunity ever permit it, to find the magistrate and thank him.

A fresh gust of wind rustled through the forest. He closed his eyes to listen as the wind made its way through the trees. He breathed in deeply through his nose and slowly exhaled, enjoying the smells, the sounds. He could hear the leaves rushing together and the branches swaying. The trees creaked and groaned with the wind.

The gust eventually abated and, with it, Marcus became aware of a disturbance. He felt it, a subtle change in the pattern of the forest. It was not unexpected. He had been waiting for it. Marcus sighed deeply. His moment of serenity and peace was gone.

He opened his eyes. His small bow lay on the ground before him. He slowly reached forward and picked it up. Three arrows were stuck loosely in the forest floor to his right and within easy reach. He quietly took one, nocked it, and then looked up.

The Vrell Road lay twenty-five yards away. Marcus could not recall the road's actual name. People simply called it the Vrell Road, as that was the only place it went.

He shifted, leaning forward to put his weight squarely on his knees. Concealed behind a stand of bushes, he was right at a spot where the road bent at a sharp angle. Around the bend came a heavily loaded supply wagon pulled by a pair of oxen and driven by a bored-looking teamster. Marcus allowed the wagon to continue past and out of view.

Undetected, he just sat and watched. A second wagon slowly followed the first. Both teamsters carefully negotiated the bend and continued on out of view. A third wagon followed and then a fourth and fifth. Marcus continued to count. When the twentieth wagon turned the bend, he calmly and coolly raised his bow and drew back, increasing the tension as he pulled.

He carefully aimed, and then released. The bow twanged. In a practiced, fluid-like motion, he nocked a second arrow, rapidly aimed, and released.

The wagon came to an abrupt halt and the teamster stared dumbly in shock at the two oxen. One had collapsed without uttering a sound. The other brayed and kicked about in pain. It seemed to take the teamster a moment to realize that an arrow protruded from the neck of the beast. Eyes wide, he was just starting to look into the forest when Marcus released his third arrow. Its flight was true and took the teamster fully in the neck. Desperate, the man grasped at the arrow, which had punched completely through the soft tissue and exploded out the other side of his neck. The teamster stood up in what appeared to be shocked panic. He teetered a moment before his legs gave out and then toppled from the wagon, landing heavily, blood spurting in jets from the wound.

Marcus grabbed his quiver, stood, and made his way deeper into the forest. Shouts of alarm from the rebel supply column rang out behind him. Marcus assumed a similar thing was happening to the next two wagons, which Todd and Davis were charged with handling. The shouts faded the farther he got from the road.

The pace he set could not quite be described as a run, but was swift enough that it was a near jog. Eli had taught him well and he was mindful to leave little evidence of his passage lest someone track him down.

It was a mile before he came to a stop in a small clearing, the rendezvous point. A few moments after his arrival, Davis and Todd appeared. They nodded at each other in greeting. Satisfied that everyone had arrived without incident or injury, Marcus said nothing but turned and immediately set out, with the others following along as they made their way to the next ambush point.

Today was the day the rebels would learn that their march on Vrell would be contested. The scouts, operating in small units, had been positioned along the road to harass, confuse, and slow the enemy. Priority targets were draft animals and teamsters, followed by officers and sergeants. Orders were to strike rapidly and disappear, shortly attacking elsewhere, making it appear that the road and advance was contested by a major force. Though the enemy would think otherwise, there were no more than thirty-five men operating under Eli's direct command, most coming from the garrison companies.

Farther up the road and much closer to Vrell, well in advance of the enemy, Captain Stiger with the Eighty-Fifth and the bulk of the Vrell garrison were preparing for the enemy's arrival. Marcus was not sure what was being planned, but he was confident the captain would be making a stand. Captain Stiger simply needed time to prepare for that stand, and Marcus was going to work hard to give it to him.

Marcus smiled as they arrived in a small clearing that they had selected earlier. He stopped and took a quick drink from his water skin, thankful once again that he did not have to wear the heavy armor of a common legionary. He wiped the sweat from his brow and took one more pull on the skin.

"Remember, three shots only and then hoof it back here." Marcus looked at the other two scouts. "No risks and no foot-dragging to watch."

The others nodded in grim understanding. They were playing a dangerous game. Taking more shots or hesitating a few moments to watch the aftermath might be tempting, but it could also prove risky should the enemy be given time to gather their wits and respond. The orders were to strike from hidden positions and, if possible, remain unseen as they melted back into the forest.

Satisfied that they were in mutual understanding, Marcus sent them on their way. Each headed off in the same general direction toward positions that had been carefully selected with an eye toward concealment. So quick had they moved from the previous ambush that Marcus judged it unlikely the enemy column they were approaching was even aware of the attack on the supply column just a few miles back.

Marcus took care to move as silently as possible. He picked his way through the forest toward the road, barely a mile away. The enemy had scouts and skirmishers of their own, of which they had seen little. The rebels appeared to not expect any resistance and, as such, had not pushed skirmishers and scouts out to screen the flanks of their march. Marcus grinned. He was about to punish them for that lapse.

As he neared his selected spot, Marcus could begin to hear the steady tromp of many feet ahead of him through the brush. He and his men were about to attack an infantry column, which would be a much more dangerous undertaking. Marcus eased behind thick brush and knelt down.

Through the brush, he could see the rebel infantry marching by, a little under twenty-five yards away. He took his bow from his back, leaving the quiver in place, and stuck three arrows tip-first into the soft forest floor, just deep enough that they would stand up on their own.

The rebel soldiers looked far from impressive. Dressed in near rags, many were barefoot. Very few wore any real type of armor, with only a handful here and there wearing the odd helmet. They were armed with long wooden spears, topped by iron tips, but more curiously, they did not carry shields. Spearmen usually carried shields. The rebel infantry kit included bags that were either slung over shoulders or hung on backs from ties around their necks. Marcus assumed these contained personal possessions and rations.

The rebels did not march in step or ordered rows as a legionary company might, but simply walked in clumps. From a professional soldier's view, they looked very much like the rabble that they were. Still, that did not stop Marcus from respecting them and what they were capable of doing. After all, it was men like these who had forced four imperial legions to retreat northward, stranding both his company, the Eighty-Fifth Imperial Foot, and the garrison of Vrell behind enemy lines.

Marcus studied the column for a few seconds before he saw what he took to be a sergeant. The man carried himself with an air of importance and authority. He was well-dressed and, unlike his men, he wore boots. He was also better armed than the others, having a shield and a short sword, worn on his right side.

In one smooth motion Marcus took an arrow, nocked it, aimed, and fired. The arrow landed with a meaty thwack and heavy grunt, taking the man full in the chest. He staggered before falling to his knees. Marcus grabbed another arrow, aimed, and released, hitting the man who had been marching next to the sergeant. So fast did it happen that the second man was hit before those around him seemed to realize they were under attack. The second man cried out as he collapsed onto the road, where he rolled in the dirt, tripping the man directly behind him.

Captain Stiger's orders were not only to strike at the enemy's supply, but also to prune the enemy ranks of their leadership. Eli had added to those orders and had made it clear that they were also to strike down those who were near the officers and sergeants so it would rapidly become apparent that being around leadership was an unhealthy proposition. This would also have the future side-effect of making it easier to spot any rebel officers and sergeants.

Marcus took his third shot as cries of alarm and screams of rage and pain began to sound up and down the column. Davis and Todd, having taken his cue, also struck. A horse somewhere up the road screamed in pain. With a deep sense of satisfaction, Marcus melted back into the forest. One of his men had found an officer.

To continue reading please purchage *The Tiger*.

CONNECT WITH MARC

Marc works very hard on his writing. He aims to create high quality books to be not only enjoyed but devoured by the reader. Late into the night he writes with a drink at his side, usually a whiskey, gin and tonic (Aviation), or beer.

It helps fuel the creativity ... *If you think he deserves one, you can help to encourage the creativity. Think of it as a tip for an entertaining experience!*
Cheers!

Go to www.maenovels.com and scroll down to the bottom of the page!

Patreon Legion: Consider supporting Marc as an author and get special access. Follow the link below to learn more about the benefits of joining the legion. www.patreon.com/marcalanedelheit

Facebook: Make sure you visit Marc's Author Page and smash that like button. He is very active on Facebook. Marc Edelheit Author

Facebook Group: MAE Fantasy & SciFi Lounge is a group he created where members can come together to share a love for Fantasy and Sci-Fi.

Twitter: Marc Edelheit Author

Instagram: Marc Edelheit Author

Author Central: You can follow Marc Edelheit Author on **Amazon**. Smash that follow button under his picture and you will be notified by Amazon when he has a new release.

Newsletter: You may wish to sign up to Marc's newsletter by visiting www.maenovels.com to get notifications on preorders, contests, and new releases. **In fact, he recommends it!** We do not spam subscribers.

Reviews keep Marc motivated and also help to drive sales. He makes a point to read each and every one, so please continue to post them.

Made in the USA
Columbia, SC
28 July 2023

20871936R00178